Copyright © 2025 Alicia Vanover

All rights reserved. No part of this book may be reproduced, stored in a retrieval system, or transmitted in any form or by any means- electronic, mechanical, photocopying, recording, or otherwise- without written permission of the copyright owner of this book.

The characters and events portrayed in this book are fictitious. Any similarity to real persons, living or dead, is coincidental and not intended by the author.

Cover design by Katie Diggle [@littlerhodyreader]
Printed in the United States of America

Save A Horse by Alicia Vanover

Save A Horse

Alicia Vanover

Contents

Copyright
Title Page
Dedication
Epigraph
Playlist

Chapter One	1
Chapter Two	5
Chapter Three	8
Chapter Four	12
Chapter Five	15
Chapter Six	19
Chapter Seven	25
Chapter Eight	30
Chapter Nine	36
Chapter Ten	40
Chapter Eleven	45
Chapter Twelve	51
Chapter Thirteen	55
Chapter Fourteen	60
Chapter Fifteen	66

Chapter Sixteen	72
Chapter Seventeen	78
Chapter Eighteen	82
Chapter Nineteen	86
Chapter Twenty	91
Chapter Twenty-One	99
Chapter Twenty-Two	106
Chapter Twenty-Three	111
Chapter Twenty-Four	116
Chapter Twenty-Five	122
Chapter Twenty-Six	127
Chapter Twenty-Seven	132
Chapter Twenty-Eight	139
Chapter Twenty-Nine	143
Chapter Thirty	147
Chapter Thirty-One	153
Chapter Thirty-Two	156
Chapter Thirty-Three	164
Chapter Thirty-Four	171
Chapter Thirty-Five	179
Chapter Thirty-Six	186
Chapter Thirty-Seven	194
Chapter Thirty-Eight	201
Chapter Thirty-Nine	208
Chapter Forty	214
Chapter Forty-One	218
Chapter Forty-Two	224
Chapter Forty-Three	228

Chapter Forty-Four	233
Chapter Forty-Five	240
Chapter Forty-Six	249
Chapter Forty-Seven	256
Chapter Forty-Eight	260
Chapter Forty-Nine	266
Afterword	271
Acknowledgement	273
About The Author	275

*For all of us who have been through some tough times,
it's okay to leave and take time to discover who you are and realize your
dreams.*

*And if your dream is like mine, a 6 foot, bearded cowboy in a pair of
wranglers and boots,
Save A Horse...
(you know the rest)*

"And the girls say
Save a horse, ride a cowboy.
Everybody says
Save a horse, Ride a cowboy.
I'm a thoroughbred
that's what she said
in the back of my truck bed
As I was gettin' buzzed on suds
Out on some back country road.
We where flying high
Fine as wine, having ourselves a big and rich time
And I was going, just about as far as she'd let me go.
But her evaluation
of my cowboy reputation
Had me begging for salvation
all night long
So I took her out giggin frogs
Introduced her to my old bird dog
And sang her every Wilie Nelson song I could think of
And we made love."
BROOKS AND DUNN

Playlist

Turquoise & Silver - Davis Raines
Long Live Cowgirl - Ian Munsick & Cody Johnson
Horses Are Faster - Ian Munsick
Lonely Eyes - Chris Young
Country Boy - Alan Jackson
Baby's Got Her Blue Jeans On - Mel McDaniel
Honky Tonk Badonkadonk - Trace Adkins
Wildflowers and Wild Horses - Lainey Wilson
Save A Horse (Ride A Cowboy) - Big & Rich
In A World Gone Wrong - Zach Top
Springsteen - Eric Church
Come A Little Closer - Dierks Bentley
Slow Hands - Conway Twitty
We're Gonna Hold On - Tammy Wynette & George Jones
God Gave Me You - Blake Shelton
Don't You Wanna Stay - Kelly Clarkson & Jason Aldean
Forever and Ever, Amen - Randy Travis
Mama He's Crazy - The Judds

Chapter One

Colt

The sun beat down on the parched Texas plains, turning the dust into a shimmering haze. As I adjusted my worn Stetson, my eyes scanned the horizon for any sign of trouble, but what I saw instead was her.

Daisy Carter, a city girl turned ranch hand, was off limits. My father, Walt, told his best friend, John, that he would teach his daughter about working hard. It was a long-overdue favor he owed. Daisy had left Garrity Valley right after graduating high school, and other than coming back for my mom's funeral a few years later, she hadn't been back here to Texas. She had never even come to visit her father.

I thought I had heard my dad and her dad talking once and mentioning something about Daisy working, but I didn't know what she did, and I never bothered to ask. Apparently, it wasn't much since she was here to learn about hard work, or at least it wasn't what her dad approved of.

We were friends as kids, but she cut all ties once she moved to the city.

"Daisy, come over here and unlock this gate." I glanced over my shoulder at my father's words. He wasn't even looking at her when he spoke.

Daisy had only been here for two days, and this task seemed to be turning out harder than my dad predicted. He thought it would be easy since he is such a hard ball, but Daisy clearly hates every minute of being here. He wasn't making it any easier on her, and I really couldn't blame him. Her attitude needed a real, hard adjustment.

Daisy wrestled with the stubborn gate, and I couldn't help but let out a small chuckle. It was fun watching her struggle. It was like a little dose of karma coming for her. If I had moved away and asked my dad for help with anything after not even bothering to ever come visit him after all he's done for me growing up, he would have slapped me upside the head or asked, 'You have brain damage, son? Did you fall off your horse?'

Daisy was still struggling, and my father wasn't going to get out of the side by side to help. One thing about my father, he would make you learn the hard way. Like I said, he's a hard ball for sure. Instead, while she struggled with the gate, my father scratched his loyal companion's head. Hank was a beagle whom my mother had given to my father during the last year of her life. Hank flopped down to the side, leaning against the back of the seat of the side by side, kicking one leg involuntarily like he always did, because to him, scratches were just that good.

"Hold on, boy. The pretty lady needs some help." I whispered, putting Shadow's lead around the fence. I walked over to Daisy at the gate, noticing my father looking at me from his comfortable seat on the side by side. I knew he wasn't going to say anything about me helping her, even if he wanted to. He knew I would help him out with teaching her hard work on the ranch this summer, as I promised him I would do, but he also knew I would never be as hard as him. I grabbed the gate, moving Daisy's hands away. With one hard heave, I unlocked the gate and opened it, moving my body to the side so I didn't get in the way. My dad put the side by side in drive, huffing as he went through.

He didn't understand why I wasn't as tough as him. Once, he told me I was like my mother in that way. I always took it as a compliment when anyone said I reminded them of my mother or that I was like her. She was the best. I wanted to help people, but I wanted to do it where there was a mutual sense of respect and understanding, with a little bit of kindness thrown in along the way.

My father wasn't always like this, but since my mother passed away seven years ago, he hasn't been around anyone or gone out like he used to. I think, after all these years, it was still hard for him to process, and he was still hurting. I tried asking him about my mother once, but he acted as if he didn't hear me. My father rarely talked about my mother anymore, but I knew he thought about her. His hardened exterior was just a cover-up for his sadness. It had been hard on me, but I came to terms with the fact that she was gone. However, I still thought about her every day and tried to keep her memory alive in any way I could.

I closed the gate back and walked over to Shadow, untying his lead from the fence. I hopped on the saddle, rubbing his neck as I always do before riding.

"Thanks for the help." I turned to look at Daisy, who was still standing by the gate, only now she had a slightly confused look on her face. I gave her a slight smile and got Shadow into gear.

I enjoyed riding, feeling the wind against my skin, and being able to not worry about anything for a couple of hours. It is something I did daily. My mother used to ride with me, and this was one of those things I did to keep her memory alive. She used to say that horses are the wings we don't have. I thought about that every time I got on a horse. She was right when she said that, and I could feel it any time I was on a horse. Riding a horse felt like soaring through the open air, where every gallop brought a sense of liberation and connection to nature. It was a perfect escape from the world.

My father doesn't ride for fun anymore, but back then, sometimes my mother would talk my father into taking a break and riding along the ranch with us. She could talk him into anything. She was his weakness. My father would go and pick her flowers every time he was out working late. She would also tell him, 'They're beautiful,' and his response was always, 'Yes, Rose, they are, but they could never be as beautiful as you.' I missed seeing my father happy.

Chapter Two

Daisy

I had already completed the grimy chore of cleaning out the stalls. The stench of manure clung to my clothes as I scraped away the muck, wishing I could escape this foul task for good. It was my father's fault I was here and doing dreadful tasks like these.

Now, I was supposed to go open the gate for Walt. I didn't understand why he couldn't ask his son, who wasn't doing anything but getting his horse ready to ride, or better yet, get off the side-by-side he was sitting on and do it himself.

I hated that my father signed me up for this. He knew I was a city girl now. I didn't want this life anymore. Yes, I had grown up on a ranch not far from this one, but I had spent the last seven years trying to forget this place. Growing up so close to here is how my father and Walt met and became friends. I guess you could say the two of them are best friends. They spent a lot of time together as Colt and I grew up, helping each other out on their ranches- my father's being a much smaller one and Walt's Texas Rose Ranch being the vast land that was as far as the eyes could see- and sometimes sharing a beer when all the work was finished. Our mothers were friends, too, and they liked to get together from time to time. Rose was a sweet person, just like my mother, Ivy.

The day of high school graduation couldn't come soon enough for me. I was already packed and ready to get out of here and to the city- somewhere new and different. The change of pace was much needed in my life. Ever since graduating at eighteen, I have been in the city and never looked back. Seven years away from this lifestyle wasn't nearly long enough.

I tried to open the gate. I could tell the chains were older by their faded color, and they were pulled so tightly. I was sweating, embarrassed that I couldn't get the chain loose to open the gate for Walt. I'm sure he is taking delight in this, though. I knew he was a tough one- he had been growing up- but even more so since his wife passed years ago. I remember the funeral. That was the only time I had come back to this place since leaving seven years ago. My father knew what he was doing, putting me under Walt's supervision for the summer. I could only hope that the time passed quickly.

I was still pulling on the impossibly stiff chains, sweat beads forming above my upper lip. I never sweat unless I mean to, like when I'm at the pool during the summer. I closed my eyes for a second, praying that I could just get the chain loose so I could end this embarrassment. It was washing over me like a wave, anxiety tightening its grip as I could feel the eyes of Walt waiting impatiently, making this simple task seem monumental and impossible.

I felt a hand brush against mine, a mix of warmth and discomfort. I moved my hands back, watching the rough, calloused hands undoing the chains and noticing the small scars. I'm sure after years of working on a ranch, you would have plenty of scars and marks on your body from all the strenuous and demanding labor. He made opening the gate look so easy, and I kind of hated him for it. I wondered why Colt was helping me. I wasn't used to that, and we hadn't spoken a word to each other since my father dropped me off here. Walt drove on with his pal by his side once the gate was open, and Colt shut the gate behind him, ensuring nothing was going to get in or out.

I turned around and looked across at the cowboy. I admired the way he swayed in those Wranglers- they fit him in all the right places. He placed his left foot in the stirrup, throwing his right leg over the horse to get on. He had a streak of sweat running down his grey shirt. I wondered how he did what he did every day. He rubbed the neck of his horse with those calloused hands of his. I wondered how many years of hard work those hands had seen on this ranch- probably as long as he could walk. That's what you do as a cowboy, especially here in Texas.

"Thanks for the help." He was sitting up so high on the horse. I hadn't been on a horse since I left Texas, and I wondered for a split second how it would feel again. The only part I ever liked about being here the last couple of years I was here was riding. I felt free. That was the only time I felt free in this place the last little bit I was in Garrity Valley.

The cowboy turned to me, giving me a slight smile. I couldn't help but notice he had some sweat forming above his eyebrows. I would have to admit that he didn't look too bad in a cowboy hat. I watched as the curls at the back of his neck blew in the wind as he rode away.

Chapter Three

Colt

Riding made me feel free. I used it to think of my mother and the times that we would ride together- fond memories- but also to be able to be with my thoughts. I loved the ranch life. I don't think I could see myself doing anything other than this. This has always been the dream.

As I rode across the open field, I could hear hooves creating a rhythmic pattern against the earth, thudding each time they landed against the grass and dirt. The wind whipped through my hair, nearly taking my hat with it a time or two when I gained a high speed. I could faintly smell the flowers - another reminder of my mother. Each gallop gave me a sense of freedom, the endless land giving me a canvas of opportunity.

The sun was no longer warming my back as it was settling. I knew it was getting late, and my dad would have supper ready soon, so I had to get back to the house. As I rode back, I kept thinking about something my mother said to me. "I want you to be happy." I was happy here, but I knew that wasn't what she meant when she said those words.

I put Shadow in his stall when I got back and rubbed his head one last time before I headed to the house. Dinner with my dad and Daisy wasn't something I was looking forward to.

My dad was sitting at the head of the table, with Daisy to his left. I knew my dad hated it when I wasn't on time, and I tried to never be late, but riding Shadow today just got away from me. I also knew that although he wanted me to always be on time, he wouldn't wait for me. I glanced at their plates, noticing there was no food on them yet, so I knew they had just sat down. At least I wasn't that late. By the time I washed up and came back to the table, they had already made themselves a plate and were starting to eat. I sat and started making myself a plate.

"I guess riding was good today?" I glanced up at my dad.

"Yes. It was good. Sorry I was late."

"Oh, you can come eat when you want. Food was hot, and we weren't going to wait until you got here and eat it cold." My dad wasn't always like this. He was a lot nicer when my mother was alive…a lot more lenient, too.

"Walt, these pork chops are very good. What did you season them with?" Daisy winked at me. She kind of saved me there.

"A chef doesn't reveal his secret."

"Well, give my compliments to the chef." We ate the rest of the meal in silence and once finished, my dad cleaned up the dishes then headed to bed. We always got up early and he didn't usually fool with staying up late. I sat on the couch and turned on the TV. Apparently, it was a John Wayne marathon. I wasn't going to complain.

"Do we have to watch this?" Daisy sat down at the other end of the couch.

"Well, you are in our home. I guess you don't have to

watch it. You could always be like my dad and go to bed. I'm sure he has lots of work for you to do tomorrow." She rolled her eyes.

"What's with you?" I took a minute, thinking of what to say.

"What is with me?"

"Um, yes. Did I stutter? Do you have a problem?"

"Do I have a problem?"

"Why are you repeating everything I say?"

"Well, do forgive me. I am trying to understand your questions." I paused for a moment as Daisy twisted herself on the couch, moving one leg up on the couch and under her body while the other hung off the couch. She had some nerve being in our house and talking to me this way. I wouldn't stand for it.

"Well?"

"Well, there isn't anything wrong with me. Not that I can think of anyway. With you, though, I'm sure there's plenty." She huffed, surprised at my words. It didn't feel so good on the receiving end of the snarky comments.

"Excuse me? You can't talk to me like that." It was our family ranch, and she was being so ill-bred. It was only fair she got a taste of her own medicine.

"Go on to bed if you don't want to hear it then, but you started it." She stood there, not saying a word, so I continued. "So, let's see…John, your dad, asked my dad for a favor, which was to keep you here to make you work on the ranch. I keep thinking about why he didn't just take you home to your family's ranch instead of this place, and all I can figure is that he knew you wouldn't listen, and he knew my dad would be tougher on you. That's probably something you need. What else? Oh yeah, that attitude of yours. That's a problem, for sure. What else am I missing? Oh, I can't forget how you seem to complain about work all the time. I mean, you moved off from here to do what?

You don't seem like one who even wants to work, so I'm not sure. Am I missing anything?" Daisy sniffed, and I looked over at her, tears forming in her eyes. Crap. Was that too much? I didn't mean to just go off like that on her. I was just so sick of her stank attitude and I didn't want to live all summer putting up with it. She got up and stood in front of me.

"I guess you covered everything." She started toward the hall, but not before I grabbed her arm.

"Daisy, wait?"

"Wait? What for?" She wiped under her left eye in a quick motion, using her hand.

"I'm sorry."

"Sure, you are." She rolled her eyes, trying to pull away, but I wouldn't budge.

"No, I mean it. I shouldn't have said those things. I've just had a lot on my mind recently, and I know that's not an excuse. You just…I don't understand you. I know my dad is stubborn and tough. I saw that earlier when you were wrestling with that gate. But…I helped you with it…"

"I thanked you for that."

"Yes, you did. It's just…you're staying here in our house. You can't have things your way all the time. I'm not sure about everything, especially not about you. I do know, though, that this attitude of yours won't work with my dad. You may hate it here for whatever reason, but you're going to have to suck it up and do it so you can eventually leave, and things will go back to how they were." I let go of her arm and walked back to the couch. When I sat, I finally heard footsteps walking farther away in the distance.

Chapter Four

Daisy

I couldn't believe the way Colt had spoken to me. Did I have that much of an attitude? I mean, I didn't want to be here anymore than he and Walt wanted me here, but this is what my dad insisted on. What choice did I have? I liked where I was living now. I wasn't happy living here, so I left after graduation. Seven years away from this place, and it seemed like somehow, I always knew that I would be back here at some point.

I think after my mom died when I was sixteen, I just had so many memories of her - memories that haunted me every place I went in this town. I wanted an escape, and the city was that for me. I knew when I left that my dad would stay. I did miss him, but the thought of being here and dealing with all the memories of my mom seemed to outweigh being away for so long. I asked him to visit. He came out once and saw my place and where I worked as a photographer. I went to a community college in the city and studied art. I was always into taking pictures and being creative, so that seemed like the best fit for me. When I found the magazine advertising for a journalist, I knew that would be a good opportunity for me. I have been there for five years now, working as a photographer and having my place. I was proud of that. My dad was so uncomfortable while in the city and looked so out of place that I just knew he wouldn't visit again, and I was right.

I watched Colt walk away, headed for the TV again. I waited for a moment and then walked down the hall to the room I had been staying in. It was decorated in beige and brown, with some black accents here and there, and a few off-whites. I liked the colors. It gave me a good memory. It was what my mom and dad had decorated their place with when they built it. I guess it was just a ranching thing to use those colors.

I shut the door, grabbing some shorts and an oversized t-shirt from a drawer. I slipped out of what I was wearing and changed into those to be more comfortable for the night. I plopped onto the bed, thinking about my past yet again. I thought about how this was not the first time I had been here.

☐ ☐ ☐

My dad and Walt were good friends, and sometimes my dad would bring me and my mom here when he was coming to help Walt out or just spend some time catching up with his buddy. Growing up, I was used to this way of life. It was fun being around the horses and riding through the open fields. Once my mom passed, though, it was hard to find enjoyment in it all.

With two years of high school left, I was dreading every second. My mom had fallen from a horse and hit her head on a rock. It was nearly instant. I remember so many things flashing through my eyes after the accident. My high school graduation, prom, going to college, getting a job, getting married, having kids...and my mom wouldn't be there for any of it. Getting away from Garrity Valley was so much easier than dealing with all the feelings that came when I saw this place. There were too many memories and too much of a painful reminder.

I remember one summer when my dad was coming to help Walt out with some cattle, and he brought my mom and me along.

We wanted to ride horses while the men worked, so Walt let us ride his. I was only eleven then, and Colt was thirteen. Colt's mom, Rose, wanted to go with us. While we were saddling up, Colt kept looking over at us. Rose gave my mom the reins of her horse and whispered, "I'll be right back." My mom and I were each sitting on a horse, waiting to go. I saw Rose pull Walt to the side for a moment, and when she came back over to us, she had Colt with her.

"Ladies, Walt thought it would be a good idea to have a man come along with us - you know, just in case we find ourselves in any trouble or need a little assistance." She winked at us both while Colt ran inside to grab a horse from the stalls. We rode for several hours around the ranch that day and stopped at a stream before heading back to give the horses a little break. Colt and I talked some while our moms talked to each other. Colt and I talked over the years of us coming here, spending lots of time together, and we became the best of friends. He helped his dad once he was old enough to do some manual labor and ranch work. His mom, though, like this time, would sometimes convince Walt to let her steal him away for some fun. That was one of my favorite memories.

☐ ☐ ☐

Chapter Five

Colt

The next day, I did feel bad about what I said to Daisy. I mean, it wasn't like I lied, but I knew it upset her. I could tell by the look on her face, even after I apologized to her, that the words I said stung. My dad had to go into town to pick up some things, and he gave me specific instructions to stay with Daisy and monitor her to make sure she was doing what chores he had her doing.

I watched her shovel out the stalls. She dropped some off the shovel onto her foot. She huffed loudly, and I couldn't help but let out a laugh. She must've heard me because she rolled her eyes. She was so miserable, and I wondered if it was because she just hated this type of work or if it had to do with her past. I knew she and I had both experienced heartbreak, and I wondered if that had something to do with it.

Daisy's mother had passed when she was sixteen. My mom passed when I was twenty. I was grateful for all the time I had with her and all the moments in my life she was there for. I could only imagine what Daisy must've gone through without her mom. She had to graduate without her mom. She moved away to college without her mom. She got a job without her mom. I knew that wouldn't be all. I mean, if she ever found someone willing to put up with that attitude, she would get engaged and later married without her mom. She would have kids without her mom. Her mom would never get to be a grandma. My mom would miss those later things, too, and that was always a hard pill to swallow. That never got easier.

"Do you want a hand?" She kept shoveling, glancing out the corner of her eye at me. "I'm offering to help you…If you want it."

"I would like that." Maybe she was trying to change after our talk last night. We finished cleaning out the stalls, not saying much to each other.

Once we finished, I did the rest of the work I did each day around the ranch while Daisy did her own thing, which was whatever my dad told her she needed to do. I wanted to go for a ride, so I saddled up my horse. I saw Daisy sitting on a step on the porch, using her hand to brush her hair out of her face. I walked over to her.

"Long day?" She huffed.

"What do you think?" That was that ever-so friendly attitude of hers.

"I think it's been a long day for me, too." I waited a moment, then made her an offer. "I was about to go for a ride on my horse, Shadow. It always helps me after a long day. If you want, you can come with. You can ride Domino. He's very calm. The only thing is that you must saddle your horse." She looked up at me, and I could tell she didn't know what to make of my offer.

"Well, I used to saddle my horse all the time. I still remember. It hasn't been that long." She rolled her eyes. "It has been a while since I have rode, though." I saw her face soften.

"I'm not sure."

"Oh, come on. Don't you miss it?"

"Maybe a little."

"Does that mean you'll join me?" She gave me a slight, cocky smile and I gave her my hand to help her up. We walked back to the stalls, and I hopped on Shadow while waiting for her to get Domino ready. I gently brushed Shadow's mane, something he always liked. He huffed and blew it all over Daisy. I couldn't help but laugh. Daisy glared at the two of us, wiping her face.

"Better watch out, Shadow. She can be a mean one." She rolled her eyes again, then turned to Domino. She paused for a moment as if contemplating on whether she should get on or not. Slowly, she put her left leg in the stirrup and threw her right leg over Domino, landing upright on the saddle. There was that strong determination of hers that I remember.

"Ready?"

"Ready."

We set off. I made sure to take things slow at first, knowing it had been years since Daisy had been on a horse. I wanted to ease her back into it.

Riding along the ranch brought me a lot of comfort. I started doing it more frequently after my mother passed. It made the feelings easier to deal with. I didn't have to face them head-on this way, and it took my mind off it all. My dad was sad for a while…I think he still is in a way…and that made it hard to talk to him because I was sad, too, but I didn't want to make him even sadder. Even now, he rarely ever mentioned my mom. Sometimes I wished he would, just so I knew he was thinking about her.

Riding with Daisy felt nice. It was the first time I had ridden horses with someone just for fun since my mother passed. I let that sink as we continued riding.

"You know...it's uh...been a while since I've ridden with someone."

"Yeah...it's been a while for me, too. It's been...years since I've been on a horse."

"You haven't been on one since you left, have you?"

"No." I knew the answer before the word left her lips.

We kept riding in silence, just listening to the sounds of the earth around us and the horse's hooves galloping across the land. I loved the ranch, and I wanted to take it over someday, but I knew my dad wasn't ready to give it up just yet. I liked the open fields, herding cattle, riding horses...all that came with having this much land and a ranch to call home.

Chapter Six

Daisy

Riding with Colt was nice. I admitted to him that it had been years since I last rode with someone... just been riding in general. Ever since I left my family's ranch, I have not been on a horse, and even before then when I was still in high school, I had pretty much stopped because that was something my mother and I did together. With her gone, it just didn't feel the same. I didn't think it ever would.

When we got back, we took off the tack and put the horses up in their stalls. We started for the house, knowing it was about time to eat, and no one wanted to be late when it came to Walt. He was one stubborn, hard-headed old man. My father was much more lenient and soft spoken. I was thankful for growing up with someone like that instead.

"Hey...um...thanks for the invite today." Colt nodded.

"I guess I could keep worse company." I playfully punched his shoulder, and he grabbed his arm as if he were in pain. We both laughed, and I couldn't remember the last time I laughed and enjoyed myself.

We looked up toward the house as we heard voices. My dad was standing beside Walt on the porch. I was surprised to see him, and I was dreading our encounter. I hadn't spoken to him since he dropped me off here. I was still mad at him.

"Are you too grown to give your old man a hug?" I shook my head and hugged him.

"It's good to see you, Colt."

"You too, John." They shook hands. I was glad to still see Colt's manners at play.

"Colt, come inside and help me set the table. John is going to join us tonight." They went inside, and I could tell that my dad wanted to speak to me alone. I was a little afraid of what he would say. This is something I had been dreading since I arrived back in Garrity Valley.

"So, how's it been here?" He propped himself up against the beam on the porch.

"Well, I've seen better times if that's what you mean. Cleaning stalls at 6:30 AM... I did not miss that." He laughed a little.

"You know why I brought you here, though, don't you?" I nodded.

"Yes. I do."

"I just want you to learn some hard work, and there isn't a harder worker than Walt Hogan." Yeah, working hard was part of it.

"He's something alright."

"Listen, since your mother died..."

"Dad, stop."

"No, you need to listen."

"Since your mother died, you've not been yourself. Sure, you graduated from high school, went to college, and got a job. You went to the city for that, and I understand...but you stayed away." He paused for a moment and I knew how much it bothered him that I had never visited, but he never visited me more than the one time either. This all didn't fall on me. "You stayed away from this place...you stayed away from me. I came to the city, which you know isn't me, just to see you. You finally come down here, and you put this whole place down like it's nothing. There are real people here. There's hard work here. I want you to learn what hard work is, since it seems you've forgotten." He didn't just want that, and I knew it.

"So, what I do isn't hard?"

"Daisy, I know you've always liked to write and take photographs...but remember what you wanted to do before everything happened...remember what you used to dream about writing about and taking pictures of...this place and the people here...that is what you always wanted to write and take pictures of. I don't want you to give up on your dream." He paused, walking a few steps on the porch. Yes, that had been my dream once, but couldn't dreams change? "We'd better go inside and eat."

The whole time at dinner, Walt and my dad were catching up. Colt spoke a few times, but I was in no mood to talk to anyone. I was frustrated with my dad. He sent me here to learn what hard work is, and then comes tonight to give me a lecture that I didn't need. I knew what hard work was. I have always known. He was also right that I always wanted to write. I wanted to write about life in the country and living on a ranch. I wanted to write about the real people who lived here. I talked to my mom about that many times. It was my dream...but dreams change. Staying here would have caused me more harm than good. I just wish he could understand that.

"Well, Daisy. I'm headed to the house." He rose from the table and I did the same, giving him a hug. I was still frustrated and mad at him, but I let it go because he was still my dad and I loved him. "I'll see you later, honey."

"Bye, dad."

* * *

I got up and started shoveling out the stalls. That was the first thing Walt instructed me to do each day. I had to get up at 6:30 AM to shovel horse manure. Man, what a way to start the day. Colt occasionally stopped by to help when he wasn't busy with his own work around the ranch. We hardly spoke to each other. I wasn't sure we would get back to being like when we were kids, but I was grateful for his help. I was even more grateful when he helped me with the bales of hay. Those things aren't easy to lift.

"So... I take it you and your day had words last night?"

"Hm?"

"Well, you were outside for a bit before you came in to eat."

"Mhm."

"Do you not want to talk about it?" I paused, remembering my dad's words.

"He doesn't think I have followed my dreams."

"Oh."

"I graduated high school, went to college, and got a job... but that's not good enough apparently." I paused, continuing to lift the bales of hay with Colt's help.

"What is it you do? I've not asked, and you've not really been forthcoming with information."

"I'm a journalist for a magazine." I took in his expression.

"And you enjoy that?"

"Yes, I do. I have always loved writing and taking pictures. You remember, don't you?" He nodded, and I knew his memory served him well. "I studied art at a community college in the city."

"I never did go to college. It just wasn't for me, and I knew that. It's good you knew what you wanted to do, though, and that you enjoy it. Everyone deserves to be happy."

"Well, my dad doesn't see it that way."

"What do you mean?"

"He doesn't think that's my dream."

"Is he right?" Curse this man and all his questions.

"When I first thought about what I wanted to do, I will admit that I thought about going to a community college to study art but then come back here and take pictures and write about the people and life here." I didn't make eye contact, hoping he would stop with the questioning, but he didn't.

"So why didn't you do that?" I paused, remembering when I had left this place and why. Those memories are still hard to process. I think about my mother every day, and I will admit that it is still a little painful. I've heard that time heals all wounds, but I don't think that's true.

"You don't have to tell me...I miss my mother, too." I looked up at him, a little surprised that he decided to share that with me. I mean, we have been talking occasionally and sometimes riding together when we finished work a little earlier in the afternoon, but I didn't know we were to the point of sharing our feelings. For a second, I caught a glimpse of what used to be. "I was twenty." I already knew, but it felt like he wanted to say it out loud.

"Sixteen." I knew he knew how old I was when my mother passed. He was at the funeral.

"It's hard to think about, isn't it? I mean...my dad never talks about her. I know he hasn't forgotten about her, but it would be nice to talk about memories from time to time."

"My dad sometimes talks about my mom. For him, I think he knows it changed us...more me than him."

"Yeah." He paused, taking off his hat and brushing his hair back before placing it back on his head. I watched those short curls in the back roll up toward the brim of his hat. I still liked the cowboy hat on him. It suited him well. "I remember when your mom died." I looked up at him, paying attention to his words. "I was 18 then. I know people say they know how it feels but believe me when I tell you...I do know how it feels." I knew he was right. If anyone knew, it was him. He went through the same thing I did, just a few years apart. We continued working in silence for a few minutes, then Colt spoke again. "Hey...I think we're about done here, and my dad went over to your dad's place for the evening. What do you say we go for a ride?" I nodded. It was becoming my favorite thing about being here.

Chapter Seven

Colt

Once we rode so far, Colt stopped, tying Shadow's lead to a tree. I got off Domino and did the same. Colt sat down, propping himself against the tree. I waited a moment, then sat down beside him.

"You know how my mom died?" I don't know why I asked that, but everything always felt so natural and safe with him.

"I do."

"I haven't ridden a horse since I was sixteen because of it. It was my fault." He turned to face me, placing a hand on my knee.

"It was not your fault. It was an accident."

"I wanted to ride that day. It had been a long day on the ranch, but I didn't care. I wanted to ride anyway. My mom didn't like me going by myself, and my dad had called it for the evening. She told him she was going to go ride with me for about an hour and then we'd be back." She sniffed. "We were riding back, and I told her I wanted to go faster. She was hesitant to do it, especially since it was starting to get dark out. She started to gain a little speed, following behind me, and I heard her scream." Daisy teared up. "I looked back just in time to catch a quick glimpse of a snake on the ground, and Mom's horse freaked. She fell off and hit a rock. I tried to get her to speak to me, but she didn't make a sound... It was instant. I made it back to the house and told my dad what happened. It was the worst day of my life."

I could see the tears starting to fall on her face. I remembered all the tears I shed when my mom passed. I usually did it away from everyone, especially my dad. I knew he was struggling, too, and the last thing I wanted was to make things harder for him. It was easier to feel the pain alone. She turned her head so I couldn't see, but I took my hand that was not on her knee and placed it on her cheek to turn her back to face me. Using my thumb, I wiped away her tears, looking into her eyes the whole time. It was an intimate connection...one that I had never experienced with anyone else.

Daisy had always been special and had taken a place in my heart from the first time I saw her as a two-year old. She had just been born and her parents brought her to visit my parents. My mom said I saw her and held her hand, saying "baby Daisy." I guess I was a goner back then.

"You were still a kid...and accidents happen. It was an accident, Daisy." She leaned over, placing her head on my shoulder. I missed her touch and our time together. It had been lonely since she left. She didn't speak for a few minutes.

"You are a good listener, you know that? You've kind of surprised me."

"Have I surprised you?"

"Well, yes. I haven't been able to talk to you since we were kids before...you know..."

"I know...we had fun as kids, didn't we?"

"Yes, we did." With her head still on my shoulder, we stayed a little while longer until I knew we needed to head back before it got too dark out to ride safely.

When we went in for dinner, my dad had already gone to bed after his long day. I went into the fridge and made Daisy and me both a sandwich while she went to shower. When she got out, we watched a little TV and ate.

"You know, I'm still the same…for the most part."

"The same?"

"As when we were kids. I still like the same things and still like to have fun when I'm not working."

"So riding is what you consider fun?"

"Absolutely. Riding has always been for me."

"It used to be fun for me, too. You know…you've kind of made riding fun again."

"I'm glad to hear that."

"I must ask…do you ever go out? I mean, you've not been out the whole time I've been here. I figured someone like you would be out with the ladies all over him."

"I don't care much for the bar scene, and truthfully, I haven't had much luck with women, so I don't date anymore. After I graduated, I went on a few dates over the years, but none of them worked out or went all that well. I just never made a connection like I wanted. My mom always tried to set me up with someone. I let her a couple of times, but they never worked out either. Once she passed, I took on even more responsibility around the ranch and haven't been on a date since."

"So, you haven't been on a date since you were 20?" He shook his head.

"Not a single one."

"I guess that doesn't make me feel all that bad, then."

"Why is that?"

"You can't judge me for this…" I could tell she was a little hesitant to share.

"This is a judgment-free zone."

"I haven't been on a date."

"Never?" She shook her head, smiling slightly.

"Not unless you count a boy coming over when I was sixteen to sit on the couch with me and both my parents to watch a movie as a date, then never." I laughed.

"How is that possible? And no, that is not a date." I looked at her. Her beautiful brown curls extended past her shoulders. Her eyes were the darkest brown I had ever seen and instantly grabbed my attention. She had the prettiest smile, one that I would do anything to see, even if that meant making myself look like a fool, which I did in the past on more than one occasion.

"I've just been more career driven I guess you'd say. My mom passed that same year, and I was depressed for a while. I stopped riding and stopped wanting to hang out with anyone or do much of anything. I graduated and kept my plan to study art at a community college in the city to expand my horizon…that's what my mom always called it."

"And you graduated, got a job, and never looked back?"

"Yeah, pretty much."

"And no one in the city even looked your way?"

"Well, maybe a couple, but I wasn't interested." I looked at Daisy. Part of me couldn't believe what I was hearing and was really questioning if she was telling me a lie.

"You could've fooled me." I looked back at the TV for a moment. What did I just say to her? She was off limits. My dad told me that when he told me he was going to do this for John. I told him he had nothing to worry about. "I think I'm going to shower and head on to bed. You want me to turn the TV off or leave it on?"

"You can leave it on. I think I'll stay up for a few more minutes anyway." I nodded, then headed to my room.

What did I mean by that comment? What did 'You could've fooled me' even mean? The way I have seen Daisy today has been different. Even the way I have talked to her has been different. I opened up to her about some things- things that I never talk to anyone about - and she did the same. Was this all too much? Daisy is beautiful, I will admit it. Her big, brown eyes and brunette hair that always seems to fall to her face have caught my eye more than a handful of times. She is also off limits. I can't go back on my word…not to my father…can I?

Chapter Eight

Daisy

I was back to the same routine that I had every day of the summer, minus a few days when Walt decided there was something else that I needed to do around the ranch. I was a little distracted by Colt's comment last night. I didn't understand why he said I could've fooled him. I told the truth. I had never been out on a date. Even after I finished what chores I had to do around the ranch, I made sure to find something else to do to occupy my mind so I wouldn't think about Colt. Our conversation had left me a bit confused.

I saw Colt around the ranch a few times throughout the day. I wasn't sure what to say to him, but I figured I'd just let him lead. He had been all over the ranch today, and I knew he had to see me when he walked from the fence where he had the cows to the house. He didn't speak, though. He didn't even look up at me. I brushed it off, assuming he was probably just busy or tired. When he came into the barn, though- where I was rubbing Domino's head- I knew there was no way he would see me. He was purposefully ignoring me, and I didn't know why. Did I say something wrong last night? I mean, I don't think I did. I scooted over in front of him when he turned to walk out.

"Can you move?"

"Can I move?"

"Yes. I need to get this back to my dad. We're moving the cattle."

"Oh…uh, yeah." I moved back over toward Domino's stall.

"Thanks. I'll be back to saddle up Shadow. I'm going to need him to help with the cattle." He nodded his head up in the way that men do. I looked back at Domino.

"That was weird to you, too, wasn't it?" Now I'm talking to a horse. I brushed my hand against Domino's nose.

When Colt got back in the barn, I wanted to ask him what was wrong, but I didn't know what to say, especially if he was mad at me for something. Saying the wrong thing could make things worse. "Colt?"

"I don't have time to talk right now, Daisy. I have to get Shadow saddled up so I can get out to the pasture to help my dad." I walked away and went into the house for something to drink instead. I knew how Walt could be, so maybe Colt was in a bad mood because he had spent the whole day right alongside his dad. That was a lot easier on me than my brain tossing and turning over the thought that I had something to do with Colt's strange behavior today. Still, it reminded me of a time when we were younger, and I was 14 and he was 16.

◻ ◻ ◻

"Colt, what is wrong with you?"

"Daisy, nothing's wrong, okay? I'm just busy."

"You keep saying that, but you can't always be busy. I thought we were friends."

"We are friends!" I flinched, realizing that he was yelling at me. Did I upset him? Did my being here bother him that much? Were we not friends anymore? What did I do that was so terrible? "Daisy, I'm sorry for yelling."

"No, you're not, and if my being here bothers you so bad, you don't have to worry about that anymore. I'll tell my mom that I don't feel good and want to go home. I'll be out of here soon." I turned and started walking toward the house where our mothers were.

"Daisy..."

"What, Colt?" I turned back toward him.

"I am sorry." I nodded, acknowledging his words but still unsure if I believed him.

"Why have you been avoiding me? And I want the truth this time." Colt was avoiding eye contact with me, his eyes fixed on the ground.

"I said something last time you were here that I shouldn't have."

"Oh?"

"Yeah...last week when you were here...I told you that it would be nice if sometimes it were just the two of us..."

"Well, Colt, it would be nice." He looked up at me.

"Really?"

"Well, yeah." I walked closer to him. "I'd like to be able to just be around my friend without anyone else around. I can talk to you about anything, Colt, and it would be nice to share things with you without having to worry about anyone else hearing. You're my best friend. I wouldn't want anything to mess that up."

"Yeah...I wouldn't want that either."

□ □ □

I knew if I had spoken another word to Colt in the barn that it would not have ended well. I wasn't the type of woman to let any man run right over me. My dad was the only one I would ever listen to, and I hadn't spoken to Colt since before my mother died. It's not like we stayed in touch after I graduated and moved, and I wouldn't call us friends now. I wasn't going to let him just talk to me any way he wanted. He did have work to do, and I wasn't going to interfere with that, but I made up my mind that I was going to confront him about this later.

I waited on the porch for a bit, taking sips of my water and looking out into the pasture where Walt and Colt were finishing up. I told Domino earlier that I would brush him, and I was going to keep my word. I went into the barn and grabbed the brush before opening his stall. He was so calm and gentle. He reminded me of my old horse.

Colt came in with Shadow, following Walt and Titan.

"Daisy, can you put Titan up for me?" I nodded.

"Yes, of course." I put Titan up, sneaking a look at Colt. I took the brush and started brushing Titan. I'm sure he would enjoy it after a long day with the cattle. I debated on what to say to Colt. He was still inside, and I turned to see him rubbing Shadow's neck. I wondered how his calloused hands felt. With each stroke, it was like witnessing a dance of strength and gentleness, revealing the deep bond he shared with his horse. It was like a silent language only they understood. I wondered how much Shadow understood about Colt. Did he know why Colt was being distant with me today? If only animals could talk, I might have my answer. I lingered for a moment more and hung up the brush, ready to go shower and eat.

"Hey, Daisy." I turned as Colt was scratching his head, pushing hair back out of his face, and readjusting his worn Stetson.

"Hm?"

"My dad said he's going over to your dads' for a drink. He'll probably be out a little later than usual."

"Oh. Okay. I can make us something to eat if you want." Was that all Colt had to say?

"Do you…I mean…if you want…would you want to go out? I mean, we could go to the bar in town and get some food there?" I smiled, realizing what Colt was trying, yet struggling so badly, to do. It had been a while for him, and for me, it had never happened. I walked closer to where he was standing, leaning against the stall.

"Colt Hogan, are you asking me on a date?" He looked up at me.

"Yeah, I guess I am. Unless you don't want to call it that, then it is two old friends getting reacquainted."

"Give me enough time to shower and I'll be ready. " I turned toward the house. "You had better clean up, too. You stink." He nervously laughed, and I left him standing there while I went inside.

I was a little shocked. I didn't want to be here in the first place, and I didn't expect to rekindle any kind of friendship with Colt. I was surprised by both of those, but this, however, topped it all. Colt Hogan asked me out. I always thought he was cute when we were kids, but we were friends, and our parents were friends…I never let anything become of it, and I sure as heck didn't ever tell him. Some things are better left unsaid.

I showered and then came the hardest part- picking out an outfit. I didn't have a lot to choose from that would fit the bar crowd, but I did have one little number that I had picked up not long before I left the city. I slipped on some tights and a tight, black dress. I added short, black boots, a thin, cream-colored sweater with black western designs all over it that I had for years and couldn't bring myself to ever get rid of, and a pair of silver earrings my mother had given me for the last birthday of mine she was here for. I looked in the mirror, wondering if it was all too much. Should I change? I didn't have a clue. I had never been on a date. I had gone out to bars and clubs in the city, but I never really danced or went out with anyone. I just liked to feel included sometimes. I walked out into the hall after hearing footsteps. Was I really doing this? Why did I agree to this? I was so nervous.

"Colt?"

"Yeah?" I looked out the door as I caught a glimpse of him taking a seat at the table, clearly ready to go and waiting for me. He had on a pair of Wranglers, the ones that fit him in all the right places. Oh, that man sure fills out a pair of Wranglers to perfection. He was wearing his boots, of course. I wouldn't expect anything less. He also had a blue and brown Aztec-designed pearl snap. I loved a man who wore those. He topped it all off with a brown jacket.

"Why are you just sticking your head out the door like that? Are you ready?"

"I don't know."

"What do you mean you don't know?"

"I think maybe I should change."

"Let me see."

Chapter Nine

Colt

She walked out of the room and stood in the hallway. I leaned back in my chair, taking her all in.

"It's not right, is it?" She looked down at her dress, fidgeting with it. "I should go change into something else, shouldn't I?" I shook my head no, trying to find the words to describe how good she looked in that dress.

"Well, darlin', you look like a breath of fresh air on a hot summer day." She stopped fidgeting to look up at me. "Are you ready?"

"I guess I am." She smiled, and I felt a feeling I hadn't felt since a teenager.

I opened the door for her, following behind her as we walked out to my truck. I opened that door, taking in how the black dress was hugging her just right. When we got to the bar, I opened the door for her and took the lead to find us a booth to sit at.

"You can wait here while I go grab us a couple of beers." I came back with one in each hand, giving her one of them. "Have you decided what you want to eat?"

"What do you usually get?" I let out a small laugh.

"I'm a cowboy in Texas. Burger or steak is my thing." She nodded.

"I'll take a burger and fries then." When the waiter came over to us, I ordered each of us the same.

"So...what made you ask me to come here with you tonight? I didn't expect it."

"No, I guess not."

"I mean, you were pretty closed off today. You barely looked my way and hardly spoke a word." I rubbed the back of my neck. She was right. I had been a jerk today, but only because I was trying to figure out how to ask someone out after it had been so long for me. That, and the fact that I was struggling between my feelings and my promise to my dad.

"I know, and I'm sorry. I shouldn't have done that." I regretted doing that to her. She didn't deserve that.

"Did that have anything to do with the comment you made last night?" She was a lot smarter than I first gave her credit for. "You said I could've fooled you..."

"I did say that, and yeah...I felt awkward after I said it. I meant for that comment to stay in my head, but it just slipped out."

"What did you mean by it?"

"You're beautiful, darlin', and it just caught me by surprise when you said you've never actually been on a date...not a real one at least, because watching a movie with someone of the opposite sex with your parents is not a real date." She tilted her head back slightly, laughing.

"Thank you." The waiter brought over our food. We ate,

talking a little in between bites. We mostly talked about the ranch and horses, reminiscing some about when we were kids and spending time together then. We talked about our parents, too, including both the good memories and the bad.

"Well, how was it?"

"Good. Do you come here often?"

"I come here from time to time to just get out, usually if my dad is gone or over at your dad's ranch." She nodded, acknowledging my response. "Have you been here before? I know you moved right after high school graduation, and you've only been here to Garrity Valley one time since…"

"First time." We sat there for a few more minutes to finish up our second round of beers. They started playing music again, and a few couples were on the dance floor. As the lively chatter and clinking of glasses filled the air, I could make out the music that was playing. *Slow Hands* by Conway Twitty, the OG panty dropper, had the kind of music that was hard to pass up. I was a sucker for 90s country.

"You want to dance, darlin'?" I offered my hand to Daisy. She nodded, taking my hand. I could feel the heat between us, and I was uncertain how the night would end, but I knew that I wasn't going to pass up an opportunity to dance with her- right here, right now.

I led her onto the floor, in between the other couples. As we swayed together, I could feel the warmth of the room, wrapping around us like a comfortable blanket. Her hands were placed over my shoulders like they belonged there. My hands found their place at her waist, and I could almost feel the steady beat of her heart matching the rhythm of the song.

Daisy was looking around at the other couples, then her eyes met mine. I stared into those big, brown eyes- the ones that as a kid didn't mean anything, but now, I wasn't sure. Now, it felt like they were ones I could pick out of any room. In this crowded bar, it felt like we were the only two people in the universe, lost in our little world.

I didn't know how Daisy was feeling. I wondered if this was too much for her. I wondered if this was only a friendship… if she wanted things to go further…all I could do is take a chance. My dad always told me if you didn't take a chance, you wouldn't know what could happen, and this was my chance.

I wrapped my arms a little firmer around her waist and pulled her in tighter. She jerked ever so slightly with my pull, and that's when I did it. My heart was racing, filled with anticipation. I smiled at her and she returned it. I threw caution to the wind and gave it a chance. I tilted her chin, my gaze searching hers for permission. I felt a rush of heat as I leaned in, our lips finally meeting in a soft, tentative kiss. Time seemed to stand still as we melted into each other. There was no one else, only us, even amidst the laughter and music at the bar, which had changed since we first started dancing.

Chapter Ten

Daisy

The dim lights of the bar were casting a warm glow around us and the other couples on the dance floor. The boots lightly tapped against the wooden floor as we swayed to the music. The atmosphere was intimate and magical. The music played softly, and I recognized the soothing voice of Conway Twitty that my parents loved and would always listen to. They danced in the kitchen to this song and others by him plenty of times throughout my childhood. It was a sweet coincidence that this was the song that Colt and I were dancing to. I could hardly believe it.

The intensity grew more and more, and I could feel the heat between us. His eyes were still locked on mine, and I couldn't help but wonder if he was going to kiss me. Maybe he wasn't sure if I wanted him to. We had just been getting to know each other again, and maybe he was afraid this would mess that up...maybe complicate things. Would it? Would a kiss between us screw up the whole summer? If my dad found out about this, what would he think? Better yet, what would he say? What about Walt? He was never one to be afraid to share what was on his mind. What would he say to Colt and me? I could only imagine how terrifying he could be when angry. And what would my mom say or think if she were here? I never wanted to disappoint her. I wish she were here so I could have talked to her about this stuff before it all happened. Maybe then I would know if this was right...if this was the right moment...if this was the right man...if this would be one, big mistake or not...if I would live to regret it all...But she wasn't here, and I had to make a decision all on my own...yet again.

I took a deep breath. I knew it. I knew what I wanted, and what I wanted was for Colt to kiss me. I wanted to feel what his lips would feel like on mine. This date was so nice, even if this was my only date and I didn't have another one to compare it to, and this dance was perfect. I could feel his hands move, and a rush of nerves and excitement ran through me. Was this it? Was this what I was missing out on? His eyes sparkled with tenderness, and his grin showed a hint of mischief, and that was when it happened.

Our lips touched, and everything else disappeared. His lips felt soft against mine while his taste was sweet. I had no idea what it would feel like to be kissed...until now. Could a kiss taste sweet? Apparently so. A perfect mix of warmth and familiarity flowed through me while our electrifying connection held strong. I felt like my heart was going to beat out of my chest with the way it was pounding. For a split second, I wondered if it was loud enough where Colt could hear. I was overcome with so many emotions all at once- joy, surprise, disbelief. I was almost ashamed to say that this was my first kiss. What 25-year-old hasn't been kissed before? It was a little embarrassing. I had imagined this moment, playing so many scenes repeatedly in my head, but experiencing this was something entirely different. It was more than I ever could have imagined.

Colt pulled back, his eyes never losing the intense gaze they held on mine. I could feel my cheeks flush, and I couldn't help but smile. He smiled back at me, with his crooked grin revealing a playful charm that made my heart skip a beat. The kiss lingered on my mind, filling me with a sense of giddiness that made me feel so alive, as if I were a teenager. I knew this moment would always stay with me, and I wondered if this could change things between Colt and me forever. Would our relationship be permanently transformed from this moment? From this one kiss?

I had a crush on Colt when I was a kid, yet I never told him. We were such good friends back then, and I never wanted to mess with that, especially seeing how happy it made my mom when she got to see her friend, Rose, and how happy they both were seeing that Colt and I had a friend in each other. He and I stayed friends until my mom died, and after that, I closed out everyone. I still spoke to my dad, but our relationship never seemed the same. When I came to Colt's mom's funeral, I didn't speak but a word or two to him. Only a few years before, it had been me standing up there, and no one knew what to say. I watched as people came through to pay their respects, some hugging me and my father, and some offering their condolences of I'm so sorry for your loss and we will be praying for you.

Colt was the cowboy I had grown up with and who had always made me laugh. He was the one I could always be myself around back then. Now, though, I was seeing Colt differently.

I saw his hair with the perfect curls- the ones that curled toward the brim of his worn-out Stetson in the back, especially after the sweat of a long day's work. That was one of my favorite things about Colt. I saw his brown eyes and the intensity within them- sparkling lightly from the glow of the bar lights. His eyes were something you would notice almost immediately about him. But I saw some other things, too. I saw a scar near his jawline, rugged like the ones I noticed on his hands after only a couple of days on his ranch. While we were still consumed by each other's gaze, I placed a hand on his cheek, rubbing the scar gently with my thumb. I wondered how he got that.

"Are you ready to go?" I nodded at him, unable to control

my smile. He let one hand fall down my side, grazing me gently, and took my hand in his. He squeezed a little as we walked outside the bar and made our way over to his truck. I got to see his truck a few times before everything became a big, sad blur. I went with him a time or two for a drive in it. When we stopped at the truck, I glanced at our hands still intertwined and saw a run in my tights. It was so embarrassing, and I placed one hand on them, but he moved it to the side.

"Colt…"

"Yes?"

"I have a run in my tights. Can we go?" He looked down, and I wondered if he even knew what I was talking about. He cocked his head to one side, almost as if he were examining it.

"Looks like a stairway to heaven to me." I playfully punched his shoulder. I was shocked by his words, but they ran off his tongue so well. I turned and reached for the door handle, but my efforts were stopped by those same calloused hands.

"Hm?" I turned around to look at him, leaning my back against the weathered, old truck, feeling the cool metal pressing against my back, a nice welcome after the heat of the day. I put one hand against the truck, feeling the faded blue paint that had seen better days. I slid my hand down until it met my waist, and I could feel the rust spots and dents- telling stories of countless adventures we had shared. My other hand was still clinging to his hand. He hadn't let go since we were inside.

"I'll get the door for you, darlin', but first…"

With one hand still holding onto mine, he raised his other arm above his head, resting it casually on the roof of the truck in one swift motion. He was several inches taller than I, and his height was perfect to look down on me. He leaned closer to me, his smile infectious. The closeness sent a flutter through my chest, and I could feel the intensity between us. His playful gaze met mine, and the world had once again faded away. I could smell his cologne-a warm, woody tone. I could only smile back at him, my mind at a loss for words as I held on to this feeling of connection to him that made my heart beat faster.

Our quiet moment was up, though, when he released my hand from his. In a swift, tender motion, he cupped my face with his hand, his other arm still resting above his head on the roof of the truck. Was he about to do what I think? This evening was turning out to be so much more than I ever could have anticipated. He tilted my head slightly upward, glancing from my eyes to my lips as if he was taking it all in, contemplating whether to let go again. I wanted him to just kiss me already, and that's when he did. He pressed his lips against mine. The kiss was gentle at first, like a sweet brush. I could feel butterflies in my stomach and sparks between us. I felt like I was melting into him, and I could feel the world around us dissolve even further as Colt deepened the kiss. We were two people in the middle of a parking lot, leaning against a truck, and it felt like there was no one or nothing around. It felt like he was pouring all of the affection he had into this moment. It was a kiss that spoke of promises and laughter, a perfect blend of comfort and excitement that left me breathless yet again. I knew this would be another one that I wouldn't forget.

Chapter Eleven

Colt

As we approached the old truck, the sun hung low in the sky, casting a warm glow that made everything feel right. I admired how those tights fit her and how the dress she was wearing hugged her in all the right places. Daisy placed a hand quickly on her thigh.

"Colt…"

"Yes?" She was a little shaky and seemed nervous. I hoped she wasn't regretting this.

"I have a run in my tights. Can we go?" I moved her hand from her thigh while holding her other, and I noticed the small, broken threads in her tights. I didn't see why she was so worried about it, but it was cute. I cocked my head to one side, saying the first thing that popped into my mind.

"Looks like a stairway to heaven to me." I stopped her efforts to open the door.

"Hm?" She turned to look at me.

"I'll get the door for you, darlin', but first..."

I took my free arm and rested it above my head against the roof of my truck, peering down into her eyes as I did so. I saw how she had her back leaning against the door, smiling at me. I felt a rush of affection, and I could feel my heart light up. I could smell her perfume, a floral tone that reminded me of the scent my mom used to wear, mixed with the earthy aroma of the truck, creating an atmosphere that felt like peace and belonging.

In that moment, I couldn't resist any longer. I had the strongest need to close the distance between Daisy and me. I released her hand from mine and gently cupped her face in my hand, tilting her chin up so her eyes were locked even fuller on mine. With a soft smile, I leaned in and pressed my lips against hers. I kissed her tenderly, wanting to bask in her and savor this moment as long as I could. My heart raced with each second that passed, and once I drew the kiss deeper, I could feel my entire body let go. I felt her hands curl around my waist, and one hand gripped the back of my shirt, sending shivers down my spine. At this point, there was no bar, no people, no music...only us. The moment was perfect. I just hoped it stayed that way.

I pulled back to gaze into her eyes once more, admiring how her eyes sparkled in the glow of the outside lights from the bar.

"What was that for?" She was barely above a whisper, still coming down from the aftershock of the kiss and wanted embrace.

"For being you." I grinned at her, remembering all the time as kids that I stole glances at her, admiring her beauty. That girl who made me laugh was all grown up now, and her beauty was redefined. Her cheeks flushed with a rosy hue now that made my heart swell.

Just then, I heard the noise of laughter, and we both turned our heads toward the bar to see a couple coming out, arms interlocked, swaying back and forth as they made their way to their car. I brushed it off, though, and turned back to Daisy.

"Now, are you ready to go?" She nodded, and I opened the door, closing it only after I made sure her legs and arms were tucked away safely inside the truck.

I held her hand on the drive, both of us stealing glances at the other, and this drive reminded me of when I first took Daisy for a drive in this truck. We were 17 and 15- the year I got this truck- and I wanted so desperately to tell Daisy how I felt back then. This felt like a second chance, a chance to make up for being too petrified as a kid to share my feelings.

□ □ □

At 17, I had saved up my money from birthdays over the years and from doing some odd jobs here and there to fix up my grandpa's old truck. I bought new tires for it and got the truck all cleaned up. It did have little, rough spots here and there from the usual wear over the years and from sitting for so long, but it was special to me. I had always dreamed about the day I got my license to drive it, and that day had finally come.

Daisy and her parents were over at the ranch, and I was so excited to show her the truck. As soon as she arrived, I yelled at her to come over to where I was.

"Hey, Colt."

"Hey. I wanted you to see the truck."

"You got it cleaned up pretty good."

"Yeah. Got new tires for it, too."

"Well, it looks sharp." She walked around the truck, looking at it all over. *"You did well."*

"Thanks."

"Well, cowboy, are you going to take me for a drive? What's the use of having a license if you aren't going to take it for a little joy ride?"

"Get in. I'll be right back. I'm just going to let my mom know." I ran inside to tell my mom, who was cooking dinner with Daisy's mom, Ivy, her smile big as she knew I was so excited about being able to drive the truck. I had driven it a few times around the ranch throughout the past few months after getting my permit, but now it was legal.

I started the truck, listening to it rumble. I put it in drive and drove it down the gravel road, listening to the sounds as the tires went across. The windows were down, the sun hanging low, and Daisy's hair was blowing in the wind. She stuck her head out the window, and I couldn't help but feel something in my chest. It was this tight feeling, like something was pressing down. I had pressed that same feeling down for years.

"Does this thing play music?" She turned the radio on and instantly recognized that the song playing was Beat This Summer by Brad Paisley. We blasted it, singing off-key and carefree, the world outside fading away.

I stole glances at Daisy, happy that she was with me and that we were sharing this time. I saw how her eyes glowed with the setting sun and how she had the biggest smile on her face. She was full of pure happiness my favorite look on her- and so was I. In this moment, nothing else mattered- just two kids in an old truck, chasing the horizon and living for laughter, fun, and adventure. I never wanted it to end.

"Daisy…" This was it. I was going to tell her how I felt. This had been years in the making, and this moment felt right. I just had to muster up enough courage to get the words out. I could do it.

"Hm?" She turned to face me again, and I slowed the truck at the stop sign, getting ready to turn around so we could head back to the ranch for dinner.

"Thanks for coming with me for the ride." The words were right there on the tip of my tongue, but that's as far as they were going. "You aren't too bad of company, Miss McClain." She smiled.

"Ah, you aren't too bad yourself, cowboy." *Why didn't I tell her? I had no way of knowing how much I would regret not telling her for all the years to come.*

"Well, let's head on back. Dinner's probably about ready."

"Good. I'm starving."

◻ ◻ ◻

When we got back, I knew my dad had already called it a night and was in bed, knowing the mornings always came early around here. I brushed a hand against Daisy's knee to let her know to hang tight while I got out of the truck to open her door. My dad taught me at a young age that although a woman could open her own door, she should never have to.

"Thanks." She started heading for the house, and I couldn't help but look at her from behind. I grabbed her arm, pushing her back against the truck. I slightly licked my lips, in awe that this whole night was real and that someone as amazing as Daisy was standing in front of me.

"You know..." I pulled her behind me, leading her to the back of the truck. I couldn't let her go in just yet-not when I wasn't quite finished and the primal urge was still inside me, not ready to be tamed. I let the tailgate down. I put my hands under Daisy's thighs and somehow they felt like a perfect fit. I placed myself between her legs, looking at those mesmerizing eyes of hers. "This dress hugs you just right, and those eyes shine brighter than the stars." My hands remained on her thighs while I planted another kiss on her, but this time on her neck. I knew what I was doing to her, and I was feeling the same. "You've got a way of making this ol' cowboy feel like the luckiest man in the world right now." I smiled mischievously. I moved a hand behind her head and pulled her in as close to me as I could, trying to soak up every ounce of her.

"Colt..." I could barely make out my name coming from her lips.

"Shh…" I continued kissing her.

"Colt…" I tried to ignore her again, but with my hands on each side of her face, I paused for a moment, looking into her eyes. "You've got to give me a chance to catch my breath or I'm not going to make it." I was making things so much more complicated by doing what I was doing, so I pulled back. Although, I couldn't help but smile with a pleased grin. I helped Daisy off the tailgate and shut it.

"Come on. Let's get you inside to bed." I led Daisy inside, my hand pressed gently against the small of her back.

Chapter Twelve

Daisy

This night had been unforgettable. Dinner was great, just getting to talk to Colt again like when we were kids. Slow dancing to the same song that my parents used to dance to in the kitchen all those years ago made me feel so close to my mom at that moment. And that kiss...well, more than one kiss, but still, they were more than I ever could have imagined or thought of. There were so many feelings I felt tonight that I hadn't in a very long time, and I had Colt to thank for that.

This wasn't the first time I had been in Colt's truck, but this was the first time that it had felt different sitting in the seat beside him, feeling the wind coming in from the window in my hair. This didn't just feel like two friends killing time and having fun with each other. This felt like more, and I was eager to see where it was going.

Most of the time, as kids, we rode horses together, but Colt occasionally took me on drives once he got his license, up until my mom died. After that, I rarely got out and didn't feel up to being around Colt or having any fun. He was so excited to finally get his license, and he loved to tell me that he could teach me to drive if I wanted. My dad had been teaching me, but I let Colt take me out a few times just because I knew he was proud of himself, and I could tell how much he wanted to. The last time we rode together in this truck was a couple of weeks before my mom passed and the heartbreak hit. I had just turned 16 and Colt was 18, almost a high school graduate. Even with the slight age gap, we still loved being in each other's company, and he was still my best friend. As a kid, I thought we would always be inseparable…but people grow up and things change.

□ □ □

"Where are we going?"

"Just wait. I know the perfect spot." *Colt drove for what seemed like forever, probably because I was so curious to know where he was taking me. He had said that it was a surprise, and as much as I enjoyed a good surprise, the anticipation was killing me.*

"Are we there yet?"

"So impatient…but yes, we're here. Stay here. Give me a minute."

I sat in the passenger seat once Colt stopped the truck and got out in a rush, waiting for him to tell me I was good to get out. The music on the radio was playing quietly, a pleasant background to the sounds of nature around us. Colt had driven us to a spot off the side of the mountain, telling me I would love it, although I wasn't sure what 'it' was.

"Come on out." *I walked to the back of the truck, and Colt had let the tailgate down and added a blanket to the bottom of the bed inside.*

"What's this?" *He plopped down on the blanket, patting it to tell me to sit down. I hopped up, sitting beside him, feeling the cool breeze against my skin. I rubbed my arms, trying to warm them a bit.*

"Here." *Colt threw a blanket around me and I took it graciously.*

"Thanks." *I wondered why he had chosen to bring me here. It felt different being at this spot with him. This seemed like such a special place, and I wasn't sure why I was special enough to be here, but I was thankful that I was who he thought of bringing along.*

"Look." He pointed toward the sky, and I turned my head in that direction.

The overlook was the perfect spot. I looked at the sky, ablaze with different colors. The pinks, purples, and oranges swirled together like a painting. It was breathtaking. At that moment, I thought this kind of view could only be seen from the country. There was no way something could look this beautiful in the city. I couldn't take my eyes off it. We sat in the bed of his truck, listening to the sounds of the crickets and other critters around us as we watched the sunset. It was another one of those times that I spent with Colt and never wanted it to end.

"This is the most beautiful thing I have ever seen."

"Yes. It is."

☐ ☐ ☐

When we got back and pulled up to the ranch, there weren't any lights on in the house, and I knew Walt had already gone to bed for the night. Colt brushed his hand against my knee and got out of the truck. I waited a moment, my eyes following him through the windshield as he walked over to the passenger side of the truck to open my door. He was such a gentleman. I guess he was a gentleman as a kid, too, always opening my door and letting me go in front of him. His parents raised him right, and I could only imagine how proud his mother would be of him.

"Thanks." I got out and was going to head for the house when that same rough hand grabbed my arm, pushing me back against the truck. He looked at me, slightly licking his lips.

"You know…" He pulled me behind him, leading me to the back of the truck. He let the tailgate down, picking me up with his hands under my thighs and placing me on it. He scooted in closer to me, placing himself between my legs. "This dress hugs you just right, and those eyes shine brighter than the stars." I could feel his hands placed firmly on my thighs. His calloused hands were rough from years of wrangling cattle and riding horses, but they felt like a warm promise against my skin, a testament to the strength and tenderness that lay beneath Colt's rugged exterior. He placed a kiss on my neck, the feel of his lips slightly tickling me, and giving me a tingling sensation that ran down my body. "You've got a way of making this ol' cowboy feel like the luckiest man in the world right now." He smiled mischievously, then moved one hand behind my head. He pulled me so close to him that we felt like one, like he was trying to devour me.

"Colt..." I let out a breathy whisper of his name.

"Shh..." He continued kissing me, each kiss making me lose myself further and further until I thought there would be no escape. This whole night had been so unexpected, but if this was any sign of what was to come, I would gladly welcome it.

"Colt..." I tried to catch my breath while his lips moved to my neck again, the feeling sucking me in and making me never want it to end. It sent shivers down my body, and I wanted his lips to linger there. Both his hands were now gripping both sides of my face. He looked up at me. "You've got to give me a chance to catch my breath or I'm not going to make it." He pulled back, still smiling with that self-satisfied grin, finally letting me breathe. He reached for me, helping me get down, and shutting the tailgate behind us.

"Come on. Let's get you inside to bed." He placed a hand behind me on the small of my back, following me inside.

Chapter Thirteen

Colt

I closed the door softly behind me, not wanting to wake my dad. I wasn't ready to deal with any of that right now. The only thing interrupting the peace and quiet of the house was the soft touches of her shoes against the floor. I stopped at Daisy's bedroom door, taking a deep breath in and wrapping my arms around her in a tight hug. I could feel her warmth, and the last thing I wanted was to leave her, but I knew I had to. I had to figure out what to do now, remembering what I had said to my dad before she came here. I pushed that thought to the side for the moment, keeping the smile on my face. I looked down at her, kissing her on the forehead.

"Goodnight, Daisy."

"Goodnight, cowboy." She had the tip of her thumb in her mouth, flirting with me, and smiling back. I had missed her calling me that. She always did when we were younger, and it was always my favorite nickname. It sounded even sweeter coming from her lips.

I made my way to the bathroom, making sure the door

didn't make a sound and turning on the shower. The sound of the water hitting the tiles reminded me of the rhythm of the horse's hooves against the earth. The steam began to rise, filling the small space. I stepped under the water flowing down and let it hit my face. I brushed my hair back out of my eyes, using both hands to do so. I had taken a shower before heading out with Daisy this evening, but taking a nice, hot shower was what I needed right now.

Once I finished, I wrapped a towel around my waist and stared into the mirror, my hands pressed against the sink. My mind was still spinning from the bar and all the little moments Daisy and I shared tonight. I thought about the way her eyes glowed in the bar lights, the way her laugh was infectious, and the way her smile nearly made me melt. I also thought about her body and how that dress she wore tonight was heavenly, how her lips tasted, and how her body seemed to fit perfectly wrapped up in mine. I could still smell her perfume and taste her sweetness, mixed with the warmth of her breath against my skin. When we touched, it was like something had been missing all my life, and I had finally found it.

The promise I made to my dad, though, was still in my mind, a weight I couldn't shake off. He told me Daisy was off limits before she came here, and I was okay with that. I told him he had nothing to worry about. I hadn't been on a date in a long time, so I wasn't concerned. Besides, Daisy and I had been friends years ago, but we hadn't spoken to each other in so long. I didn't expect anything to happen. Boy, was I wrong. I swore I wouldn't touch her or let things become anything more than her spending the summer here to learn hard work, per her dad's request. I made the promise out of respect, and yet every time I closed my eyes, I could see Daisy.

I couldn't help but wonder what she looked like lying in bed in the room just across the hall. I wondered what she was wearing, if she snored, if she was a heavy sleeper or not...I wondered if I could hold on to the promise I made. The night had been electric and captivating, and I felt a pull toward Daisy that was so hard to resist. Deep down, I knew I would have to stay true to my word, keeping my feelings hidden deep inside, a familiar feeling for me from years gone by. I would have to do it, but hurting Daisy was the last thing I thought I would ever do.

Lying in bed, my mind wandered to what the woman in the room across from me was thinking, and how times used to be with us.

□ □ □

I could hear her laughter, a constant state for us. It always brought a smile to my face hearing her laugh. We spent so many afternoons chasing each other, playing hide and seek. She was ten and I was twelve one summer, playing out toward the barn.

"Come on, slowpoke!" I ran after Daisy, almost running over her when I finally caught up.

"Okay. Now what?" Daisy pointed to a tree.

"I dare you to climb the highest branch of that oak."

"I don't know, Daisy." I looked up, seeing how tall the tree was. "It looks pretty high. I don't think that would be safe."

"Safe? Colt, when did you ever skip out on something because it wasn't safe?" She was right, but that still didn't take away my fear and hesitation. Out of the two of us, though, she was the daredevil.

I looked at her- those big, brown eyes glowing in the sunlight, sparking with mischief- and I couldn't back down. I couldn't let her down. Not this girl. I wedged my foot between a forked spot in the tree, using a branch to pull myself up. I climbed higher than I ever thought I could, and when I reached the top, I looked down and for a moment thought I saw an angel. Daisy was there, cheering me on, her hair blowing in the wind. She was the prettiest thing I had ever seen. She had a way of making me feel invincible, and I had never felt it as much as I did at this moment. With Daisy by my side, I could be brave and do anything.

It wasn't just the adventures that defined our childhood; it was the bond that we shared. Daisy and I would sit under the stars countless nights after dinner while our parents talked or sat on the porch, sharing our secrets and dreams. I believed, in those moments, that we would always be there for each other. In my life is where I always wanted her to be.

☐ ☐ ☐

The innocence of our time together as kids felt like a lifetime ago, yet the memories were still so vivid, etched into my heart.

I didn't want to hurt Daisy. I didn't want to hurt my dad either. I could feel the weight of the heavy decision. There was so much turmoil in my heart; both sides were fighting, both ready for battle. The moonlight seeped through the curtains, casting shadows in the room, but instead of falling asleep in preparation for the early morning ahead of me, I was faced with so many thoughts racing through my mind. My heart kept telling me I had to choose.

On one side, I saw Daisy. She was sitting on the tailgate of my truck, laughing. Another image came to mind; this time, she was in the barn brushing the horses. I saw her riding horses with me, her hair blowing in the breeze, and I saw her riding beside me in my truck, her skin on mine, and the prettiest smile I ever saw on her face. She was like a piece of art, every curve and contour told a story that captivated me, making me want to look every inch of her over. She had a strong presence around her, making anywhere she went full of life. Every glance at her left something else to be admired. She was a dream, and I didn't want to let this dream go.

On the other side, I saw my dad. I saw moments of him talking with and dancing with my mom- all the good times they shared. I saw him working around the ranch day after day, and I followed him around ever since I could walk because I wanted to be just like him. I wanted to run this ranch someday and make him proud. I heard his stern and unwavering voice. I heard myself speaking to him, promising him he had nothing to worry about, that there wouldn't be anything between me and his best friend's daughter. We were in the past, after all.

But now, what if Daisy could be my future?

I rolled over in the bed, facing the windows. 'Am I going to hurt her?' I whispered. It felt like the weight of the world was on my shoulders. I rolled over again, this time spreading my arm out, realizing how much space was on the other side of me in the bed. What if something could fill that space…or someone?

I knew I had to make a choice, and the thought of losing Daisy felt like I would be empty once more, just when I was starting to be myself again. The thought of hurting my dad and going back on my word made me feel like I was letting him and my grandfather down. Our word was religion around here, and without that, what did we have?

With a sigh, I closed my eyes, trying to quiet the storm within me. I needed clarity, just a single moment of peace to figure out what to do in this impossible situation. I needed to know what was really in my heart and what I wanted for my future. I only hoped that whatever was in there, I would have the courage to follow it and not let fear dictate my path. If my dad and Daisy had one thing in common, they both taught me to face my fears head-on, no matter how hard it was.

Chapter Fourteen

Daisy

I lay in bed, wondering what was running through Colt's mind. The last thing I expected when my dad told me I needed to come here, and pretty much forced me to stay here for the summer, was to end up reconnecting with Colt. I especially didn't think we would reconnect in this way. I was sure my dad wouldn't love the idea of me off with someone instead of keeping my focus on the ranch and working. I don't know what I would say to him if he were to find out.

I rolled over in bed, picturing the magical night I had with Colt. I let peace come, focusing on the silence, knowing whatever was going to happen could happen in the morning.

***

I got up the next morning, quickly changing, and ran into the kitchen for some coffee. I noticed a note on the counter, letting me know Walt and Colt were out in town getting some supplies and would be back in a few hours. I enjoyed the serenity around me while I finished my coffee, then I rinsed out my cup and walked out to the barn. I wasn't eager to clean out the stalls, but I was eager to see the horses. I hadn't realized how much

I had missed being around horses while I have been away. I cleaned out their stalls, made sure they all had food and water, then took down the brush. One by one, I brushed them- Titan first, then Shadow, and then Domino. It had only been about an hour and a half, and since I didn't have a list made for me or Walt here to tell me what all I needed to do, I decided to go for a ride.

"Hey, Domino. Do you want to go for a ride?" I grabbed the saddle, ready to feel the wind in my hair.

* * *

When I started, I kicked Domino into high gear so I could feel nothing but the wind blowing against my face, moving my hair every which way. I pulled the reins to slow Domino down, taking in the scenery around me. The sun was casting a bright light across the open fields, and the sounds of hooves against the soft earth were soothing, like a gentle heartbeat that matched mine. I stopped Domino so I could admire the view around us, closing my eyes briefly to absorb it all. I took a deep breath, smelling the flowers and grass. As we continued, I could feel all my tension seep away. The world around me was so alive, and after the night I had, I was ready to take on whatever the day would bring.

I began to make my way back to the ranch, the sun now fully lighting the path. The familiar sights of Texas Rose Ranch brought joy to my heart and a smile to my face, but the sounds of voices caught my attention.

Rounding a bend, I spotted Colt, my cowboy, and Walt unloading items from the back of their truck. They were chatting about something- probably about what needed to be accomplished for the day. I could see some bags and feed for the animals as I arrived closer to the barn to put Domino back in the stall.

I felt a warmth in my heart as I watched Colt and Walt work together, remembering all the times I sat on the porch or various places around the ranch through the years as kids, watching them two together. Colt had always wanted to be like his dad and take over someday, and I knew this was his element. He was made for this. I hopped off Domino, taking the lead in my hand, and walked him into the stall. The smell of hay and leather surrounded me. I rubbed his nose once I closed the stall door, pressing my forehead against him, feeling his warmth. He was so gentle, and I was glad Colt had suggested I ride this horse.

I turned and hadn't noticed that Colt had made his way inside the barn. He was organizing the supplies he and Walt had picked up in town this morning. I steppedcloser to him, trying to get a look at him. We had shared such a close bond as kids, and I could feel how close we were starting to get after this time being back here, especially after last night. I approached him, trying to catch his eye.

"Hey, Colt. How was the trip?" I was trying to keep it casual, not trying to get ahead of myself or let any anxiety creep in.

Colt turned to look at me for a moment, giving me a small smile, but then he quickly turned back to continue unpacking things from the bags and boxes.

"It was good. Just got what we needed." His response was quick, not giving me much room to continue the conversation. I furrowed my brow, twisting a piece of my hair through my fingers.

"I saw you and your dad talking when I got back from riding Domino. You two seemed like you had a good time. Did you find anything interesting in town?" I placed my hand against his back, wanting to have a little reminder of our time together and the way it felt when we touched. I hoped pressing him further would help him open up and continue the conversation.

Colt shifted his weight just enough so my hand was no longer touching his back. He glanced around the barn like he was looking for something. I turned, unsure if he was going to speak or not.

"Yeah, just the usual stuff. Just a typical trip." He was still avoiding my gaze, and I could feel the anxiety creep up on me. A lump formed in my throat and I felt sweat form on my hands. I wiped them on my jeans. I took a step closer to Colt, trying to remain calm.

"Colt, is everything okay? You seem...different." I spoke softly, hoping that he couldn't sense all the emotions I was currently trying to suppress. "Did you and your dad get into a disagreement while you were in town or something? If you did, you can tell me. You can talk to me about it, whatever it is."

He finally looked at me, and for a moment I caught a glimpse of the same man that asked me to dinner yesterday. The same man who took me on what apparently was my first date. The same man that had so much gentleness in him, despite his rugged exterior. The same man that touched me so gently and softly, making me crave something I had never felt before. I hoped his expression would lighten up, but when he turned again, I was filled with so much uncertainty.

"I'm fine, Daisy. Just tired, I guess." His words felt rehearsed. I folded my arms, contemplating my next words.

"You know you can talk to me, right? We always used to talk to each other about everything. If something is bothering you..."

"It's nothing. I'm fine. Just busy. There's a lot to get done today." I felt worried, hating the way this was going. I just wanted a conversation with him, and this was not how I expected our first interaction to go after last night. I didn't want to keep prying, but I knew I deserved more than this. He tried to shut me down once when we were kids, and another time since I had started staying here, and I wasn't about to let him do it again.

"Colt, I'm just...worried. I don't want you to feel like you can't tell me things or need to hide stuff from me. I want to be here for you. After last night, I thought there was something between us." When he didn't give me a response, I continued. "Was it only a one-time thing? Was it just a way for you to get a little action since you don't get much? If you were just using me, then at least be man enough to tell me." He turned quickly, his expression dark.

"You know dang well that I'm not like that."

"Then tell me the truth." He sighed.

"Will you please just let this go? I don't want my dad to see us talking like this."

"Like what? We're just having a conversation." I was so frustrated, but I tried to keep calm and not raise my voice to where Walt could hear.

"Yeah, but if he saw this right now, he would be able to see that this isn't a friendly conversation. He would know something's up, and I'm not ready to deal with that. I still haven't figured out what to say to him…how to explain this."

"Explain? Can't you just tell him that we're seeing each other?"

"You don't understand. It's not that simple."

"You're right. I don't understand. I don't understand because you won't tell me anything." I paused, trying to catch my breath. "Colt, you have to know that I'm just worried about you."

"I know, Daisy." He rubbed the back of his neck.

"So? Are you going to tell me?"

"When my dad told me he agreed with John to let you stay here, he made me promise him something."

"Okay?"

"He told me you were here to learn hard work."

"I'm so sick of hearing that."

"Will you let me finish?" I nodded. "He told me that he was doing this as a favor to your father, one that he owed him. I told him he had nothing to worry about."

"That still doesn't explain this…"

"He told me to leave you be." I could feel my blood boiling. Was Colt saying what I thought he was saying? "He told me that I was to leave you alone…I wasn't supposed to let anything happen between us. This was supposed to be strictly business."

"So, let me get this straight. Your dad basically told you to keep your hands off me? Is that it?" He nodded.

"Daisy…" He reached out to touch me, then stopped himself.

"Tell me one more thing. Did you agree?" He nodded. No. It couldn't be. How could he do something like this to me? He swore he'd never hurt me and now look at this. Look at what he's done.

"Daisy, I'm sorry."

"Are you sorry that your dad told you to do that, although he had no right to? Are you sorry that you agreed? Or are you sorry that you asked me out last night and things ended up getting heated between us?" He didn't answer. All he could do was look at the ground, keeping his eyes off me. I felt tears swelling in my eyes. I wasn't weak and I wasn't going to let him see me like this. I took off toward the house, not looking back.

Chapter Fifteen

Colt

The whole drive with my dad, I was trying to figure out what to do with the situation I was in. I tried to talk to him, but I couldn't find the words. He spoke a little to me, only to give me orders to grab this and load that. I didn't mind. It was the only thing keeping my mind from racing with all the thoughts. I was dreading seeing Daisy when we got back because I knew she would want to talk, and I wasn't ready.

* * *

When we got back to the ranch, I got out and started helping my dad unload everything from the truck bed.

"Take that box and bag to the barn and put that stuff away."

"Right on it." I heard hooves approaching us, and I knew it could only be one thing. I didn't look up, though, keeping my mind on the task at hand. I carried everything into the barn, my dad going toward the fence. I saw Daisy hopping off Domino. She looked stunning on the horse. She didn't notice me, and I was kind of hoping she wouldn't. It would make this a lot easier for me because I wasn't yet ready to make any decision.

"Hey, Colt. How was the trip?"

I turned to give her a quick smile, then got back to work.

"It was good. Just got what we needed." I was hoping I could cut the conversation short and Daisy would take the hint.

"I saw you and your dad talking when I got back from riding Domino. You two seemed like you had a good time. Did you find anything interesting in town?" She placed her hand against my back. It felt so nice to feel her touch again, but I knew it was only making things harder. I moved my body so her hand would leave me.

"Yeah, just the usual stuff. Just a usual trip." I avoided making eye contact with her, trying to make it easier.

"Colt, is everything okay? You seem…different. Did you and your dad get into a disagreement while you were in town or something? If you did, you can tell me. You can talk to me about it, whatever it is." I appreciate her wanting to be there for me. It reminded me of when we were kids. But this was not the right time. This was not what I needed right now. I needed some time and space to be with my thoughts and think this all through.

I finally looked at her, unsure of what to say or do.

"I'm fine, Daisy. Just tired, I guess."

"You know you can talk to me, right? We always used to talk to each other about everything. If something is bothering you…" She was right. As kids, we would talk for hours about anything and everything. But this was not just a carefree day, and we are not kids with our little problems. We are adults now with grown-up problems.

"It's nothing. I'm fine. Just busy. There's a lot to get done today." I had no idea what she was thinking, but I could only imagine how she was feeling right now. I was cutting her short, and after the night we had, I'm sure she felt things were off. I didn't want this, but what else could I do without talking to my dad?

"Colt, I'm just...worried. I don't want you to feel like you can't tell me things or need to hide stuff from me. I want to be here for you. After last night, I thought there was something between us." I didn't respond and she kept talking. I could tell she was probably scared. "Was it only a one-time thing? Was it just a way for you to get a little action since apparently you don't get much? If you were just using me, then at least be man enough to tell me." I couldn't believe those words. There was no way she could really believe that, could she?

"You know dang well that I'm not like that."

"Then tell me the truth." I sighed, knowing I had to come clean. Seeing her like this was breaking my heart and the last thing I ever want to do is hurt her or cause her any pain.

"Will you please just let this go? I don't want my dad to see us talking like this." I hoped the truth was better for her than letting her mind wander.

"Like what? We're just having a conversation." I wanted her to keep her voice down. The last thing I needed was for my dad to hear any of this or even catch a glimpse of this argument. I had no idea what he would say or do. I wasn't ready for that discussion.

"Yeah but if he saw this, right now, he would be able to see that this isn't a friendly conversation. He would know something's up, and I'm not ready to deal with that. I still haven't figured out what to say to him...how to explain this."

"Explain? Can't you just tell him that we're seeing each other?" If only it were that simple. I could only wish.

"You don't understand. It's not that simple."

"You're right. I don't understand. I don't understand because you won't tell me anything. Colt, you must know that

I'm just worried about you." She always did care so much about me. I loved that side of her.

"I know, Daisy." I rubbed the back of my neck.

"So? Are you going to tell me?" I had to come clean with her. I only hoped it didn't hurt her.

"When my dad told me he agreed with John to let you stay here, he made me promise him something."

"Okay?"

"He told me you were here to learn hard work."

"I'm so sick of hearing that."

"Will you let me finish? He told me that he was doing this as a favor to your father, one that he owed him. I told him he had nothing to worry about."

"That still doesn't explain this…"

"He told me to leave you be. He told me that I was to leave you alone…I wasn't supposed to let anything happen between us. This was supposed to be strictly business." Maybe he remembered how close we were as kids, and he was afraid now that we were adults something would happen? I wasn't sure why he did what he did, but that was besides the point.

"So, let me get this straight. Your dad basically told you to keep your hands off me? Is that it?" I nodded.

"Daisy…" I reached out to touch her, just wanting to wrap her in my arms, then stopped myself.

"Tell me one more thing. Did you agree?" I nodded, and I knew it was hurting her. I could see it in her eyes.

"Daisy, I'm sorry."

"Are you sorry that your dad told you to do that, although he had no right to? Are you sorry that you agreed? Or are you sorry that you asked me out last night and things ended up getting heated between us?" I didn't answer. I didn't know what to say. I looked at the ground but caught a quick peek long enough to see tears forming in Daisy's eyes. I had only seen Daisy cry on one occasion- her mom's funeral. I knew at that moment that I had not only broken a promise to my dad, but also to her.

◻ ◻ ◻

"Colt?"

"Daisy?"

"You know how much you mean to me, don't you? We've been friends for fifteen years."

"Yeah, it's been a long fifteen years of me putting up with that sass of yours. I guess my first two years of life were to prepare me, but there's no way anyone could ever be that prepared." She punched my shoulder and we both laughed. "No, but... seriously, Daisy. I'm glad you've stuck around all these years." She smiled, and it nearly took my breath away. Every dang time she smiled, it made me feel a way I had never felt before. I never knew seeing someone else happy could bring myself so much happiness at the same time.

"It hasn't always been easy." We laughed again. We stayed in this constant state, and it made me always want to be around her. Any time she was at the ranch was a good time.

"Hey. You know I always got your back, don't you?

"Always."

"No matter what happens, I'll never hurt you, Daisy."

"I know."

◻ ◻ ◻

I leaned against the barn door, staring blankly out at the fields. My heart was so heavy. I could still hear Daisy's words and the look on her face when I told her the truth. How could a night so perfect and with so much heat lead to a morning like this? Now, everything was just overshadowed by the weight of my promise to my dad.

I ran my fingers through my hair. Why did I let it go

that far? Why didn't I just tell her last night before all of this happened? I was the one who asked her to go to the bar, so this was all on me. I promised I would keep all this as strictly business, and now my mind was occupied with the thoughts of Daisy and me as kids and the way I felt about her then. But after last night, the feelings I had for her as a kid couldn't compare.

My phone buzzed in my pocket, and I was hoping I would see Daisy's name. Instead, it was a weather notification. I didn't mean to hurt her. I was never supposed to hurt her. Her leaving was hard enough on me, but I still never wanted her to feel the same pain I felt then. I can't do this.

I knew I wanted to be with Daisy, but what if we continue with things like last night, and once summer ends, she decides to go back to the city? She could very well leave here again. She had a life in the city. She had a job. Why would she just leave that? Was that a risk I was willing to take?

I felt torn between two worlds- my heart yearning for one of the most amazing people I have ever known and my loyalty to my father pulling me back to reality.

Chapter Sixteen

Daisy

I ran into my room, plopping on the bed. I pulled my legs up to my chest and let myself cry for a little bit. I hadn't cried in so long- not since my mom's funeral. I wasn't an emotional person like this, and I hated crying. I sat up on the bed, letting the tears I had left flow down my face.

His words echoed, 'He told me to leave you be. He told me that I was to leave you alone…I wasn't supposed to let anything happen between us. This was supposed to be strictly business.'

How could Colt do this? How could he not even bother to tell me? He asked me out. If he made a promise like that and had an intention of keeping it, then why did he ask me to the bar? Why did he dance with me? Why did he touch me or kiss me… more than once? This was on him. He was at fault, not me. I only followed the signs. I guess the only thing I could blame myself for was letting my guard down.

I hugged my knees to my chest, feeling the weight of his words. What kind of promise is that? Why would his dad ask him to make a promise like that in the first place? That part didn't make any sense. I couldn't wrap my head around it.

The memories of our laughter and smiles as kids when we played, talked, rode horses together, and went for a joy ride in his truck came flooding back. How could we ever go from that to this? It didn't seem real. All the sweet memories we shared were now overshadowed by this one... this one stupid thing that might just be the absolute breaking point.

The room was quiet, but inside I felt a storm passing through. I wanted to scream but knew not to because the Lord only knew what Walt would do in that case. There would be no denying that something was wrong then. I wish Colt could see how I was last night. I wish he could see how I have been when riding through the fields with him while I've been here and feel how I have felt. Maybe then he would see how much he means to me.

Even after all these years apart, Colt was still a steady presence. But now, I wonder how much longer he will hold a place in me. The fear of losing him again broke my heart, and all I could do was cry.

I finally went into the bathroom, wiping away my tears. I cleaned my face and gave myself a little pep talk, taking a deep breath. 'You've got this. You're strong. You've gone through a lot harder than this and still came out on the other side.' I took another slow, deep breath and walked outside, stopping myself for a moment on the porch to feel the breeze.

"Hey, Daisy." I looked at Walt standing there with his dog, Hank. "I'm headed to give the cows some hay. Come along. You can help unload."

"Yes, sir."

I was happy about the distraction. Somehow, Walt was always right on time, and I appreciated it. We drove to the field, Hank sitting in the back and wagging his tail. I rubbed his head, him clearly enjoying himself.

I walked over to the bed of the truck where Walt was

tossing bales of hay onto the ground. Hank was running, barking excitedly at the sight of the cows in the distance. The thudding of the hay hitting the ground was oddly soothing. For the first time since I've been here, I was thankful that there was so much work to be done.

"Come on, Daisy! Grab a bale!" I did as Walt instructed, making sure to drop the bales where he wanted me to. It felt good to be out here and away from everything. It was good to be away from Colt right now.

I reached for another bale, feeling its roughness. I let out a grunt with the weight of the bale pressed against my chest as I walked it to the fence where some of the cows were now coming closer. I tossed the hay down, letting the animals come even closer to the food. For a moment, I forgot about everything.

"Look at them go!" I turned to Walt, seeing a slight smile on his face.

I wondered how many times he has smiled since Ivy passed. After losing my mom, I could only imagine what it would feel like losing your absolute best friend. That must have been so hard on Walt. I knew it was hard on my dad, especially with how sudden it was. I couldn't help but smile, though, loving the fact that I could see Walt like this. Maybe he needed this as much as I did.

"Thanks for this." I glanced at Walt. "I needed a break."

"Hey now. This is still work." He slightly smiled at me, and I gave him one back. In that moment, I felt a little lighter, and I saw Walt in a different light.

We stood by the fence for a while longer, watching the cows munch on the hay, enjoying every bite. I smiled as I watched them, their movements bringing me a bit of calmness. I thought of how I used to do this with my dad. I always enjoyed those times, and sometimes, I wish I could have them back.

"I used to do this with my dad."

"I remember." He paused for a moment. "He's a good man."

"Yeah. He is."

"It's not hard to be a little jealous, is it?"

"Hm?"

"They get to take it easy and just enjoy life."

"Yeah, they do."

"That must be nice."

"Walt, can I ask you something?" He turned to look at me. "Do you ever think about retiring?"

"Does your dad ever think about it?"

"I wouldn't know what he thinks about." I hadn't had a good, heart to heart conversation with my dad in a long time.

"You haven't spoken to him in a while." It was a statement rather than a question. "He is proud of you, you know. He just wants you to be happy." I was unsure what to say to him. "But to answer your question, I do think about it sometimes. Honestly, though, I would still want to stay here…maybe live in the cabin at the far end of the ranch. I'd still do work around here, but… I think Colt could handle the responsibility of taking on this place." I nodded, still unsure what to say to him. "Do you think so?"

"I don't know if I'm the best person to ask about this."

"You two were friends growing up. I know you didn't come around as often after…you know…but almost sixteen years of a friendship like the two of you had has to count for something. You don't spend that much time with someone and not learn things."

"He'd take this on. This is where he's meant to be."

"Well, we should head back to the house before it gets any later. I don't know about you, but I'm about to starve out. What do you say we go to the house and grab a sandwich? You have to keep up your appetite for everything else we have to accomplish today."

"Good thinking."

We got back in the truck, Hank taking his place in the back seat. He was so well-trained. We didn't talk on the way back, so it gave me time to think about what Walt said. 'Almost sixteen years of friendship like the two of you had has to count for something. You don't spend that much time with someone and not learn things.' I knew Colt. Even after this time, I was sure I still knew him. You don't just get up one day and change everything about yourself.

Being back here, I have slowly seen that same boy I wanted to spend every minute with come out and open up to me again. It was like our friendship was a flower needing water, and it was starting to bloom again. But what was I going to say to Colt? I honestly had no idea. Maybe all I needed to do was give him time to explain. I still couldn't believe Walt asked him to promise him something like that, and I couldn't believe that Colt had agreed. I wasn't sure how I'd react to any sort of explanation from Colt, but if he offered one, I would at least listen.

Forgiveness would be hard, no matter what his reasoning might be.

And if he didn't come to me to explain, then I would know that whatever happened between us was a one-time thing, and I would let it go, keeping this summer as what was meant to be… strictly business.

As we approached the house, I could feel my stomach growling. Walt parked the truck next to the house, and he opened the door for me.

"Thank you." He opened the door of the house for me, too, and there was never a time I could remember when Walt ever let Rose, or any other woman, open their door if he had any kind of say.

"I'll grab the bread, cheese, and lunch meat. You get the fixins?" I nodded, knowing exactly what he meant and what I wanted. I grabbed the mayonnaise, tomato, and lettuce from the fridge, then sliced and cut up everything. I could taste the sandwich; I was so hungry. Walt put out two plates with the start of a sandwich for each of us, and I layered on the toppings.

"Good?"

"Didn't you get the pickles?"

"No, but I will."

"You can't have a sandwich without a good pickle on the side. I canned them myself. They're good. You have to try them." I got a fork out from the drawer and dipped it in the jar, pulling out a few and adding them to my plate. I ate one of them.

"They are good."

"Come on, now. Don't be stingy with them. Pass me the jar." I did and took a bite from my sandwich, hearing a small whimper. We both turned to look at Hank, who was sitting by the door. "His food is in there by the door. There's a scoop already in it. Get him one."

"Of course. We can't forget about you, Hank." I scooped up some food and poured it into Hank's food bowl. He went to eat as soon as the first bit of kibble hit the bowl.

"Looks like he is as hungry as we are."

Chapter Seventeen

Colt

I stood in the barn, putting away what was left in the box and bag. My hands moved mechanically, knowing every action that needed to be done. There wasn't any thinking involved.

The argument with Daisy replayed over and over again. Her words cut so deep.

I was supposed to go out and check on the cows on the other side of the ranch. I tightened the saddle up on Shadow, glancing out the barn door to see if I could spot Daisy anywhere, but she was nowhere to be found. I wondered if she had run off somewhere to be alone for a while or if my dad had told her something to do. Either way, I was worried.

What am I supposed to do now? I apologized, but she didn't want to hear it. I'm sure I would be mad, too, if the roles were reversed. I honestly couldn't blame her. I probably wouldn't want to hear any explanation either…at least not yet, when it was still so fresh. Maybe she was taking some time to process it all, and she would come find me later to talk…just maybe.

I took a deep breath, deciding to focus on the work I needed to do instead. I could control this, but I couldn't control Daisy. I hopped on Shadow and let him go, feeling the adrenaline as we set off through the fields toward the far end of the ranch. I guided Shadow, giving him gentle nudges.

As we rode, my thoughts still drifted to the argument with Daisy. I could still feel the tension between us, and the weight of knowing this all fell on me was so heavy.

I focused on the nature surrounding me, bringing me some calmness when I thought of the simple joys that this way of life brings.

□ □ □

My mother and I rode on occasions together, just the two of us. The sun was shining brightly, and the wind was blowing with a gentle breeze. I could smell the flowers.

"Colt?" I looked at her, listening to her soothing voice. "You know I want you to be happy, don't you?" I nodded. "If this place here brings you happiness, then stay." She waited a minute and spoke again. "Happiness isn't something you find. It's something you create. I want you to create your own happiness, baby. I want you to find your reason and love."

Her smile was beautiful. Her eyes sparkled with so much wisdom. My mom was the kindest person. She always gave the best advice, but this lesson stuck with me more than any other.

"Colt, whenever you're feeling lost or unsure, remember to look around you. Find joy in the little things. Do things that give you peace. That is where you will find your answers and comfort."

□ □ □

I missed my mom so much. It was times like these that I wish she were here to lend me an ear and give me some of her wisdom.

When we reached the pasture, I scanned the herd. I hopped off Shadow, wrapping his lead around the fence. I went inside the fence, trying to get a better look. I counted heads to ensure everything was there. The cows were munching on the field in the grass, some lying around to get in a nice nap. I felt relief when I counted thirty heads. At least everything was good for someone.

As I turned to head back to Shadow, I rubbed my head. My head was starting to thump, and I knew a headache was coming- one caused by pure stress.

As we rode back, I wondered if I needed to be the one to speak up and talk. It was my fault, after all. But, knowing Daisy, she needed time. Wouldn't she come to me when she was ready? I could wait.

The familiar image of the house came into view. I was anxious and worried, but I was trying to keep calm. If I freaked out, that's when everything would go south. My heart sank as her perfect silhouette came into view, making her way outside the house, my dad following behind. He was obviously keeping her busy, and I wasn't about to approach her at this time.

I made my way out of the barn after putting Shadow back in his stall and heard my dad's voice.

"Colt!" I turned toward the house, then started walking to get closer to him. "How are the cows?"

"All counted for."

"Great. No issues?"

"Nope. All looks good."

Daisy had moved past us and was now walking toward the barn.

"Daisy and I are headed to feed the horses. You go on inside and get you a bite to eat, then I need you back out here." I nodded.

As I moved inside the house, I lingered for a moment on the porch, peering over my shoulder to catch a glimpse of Daisy and her untamed curls. My dad was walking over to Daisy, and it almost looked like he was smiling.

I wish she were ready to talk, or that I could muster up enough courage to just tell my dad what happened last night and then this morning. Maybe he would understand? He was a hard ball, but he had to remember what it felt like to have feelings for someone.

Chapter Eighteen

Daisy

"Alright. Let's clean this up and get on with it. We need to go feed the horses and do a stall check."

"Yes, sir." We walked out the door, and I spotted Colt riding into the barn on Shadow. He looked so majestic riding. It had always suited him so well.

"Colt!" I jumped a little. I didn't want Colt over here.

As he made his way closer to the house where Walt and I were, I could feel his eyes on me. I made my way past them and headed toward the barn to get started on the next task at hand. I had fed the horses by the time Walt came into view.

"Need any help?'

"Just need to check the stalls. Looks like Titan's stall needs some shoveling."

"Well, make sure you get it all. Double-check the others again, too. I think we got most of the work done yesterday after the long day, so once you're finished here, take the afternoon off."

"You sure?" Walt nodded.

"You just be inside for dinner." I nodded back at him. What would I do with a whole afternoon off?

I killed some time in the barn, brushing the horses not only to make them feel good, but also to make me feel better. I decided to go for a walk through the fields to a secluded place where we had come a couple of times as kids. My boots crunched against the grass as I made my way through the grass and thicket. I finally reached my destination- the secluded spot- the same as when I had last seen it. There was a clearing with a small pond surrounded by trees. It was beautiful, and it was a great place to come and think. I hoped it would give me answers and bring me some peace.

The sun began to dip below the horizon, the warm orange hue filling the sky. I sat in a tree that had bent over, the same as when we were kids, and watched as the water shimmered in the fading light. I took a deep breath, trying to relieve some of the pressure I felt in my chest. This spot was the perfect place to be to get away from the noise, expectations, responsibilities, and most importantly, Colt. The only sounds I could hear were from the animals in nature, frogs croaking, crickets chirping, and leaves rustling. My mind started to calm down, the jumbled thoughts subsiding.

I closed my eyes, letting the peace come over me as I felt the cool breeze against my skin. I remembered who I was. I remembered my strength and what I have been through. I remembered how I never let fear take over and was never scared of anything. I remembered how I always wanted to be around the people I cared about.

This spot was my refuge, a place to come and recharge whenever I needed. It hadn't changed, and in that, I felt comfortable.

I knew I couldn't avoid Colt and Walt any longer. It was almost time for dinner and Walt told me to be there. I wasn't going to be late. As I walked into the kitchen, I could smell the delicious food. Walt was at the stove stirring a pot, while Colt leaned against the counter, arms crossed. My chest felt tighter, but I tried to subdue it. It was only dinner, and I could handle a meal.

"Hope you're hungry."

"It smells good." I kept my tone neutral, not going to give Colt the satisfaction of knowing how distraught I've been. I watched as he grabbed a bowl and sat at the table.

"Here's you a bowl, Daisy."

"Thanks." I took the bowl from Walt, taking a seat at the table. Walt finally joined us and it felt like the tension could be cut with a knife.

"So, what'd you do with your afternoon?"

"Nothing. Brushed the horses and went for a walk."

"There's plenty of walking you can do here." I nodded, faking a smile.

"Sure is."

"Well, I hope you enjoyed some time to yourself."

"Yes, I did. It was nice."

I picked at the food in my bowl, stealing a glance at Colt. He hadn't looked up once since I sat down. I could feel the tension. It was so strong and I was afraid Walt would pick up on it. We were almost finished with our food, and none of us had spoken since Walt's last comment.

"Everything okay?" I looked up from my bowl at Walt.

"With me?"

"With either of you. You ain't speaking. Cat got y'alls tongue?"

"No, sir. Everything's fine."

"It's all good, Dad."

"Well, I'm off to bed. Y'all be sure to get some sleep and be ready to go in the morning. Don't stay up too late now."

I took a deep breath, realizing that Colt and I were now alone. This is the one thing I didn't want to happen. Not tonight.

"Daisy, I know you need some space." I didn't answer him. "I am sorry."

"No worries. You want me to do the dishes, or do you have it?"

"No, I can do it."

"Alright. Well, I'm going to bed."

I wanted Colt to make the first move, but not just by apologizing again. He owed me an explanation. I deserved that much. If I had to wait, I would.

Chapter Nineteen

Colt

I got back outside after grabbing a quick sandwich and headed to the barn. I knew my dad said we needed to shoe Titan, and he'd need help doing so. I squatted beside the horse, knowing I was only moments away from breaking a sweat.

"Hold him steady, Colt. He doesn't need to be moving around too much while I'm trying to do this."

"Got it, Dad." I put a hand on Titan's neck. I could sense his nervousness, and in that sense, we were the same. I rubbed my hand down his neck, speaking softly to keep him calm while my dad was at work. "Easy now, boy. Just a little bit longer." My dad continued to work while I tried to ease Titan's anxiety. He fit the shoe on, driving the nails with precision. I had never shod a horse, but I was sure that after seeing my dad do it for so many years that I could.

"You know, Colt, this is a good skill to have." My dad looked over his shoulder at me. My dad had his wisdom, too, but he didn't share it as often as my mother used to. "This takes practice, but patience is key." He wiped the sweat from his forehead.

"I get it. Wish it didn't take so long, though." This was one of those tasks that weren't my favorite on the ranch. I was glad my dad still handled this, and I was only needed for some assistance.

"Son, you have to remember that you can't rush things." I guess he did know the right words to say sometimes. He was right. I needed to be patient with Daisy, even if all I wanted to do was run and find her, squeezing her tight and kissing her with all the passion I had in my body. I wanted to make her feel the way I felt, and I knew she felt at the bar. "You have to build trust."

"I know, dad." We finished with the shoeing. It seemed like it took forever, and I was so happy for it to be over.

"We need to check their water." I nodded at him, making sure each horse had their water trough full. My dad had started checking with me, but he ended up propping himself against Titan's stall, rubbing his head.

"All good."

"Great. I think we're finished for the day. I know yesterday was a long one, so let's call it." He headed toward the barn door." I'm going in to make some dinner. Why don't you help me?" I nodded, shutting the barn doors behind us and following him inside. We each took a shower first, making sure to clean up before touching any food or doing any type of cooking.

"What are you making?"

"You remember that fancy chicken soup your mom used to make?" I nodded, licking my lips a little at the thought. It was our favorite meal my mom used to make, and any leftovers were sure to be eaten the following day. It was one of those meals that you just remember from your childhood. It's a part of who you are. "Here. You cut up this and add it to the pot while I get the chicken going." I did as I was told, taking the vegetables from my dad and then moving around to find a knife and a cutting board.

The smell of the food made my mouth water. I leaned against the counter, taking in the smell. My stomach growled, and all I wanted was a big bowl to devour. I tried to focus on the food rather than what else was on my mind. I knew it was only a matter of time before Daisy showed up.

"Looks like it's ready. You hungry?"

"Starved." I heard the door creak open, and I knew it could only mean one thing. I didn't turn around, keeping my eyes on the food. I was completely clueless about how this interaction would go. This would be the first time we were confined to one space since our argument. I just hoped it didn't go south right in front of my dad. That probably wouldn't end well. It would be a whole lot better if my dad learned about what happened between Daisy and me from me instead of her. At least owning up to it might make it a little better...I could only hope.

"Hope you're hungry."

"It smells good." I couldn't sense any emotion in Daisy's tone, but I knew she still had to be upset. If she weren't, she would have come to me to talk at some point today. I grabbed a bowl and sat at the table.

"Here's you a bowl, Daisy." My dad handed her a bowl. I still didn't look at her. Instead, I started eating.

"Thanks." Daisy took a seat at the table, bowl in hand. My dad finally sat down, and I was a little relieved.

"So, what'd you do with your afternoon?" He was looking at Daisy. I knew he had given her the rest of the afternoon off, and I couldn't help but be a little curious about what she did with her free time. You didn't get much free time around here, so when you did, you usually made sure not to take it for granted.

"Nothing much. Brushed the horses and went for a walk." I knew she was cutting it short for a reason, but I wasn't going to say anything. I kept quiet.

"There's plenty of walking you can do here."

"Sure is."

"Well, I hope you enjoyed some time to yourself."

"Yes, I did. It was nice."

I noticed her picking at her food and saw her take a quick look at me. I still hadn't looked her way. After my dad's words, no one spoke again. It was awkward.

"Everything okay?"

"With me?" Daisy spoke first.

"With either of you. You ain't speaking much. Cat got y'alls tongue?"

"No, sir. Everything's fine."

"It's all good, dad. Just enjoying the food." I titled my bowl so he could see the last bite or two left inside.

"Well, I'm off to bed. Y'all be sure to get some sleep and be ready to go in the morning. Don't stay up too late now." Daisy and I were now alone. I wondered if I should say something. I wasn't sure what, but could it make this worse?

"Daisy, I know you need some space." Of course, no answer. "I am sorry. The last thing I wanted was to argue with you, especially after a night like we had."

"No worries." She rose from the table. "You want me to do the dishes, or do you have it?"

"No, I can do it."

"Alright. Well, I'm going to bed."

I cleaned up the dishes alone.

What did I do wrong now? It didn't make any sense. Something was off. Daisy was off. I went into my room, taking off my jeans and t-shirt and adding pajama pants to get comfortable. I sat on the edge of the bed, hearing nothing but silence. Daisy glanced at me once at dinner, but that was it. She barely spoke to me. It felt like there was a wall between us, and I wasn't sure how to break it down.

I thought about how Daisy and I used to talk for hours, her laughter spilling out like sunlight. She made me feel something inside that I had never felt. Back then, I was always on the inside with Daisy, us sharing every little detail.

Now, it felt like I was on the outside, looking at a time in the world that was nearly perfect. Daisy and I were best friends, my mother was still here, and life was so good.

Daisy got up and left so quickly to go to bed, and it stung. I just wish she had talked to me. I wish she had at least asked me why. Something was better than nothing.

I sighed, running a hand through my hair. All I did was try to give her some space and apologize…again. What was she expecting me to say? What else was I supposed to do? If she wanted something, why couldn't she just tell me or ask me? I hated what I was feeling. It felt like I had a hole in my heart, and I was so afraid of losing Daisy…again. My heart felt hollow, and I wanted it to be filled again. What could I do to bridge the gap that had formed so suddenly between us? My first step was to figure out how to break through the barrier she had built.

Chapter Twenty

Daisy

For the better part of the last few days, I have kept my mind on the work around the ranch. I moved with a sense of purpose to complete my duties and anything Walt told me to do, without question or any attitude. Walt seemed to be in a particularly good mood this morning and his spirit hasn't faltered. He had been giving me plenty of tasks to do around the ranch, though, but I still didn't complain. Happy Walt was much better than the alternative.

Colt and I still haven't talked. I want him to be the one to come to me, and I still don't want to give up on that. I don't want to give in. I didn't do anything wrong, unless agreeing to go out with someone was wrong. I guess to Walt, it would be considered wrong in this case. I still didn't understand why he asked Colt to promise him that. It's just a weird thing to do. I'm an adult, and so is Colt. If we want to go out, then who is to stop us? I know how much Colt cares about his dad, though, and wants to please him, so it couldn't be as simple as going against his dad's wishes.

The sun was casting a warm glow over the fields as I

continued working. I checked the fence line, as Walt instructed, saying how important a task it was. I made sure there were no gaps where the cattle could get out and wander off. I had chased cattle before, and that was not as fun as it may seem. My boots crunched against the ground with each step I took.

Nonetheless, I could still feel the tension inside me from the conversation with Colt. Yes, I had been short with him at dinner the other night and we haven't spoken a word since, but why was I supposed to be the one to make the first move for any sort of reconciliation when the fault was on him?

I couldn't shake the uneasiness from it all. There was no denying that Colt was being distant, and I was being reserved. It was hard to figure out how to navigate the shifting dynamics between us.

"Daisy, how's that fence look?"

"Looks good, Walt."

"Well, good. Your dad called."

"Oh?"

"He needs some help replacing a few pieces of his fence. I'm going over to help him. You stay here. There's plenty of work to be done. You need to go feed the horses and check their water. I'll be back later."

"I'll get right on it."

I missed my dad. I wished he had come to visit me more in the city, but I knew why he wouldn't. He felt too out of place there, and my dad hated to be anxious. It would be nice to spend more time with him, though. We saw each other at Rose's funeral and the one time he came to see me, but we haven't seen each other besides those two times. I did call him occasionally to check in, but it wasn't the same.

I went to the barn and checked on the horses, rubbing each of their heads and giving them the right amount of feed that

Walt had shown me, and filled up their water troughs. Being with the horses gave me so much peace and comfort. It was like my problems faded away any time I was near them.

I heard a noise in the distance and I turned to see Colt with his hands in his pockets. He walked with a purpose, but his stride slowed momentarily, and I sensed some hesitation. My heart raced. Was he finally going to come to talk to me? I missed hearing his voice. I missed the way we were. I was stopped dead in my tracks. I wiped my face, feeling the sweat. As he drew closer, I met his gaze.

"Hey, Daisy." His voice had a mix of uncertainty and determination. "Can we talk for a minute?" I nodded, trying not to let my face reveal any emotion.

"Sure." Colt shifted his weight, rolling his neck from one side to the other, as if trying to figure out how to start the conversation.

"I wanted to talk to you about all this."

"Okay?" It came out as more of a question than a statement.

"This is my fault, and I own up to that."

"Okay."

"Daisy, could you stop it with the okays? I want you to know why I promised my dad what I did."

"Alright." He roughly rubbed his head, wishing I would stop with my antics, but he knew I was never going to change. I crossed my arms, feeling my chest tighten. I have wanted him to come to me and talk for days now, and now that he finally was, I was so nervous and anxious. "So, why did you promise him that? I mean, do you have any idea how that made me feel? And you telling me that after the night we had…it just felt like you were trying to put distance between us. I don't like that. I don't want there to be any distance between us." He opened his mouth to respond, then closed it.

"It's not like that. I just…this place is my life. It's my legacy, too, not just his. I want to take over someday. You know that. At the time, you and I hadn't spoken since right before your mom died, and I barely thought we would talk and be able to get along again once you got here…at least not like when we were kids. And I didn't expect anything else. I figured work was all both of us would be doing this summer."

"So that makes it okay? You didn't think about how this could affect me."

"You're right. I didn't. I thought it would be good for both of us, you know…to not have anything complicate you being here."

"Good for both of us?" I raised my voice, anger coming over me. "It seems like you were making decisions for me, like I couldn't make them on my own. You didn't consider how I would feel at all." Colt stepped closer, attempting to touch my arm, but I wouldn't let him.

"I'm sorry, Daisy."

"That's all you keep saying, Colt."

"Because I don't know what else to say." Colt never raised his voice, and I knew he wouldn't, even if he wanted to. "I didn't mean to hurt you. I care about you so much. I always have. But I can't let my dad down. It's just…complicated."

"Complicated doesn't even begin to describe this." I was starting to get frustrated with him. "I know you don't want to upset your dad, Colt. I know that. But where does that leave me? Where does that leave us?" I choked a bit with those words.

"Daisy…"

"Spit it out already, Colt, because I'm getting tired of hearing I'm sorry. Give me more than that."

"I had feelings for you as a kid, and I have feelings for you now." He came closer to me.

"You had feelings for me back then?" He nodded. I couldn't believe I never knew that. We always had this special bond, and he looked dang good back then so of course I had feelings for him. But he liked me? How did I never know that? Did I miss every single sign?

"I don't want to pick a side, Daisy. I want to find a balance. We can figure this out together, but there's something I have to do first."

"In the middle of a conversation like this, what could you possibly have to do?" He came so close to me that I could feel his breath against my neck as he whispered.

"This."

He cupped my face in his hands, bringing my lips to meet his in a heated kiss. This kiss felt different from the last one. His eyes were dark, filled with hunger. There was a fire igniting between us, and I wasn't sure how to put it out. He backed me against the barn doors, kissing me from my lips to my neck, making me tingle all over.

"Come on." He took my hand and led me out of the barn toward the house.

"What are we doing?"

"You'll see." We went into the kitchen and I felt a rush of excitement. Colt was intriguing me, making me wonder where his mind was going and if his heart was racing as fast as mine. "How about a little fun?" He winked, and I felt like drowning in every piece of him. I giggled, unable to contain myself. Colt grabbed the ice cream from the freezer, and I was starting to get a hint at where he was going.

"Let's make this interesting." I grabbed the can of whipped cream from the fridge. "Take off your shirt." He whipped around to face me, his face showing a mysterious grin, and I knew he was about to love this. He took it off, his shirt sticking to him slightly as he pulled it off to reveal his toned torso.

I sprayed a generous amount of whipped cream onto his chest. He flinched a little when the cool cream touched his skin. He laughed and leaned against the counter. The whipped cream glistened off his chest.

"You think you can handle this? He teased.

I bit my lip, my heart racing as I took a step closer to him. I placed a hand behind his neck, moving in so close he thought he was about to be kissed before pulling away. I could be a tease, too. Using my fingers, I drew circles on his skin where the whipped cream was.

"Maybe I want to add more." Colt's eyebrow rose, and I knew exactly what I was doing to him. I had him exactly where I wanted him.

"Oh, really? Show me what you got."

I leaned in again, this time licking off some of the whipped cream from his chest. Colt's laughter echoed through the kitchen, and I was starting to get turned on. I knew he was, too. I was lost in the moment, the ice cream forgotten as I was enjoying this way too much. As the whipped cream disappeared, Colt took my hand and pulled me closer. Our bodies were touching, and I had almost forgotten what his skin felt like against mine.

"What's next, Daisy?" His words seemed like a challenge. I smiled, leaning in so I could whisper in his ear. I grabbed the tub of ice cream.

"I'm not done just yet."

I held up the ice cream like a trophy. Using a spoon, I plopped some down on Colt's bare chest, raking the spoon down his chest. I heard him gasp, stiffening his body a little with the temperature contrast. I ran my fingers through it, the ice cream feeling icy against his skin.

"How's this working for you, cowboy?" I missed calling him that. He moaned a little as I licked the melting sweetness off his chest.

"You're going to pay for this." I laughed, finishing clearing his chest. Colt leaned down, kissing me passionately. The kiss felt like he was trying to suck up every ounce of me, leaving nothing behind. "Alright, it's your turn now." He lifted me, placing me onto the counter when he was just sitting. He took the tub of ice cream from my hands, using the spoon to scoop some out. He pointed the spoon at my shirt. "Come on now. Don't make me beg. You know I will." The way he looked into my eyes at that moment, I felt nothing else. I was drowning in him, and he was drowning in me.

"Maybe I want you to beg." At that moment, he got on his knees. He peered up at me, making me feel so in control.

"Come on, darlin'. Let me get a little taste." Those words left his lips so smoothly. I was falling hard and fast. I pointed at the tub of ice cream still in his hands.

"What are you going to do with that?" He winked at me, getting back up on his feet. He moved in closer to me as I took off my shirt. He plopped the spoonful of ice cream on me, starting from my neck and ending at my chest. The feeling of the cold, melting cream against my skin was enough to balance out my body temperature, which had risen from this encounter with Colt.

"Don't worry. You'll enjoy this as much as I did."

He set the tub on the counter beside me. Then he leaned in closer, propping himself on opposite sides of my body. He looked at me, then moved closer, and I knew he was about to kiss me. But he played the same teasing game I had with him and pulled away instead, right when I could feel his breath against my skin. I felt his touch against my neck, licking off the start of the ice cream. He stayed there for a few minutes, and I enjoyed every second of him sucking and licking every drop of stickiness from my body.

"I have one last surprise for you." I leaned back on my hands and turned my head as he went over to one of the cabinets and pulled out a bottle of chocolate sauce. I took the moment to admire the way his jeans hugged him in all the right places. "You didn't think I'd let you get off so easily with being a tease earlier, did you?"

He squeezed the bottle, letting the syrup drip down my chest. Before it rolled too far down, Colt stopped it with his lips. He kissed me on my chest where the sauce stopped, then licked me in one motion up and back down again.

In that moment, Colt slid the bottle across the counter and pulled me so close to him that we felt like one and the same. He kissed me, every wall I had put up being torn down. I wanted to fall into him and I could feel it.

I was falling.

Chapter Twenty-One

Colt

I had woken up with a migraine. I helped my dad with the cows, and then he told me to go lie down for a bit. I was really struggling. I knew stress was causing this one, and those were always the worst.

"John called. He needs help with repairing a fence. I'll be back later. I'll let Daisy know on my way out."

"Okay, dad."

Daisy and I still haven't talked. I wanted to give her space, and all I have been doing is hoping that she will come to me when she's ready to talk and hear me out. I did mess up and I would tell her that and own up to my mistake.

I wanted to be back in her presence more than anything. That was all I ever wanted, even as a kid. Hopefully, we can work this out together.

☐ ☐ ☐

"*Hey, Daisy.*" *Even at seven years old, Daisy had my heart. I* was one smitten nine-year-old, and she had no idea.

"Hey, Colt."

"Whatcha doin'?"

"I'm going on an adventure!"

"Can I come?"

"You're always invited!" She smiled at me, and my heart skipped a beat. I smiled back at her. Her happiness fueled my own. I felt every emotion she felt.

We started walking through the fields. Our parents never really worried about us running off somewhere. We always listened and knew how to get back. It was one of the perks of growing up on a ranch, knowing where everything is because you literally spent every waking moment outside.

"Check it out!" Daisy bent down, picking up a rock.

"A rock?"

"Not just any rock, silly."

"Huh?" I was so confused. All I saw was a rock in her hand.

"Look at it." She raised the rock up, her fingers grasping it. I took it in. "It looks like a heart. Do you see it?" I looked at it again and saw what she saw.

"Yes! I see it!"

"I wonder how big our hearts are. Do you think they're this big? Or bigger?"

"I don't know. I think mine's bigger."

Of course, mine was bigger. It had to be so much bigger than the rock Daisy was holding because of all the love I had for her. She was everything to me. She just didn't know it yet."

□ □ □

The sun was beaming in through the window and I lay on my bed, thinking of Daisy and wishing that this migraine would ease. Daisy had been hard at work the last few days, even more so since before the argument. I knew what she was doing. She was running away from her problems instead of facing them head-on. That was typical character for her, but I wasn't going to say anything about it. I knew better. I lay there a while longer and couldn't scratch the feeling in my chest. I needed to see her, and with my dad being gone and not coming back for a while, this was my perfect opportunity.

I stepped out on the porch, looking around. I didn't see Daisy anywhere, which usually meant only one thing. With my hands in my pockets, I made my way to the barn. Once I got into the line of sight, I could see her. I took her in as I walked, seeing her perfect curves and the way her body fit in those jeans. She was a sight for sore eyes.

Still, I was uneasy.

"Hey, Daisy. Can we talk for a minute?" I was so nervous that I thought I might faint, but I had to have this conversation, and it had to be now. It couldn't wait any longer. Time was up. She nodded.

"Sure." I rolled my neck from one side to the other, breathing out. After all this time has passed, I should know what to say by now. I should have it all planned out.

"I wanted to talk to you about all this."

"Okay?"

"This is my fault, and I own up to that." Boy, was I stating the obvious.

"Okay."

"Daisy, could you stop it with the okays? I want you to know why I promised my dad what I did." Gosh, she was so infuriating sometimes.

"Alright." I rubbed my head with frustration. She crossed her arms and continued. "So, why did you promise him that?

I mean, do you have any idea how that made me feel? And you telling me that after the night we had…it just felt like you were trying to put distance between us. I don't like that. I don't want there to be any distance between us." I tried to respond, but I couldn't get the words out.

"It's not like that. I just…this place is my life. It's my legacy, too, not just his. I want to take over someday. You know that. At the time, you and I hadn't spoken since right before your mom died, and I barely thought we would talk and be able to get along again once you got here…at least not like when we were kids. And I definitely didn't expect anything else. I figured work was all both of us would be doing this summer."

"So that makes it okay? You didn't think about how this could affect me." Her words were breaking me.

"You're right. I didn't. I thought it would be good for both of us, you know…to not have anything complicate you being here."

"Good for both of us?" She was mad, her voice getting louder. At least my dad wasn't here to hear this. "It seems like you were making decisions for me, like I couldn't make them on my own. You didn't consider how I would feel at all." I could hear the catch in her throat as she spoke. I stepped closer, wanting to touch her, but she rejected my embrace.

"I'm sorry, Daisy."

"That's all you keep saying, Colt."

"Because I don't know what else to say. I didn't mean to hurt you. I care about you so much. I always have. But I can't let my dad down. It's just…complicated." I wish she would just tell me what she wants…what she needs. I'll tell her anything she needs to hear to get us back to the way we were. I just can't lose Daisy again.

"Complicated doesn't even begin to describe this. I know you don't want to upset your dad, Colt. I know that. But where does that leave me? Where does that leave us?" I knew she was hurt, and this was breaking my heart so much to see her in this kind of pain. I wanted it to end.

"Daisy..."

"Spit it out already, Colt, because I'm getting tired of hearing I'm sorry. Give me more than that."

"I had feelings for you as a kid, and I have feelings for you now." I had finally confessed the feelings I had buried deep inside. It felt like a proclamation.

"You had feelings for me back then?" I nodded. I waited to see if she would say anything, but she didn't, so I continued.

"I don't want to pick a side, Daisy. I want to find a balance. We can figure this out together, but there's something I have to do first." I wanted her...right then, right there, right now.

"In the middle of a conversation like this, what could you possibly have to do?" I came so close to her, whispering in her ear.

"This."

I cupped her face into my hands, bringing her lips to meet mine. I wanted every ounce of her at thismoment, and nothing was about to stand in my way. I backed her against the barn doors. I kissed her, starting from her neck and working my way down to her lips. They were still as soft as ever.

"Come on." I took her hand and led her to the house, making our way into the kitchen for what I had on my mind.

"What are we doing?"

"You'll see." I gave her a minute to figure out what was going on, then replied. "How about a little fun?" I winked at her and she giggled. I took the ice cream from the freezer, all part of my plan.

"Let's make this interesting." She grabbed the can of whipped cream from the fridge. "Take off your shirt." I whipped around to face her, realizing that she was catching on. I slipped my shirt off, feeling a little sweat as it lightly stuck to my body.

She sprayed a generous amount of whipped cream onto my chest. It was cool against my skin, and I laughed a little.

"You think you can handle this?" I teased.

She bit her lip and placed a hand behind my neck. I wanted to kiss her, but she backed away right when it was about to happen. Gosh, she was being a tease, and it was working. She drew circles on my skin where the whipped cream was.

"Maybe I want to add more."

"Oh, really? Show me what you got."

She leaned in again, licking off some of the whipped cream she had put on my chest. I laughed. I was really turned on right now, feeling her touch and seeing her worship me like she was doing. Once she cleaned the whipped cream from me, I took her hand and pulled her closer. I loved the way it felt to touch her.

"What's next, Daisy?" She grabbed the tub of ice cream.

"I'm not done just yet."

She held up the ice cream like a trophy. She took the spoon and plopped some down on my bare chest, and I gasped. She ran her fingers through the ice cream.

"How's this working for you, cowboy?" She has started calling me that as a teenager, and it was my favorite nickname. I moaned a little as she licked the remnants off my chest.

"You're going to pay for this." As she finished cleaning my chest, I laughed, then kissed her. I kiss her hard, wanting to taste every single bit of her. "Alright, it's your turn now." I picked her up and put her on the counter. I needed her there. I took the tub of ice cream from her hands, using the spoon to scoop some out. I pointed the spoon at her shirt. It had to come off. "Come on now. Don't make me beg. You know I will." I would beg. I would worship her if she asked me to.

"Maybe I want you to beg." I got on my knees and peered up at her. She was hitting all the right buttons.

"Come on, darlin'. Let me get a little taste." She pointed at the tub of ice cream I was still holding.

"What are you going to do with that?" I winked at her, getting back up on my feet. I got closer to her and watched her closely as she took off her shirt, examining every layer of her bare skin.

"Don't worry. You'll enjoy this as much as I did."

I put the tub on the counter beside her and leaned in closer. I propped myself on opposite sides of her, moving closer to her. I went in for a kiss and pulled back just as I was centimeters away, just as she had done to me. I started licking off the ice cream from her body, starting with her neck. I remained there for a bit, loving the taste.

"I have one last surprise for you." I walked over to a cabinet and pulled out a bottle of chocolate sauce. "You didn't think I'd let you get off so easily with being a tease earlier, did you?"

I squeezed the bottle and let the syrup drip down her chest. I stopped it with my lips before it rolled down her body too far. I kissed her chest where the sauce stopped, then licked her in one motion all the way up to her neck and back down again. Her taste was indescribable.

I slid the bottle across the counter and pulled her close. I wanted to consume her...devour her. We fit perfectly together. I was so glad to have this back.

Chapter Twenty-Two

Daisy

I leaned against the counter, letting the coolness of it cool me off slightly from all the heat we had just caused. My heart was still racing. I missed Colt even more than I thought possible to miss someone. Colt was propped against the counter across from me now, and I kept picturing the steamy scene that just played out. It was straight out of a movie, and it was a little hard for me to believe that this was real life…my life. I could still taste the whipped cream and ice cream I licked from his body. The messiness was totally worth it. Just a taste of him and I was a goner.

I crossed my arms, knowing that although what had just happened was absolute perfection, there was more to the conversation that had to be discussed. I was afraid of what might be said, but our talk wasn't over just yet. The playful banter we had shared was slowly fading away, and this time, I needed to speak up first.

"Colt?"

"Hm?"

"We really need to talk about what happens next. I can't

pretend like everything's fine."

"I know."

"We need to figure out where we go from here." He nodded. "You and I both know we aren't just friends...I mean, after a scene like that..."

"Yeah, but that's what my dad thinks. He thinks we're just friends...or at least we can get along sort of like we used to. I don't think he knows the full extent of our friendship...before things started heating up between us." He ran a hand through his hair. The light from the window cast a warm glow on his face. I could see the wheels turning in his head. "If we tell him now, I'm afraid it will complicate things."

"What do you think will happen?"

"I'm not sure...but what if he doesn't take it well? I don't want to lose this summer with you because of a misunderstanding." I sighed.

"I hate hiding this." I had to come up with a solution, and fast.

"I do, too, Daisy."

"Maybe we can have it all."

"What do you mean?"

"Maybe we can be together when your dad isn't around, and we can go out sometimes and go riding...and we don't have to tell him."

"I do want to enjoy this time with you...that sounds like a plan...because honestly, I just can't keep my hands off you." He moved closer, his movement like a lion on the prowl, and I was his prey. He wrapped his calloused hands around the back of my neck, pulling me in to meet his lips. "I kind of like having you as a secret."

"It might be kind of fun." I winked playfully at him. Our minds were definitely on the same wavelength. "So, let's just take it one step at a time."

"Deal." He slid his hand down my leg, running a wave of heat through my body. This man knew all the right ways to get to me.

"So…we can have our own little adventure with this?"

"Whatever you want, darlin'." Those words rolled off his tongue so smoothly.

"Sounds like something out of a movie, like we'll be in our own little world." I liked the idea of it. No one would know, so there would be no one to complicate things. I was never a fan of having people nose around in my business.

"You always did like a thrill." I grinned, knowing he was right.

☐ ☐ ☐

I stood at the edge of the creek, watching the sun hit the water's surface. At sixteen, I felt limitless. I was full of adventure, and Colt was always there to be a part of it, usually with no questions asked. Colt was eighteen and pretty much my partner in crime. He was up for anything, just like me.

"Come on, cowboy!" I looked back at Colt, motioning for him to come closer.

I took hold of the rope. Ready to take off, I pulled back a little then let go. The wind blew my hair and I went flying into the air. I let go and landed right in the water with a splash. When my head bobbed up, I could hear Colt laughing.

"Don't worry. I'm coming to join you." Colt walked over and grabbed the rope.

"Hold onto it and pull yourself back a little, then lift off. It's so fun!"

"Better watch out!" Colt did as I told him and plopped right into the water, only a couple of feet from where I was. I watched as his head came out of the water, his hair slicked back.

"Wasn't that fun? Let's go again!"

"You're crazy, Daisy."

"Yeah, but you like my craziness." I saw that cute smirk come across his face, but I brushed it off.

I got out of the water and headed back to the rope to go again. I looked down at Colt and noticed how the sunlight was dancing in his hair. He was the perfect image. He would make the perfect boyfriend...and husband one day. I only wish it were me. I couldn't help but smile, knowing whoever that woman ended up being would be the luckiest woman in the world.

Colt was exceptional, raised to be a gentleman. Since he and I were friends, he always looked out for me. I knew he always had my back. He was a free spirit like me, but that was a side that only I really saw. Back on the ranch, he was grounded by the work and the responsibility. Sometimes, I felt bad for him. I had work to do on my family's ranch, too, but I know being a girl that my dad didn't assign me the same tasks he would if I were a boy, so I could only imagine how hard it was for Colt. Plus, our ranch was much smaller. It was just enough to suit my mom and dad well when they bought it.

I looked down, seeing his eyes locked on me, and felt comforted. When we were together, it was just the two of us. The world always seemed to fade away. There was a spark between us- there always had been- but neither of us has ever done anything about it, and quite honestly, I didn't think either of us ever would. I guess some things are just supposed to be this way, but at least Colt was in my life in some capacity.

I took in a deep breath, remembering all the quiet conversations sharing secrets and dreams, the laughter that was nonstop for us, the adventures we had been on, and so many other things that bonded us. I saw the encouragement in his gaze, but also something more lingering there- an understanding far greater than words.

"Daisy, are you coming?" I snapped back to reality, realizing I was still holding onto the rope.

"Yeah, I'm coming. Hold your horses." I pulled back on the rope, letting my body move backward to get more momentum, then lifted my feet off and went flying into the air a second time. I let go when I was near where Colt was in the water, landing with a splash beside him.

"You almost landed on top of me!"

"Should've moved out of my way, cowboy."

□ □ □

Chapter Twenty-Three

Colt

Daisy was leaning against the counter and I was leaning against the one across from her, licking my lips and taking in her gorgeous body. Neither of us had put our shirts back on yet, and I was very easily distracted. She took my breath away. The mess we just made was completely worth it. I would have made that mess to get even one little taste of her.

She crossed my arms and I was afraid of what was to come, knowing that her folding her arms meant one thing- that she wanted to talk. I hated those words. I'm sure they might just be the most dreaded words for any man to hear. Usually, they didn't mean anything good.

"Colt?"

"Hm?"

"We really need to talk about what happens next. I can't pretend like everything's fine." I wish we didn't have to talk about anything. I wish this could be our life and we didn't have to worry about anyone else. I just want us.

"I know."

"We need to figure out where we go from here." I nodded. "You and I both know we aren't just friends...I mean, after a scene like that..."

We aren't just friends. We are so much more than that. We were almost more than that as kids, and we probably could have been more if I hadn't been so stupid and backward and just manned up and told her how I felt. I could tell she longed for me as much as I did for her back then, but I never got around to sharing how I felt.

That is still my biggest regret to date.

We lost so much time and maybe if we had been together, she would never have left.

And then I wouldn't have missed her as bad as I did.

I wouldn't have shed tears for her.

But this is now, and I can't change the past. I have to make up for what happened before and do what I need to do this time to hold onto her. My heart longed for the beautiful and stunning, curly headed, brown eyed girl that took my breath away and always made me turn my head.

"Yeah, but that's what my dad thinks. He thinks we're just friends...or at least we can get along sort of like we used to. I don't think he knows the full extent of our friendship...before things started heating up between us." I brushed my hair back. "If we tell him now, I'm afraid it will complicate things."

I made a promise to my dad, and I was so afraid of hurting him that I was terrified to tell him the truth. I have never, not once, broken a promise to my dad. My word meant something, and now what was I to do?

"What do you think will happen?"

"I'm not sure...but what if he doesn't take it well? I don't want to lose this summer with you because of a misunderstanding."

She sighed, just barely where I could hear. The thought of not having Daisy here all summer hurt me. This was the first time I had seen her in seven years, other than at my mom's funeral, and it was really starting to feel like old times...you know, without all the kissing and touching we've done. But I'm sure that would have been done back then, too, if only...

"I hate hiding this."

"I do, too, Daisy."

I wanted to shout the way I felt about her from the rooftops. I wanted everyone to know how I felt, especially Daisy. I wanted people to know she was mine, and I wasn't going to let go this time.

"Maybe we can have it all."

"What do you mean?"

"Maybe we can be together when your dad isn't around, and we can go out sometimes and go riding...and we don't have to tell him." Would she be my secret? Did I want her to be hidden? I really didn't, but what other choice did I have? I couldn't lose her again.

My heart couldn't take that heartbreak again.

"I do want to enjoy this time with you...that sounds like a plan...because honestly, I just can't keep my hands off you." I was looking at her, glancing down at her body once more, and I just couldn't help myself. I knew my dad would be back soon, and I needed one last touch. I moved closer, wanting to feel what was mine. I grabbed her neck from behind and pulled her in to steal one last kiss. "I kind of like having you as a secret." Honestly, the sound of that was starting to grow on me. Maybe it was turning me on a little bit, or maybe I still hadn't come off the high from our fun just a little while ago.

"It might be kind of fun." She winked, and I could tell she

was enjoying this. "So, let's just take it one step at a time."

"Deal." I slid my hand down her leg, tempting her. I knew what I was doing. I loved to watch her as her body took over.

"So...we can have our own little adventure with this?"

"Whatever you want, darlin'." I meant it. Whatever she wanted, as always, I would give her. I would give Daisy the world.

"Sounds like something out of a movie, like we'll be in our own little world."

"You always did like a thrill." She knew I was right, and her grin said it all. "My dad should be home soon. I can make dinner if you want to go shower."

"Wouldn't suppose you have time to join me, would you?" Oh, she has no idea how badly I want to take her up on the offer, but my dad could be back at any minute, and the only thing worse than me telling him I broke my word to him is for him to come home and find it out by us showering together.

"Better not...you know..." The look on her face said she knew what I meant, and she got off the counter, picked up her shirt, and headed toward the bathroom. I grabbed a rag and dampened it to wipe off my body, then put my shirt back on and heard the water running.

I hadn't heard my dad pull up yet, so maybe I could spare a minute or two. I knew I didn't have time to do what I wanted and hop in there with her, so instead I leaned against the door frame, listening to the soft sounds of the water cascading down her body. My mind drifted, picturing Daisy inside. If I were in there right now, I would find ways to make her laugh, listening to her laughter echo off the tiles. I could see her splashing me for trying to touch her- playfully of course. I would splash her back, then my urges would take over, and I would pin her against the wall, taking in her whole body and kissing her until I could no longer breathe. Daisy's appeal was undeniable, and I could only imagine what it would be like to be in that shower with her, feeling the water's warmth against my skin, and I feeling her touch.

I shook my head slightly, knowing I needed to snap out of it and cool off before I got myself into trouble.

I made my way back into the kitchen and pulled out some steaks from the fridge.

Chapter Twenty-Four

Daisy

I let the warm water run down my body as I thought about what had just unfolded between Colt and me. I never thought something like this would happen. After all this time, I didn't think that coming back here would change anything, especially not in this way. I had just stopped talking to Colt once my mom died. I shut everyone out after that. I was a little surprised at how Colt was trying to reconnect a little at the start of my stay here, and thinking about how that little girl once could only dream of being with him made my eyes swell. To that little girl, this was a dream come true. Now, we just had to keep pretending like we were friends, keeping our relationship a secret from Walt. It was my idea, but it was the only thing I could think of to keep us together. That was all that mattered to me at this moment. Maybe keeping this relationship hidden from Walt would give an exhilarating edge to it.

I rubbed over my body with my hands, trying to wash away all the stickiness. I felt like someone was watching me, and I kind of hoped it was Colt out there. Just the thought of him standing out there, wondering what it would be like to join me in this shower, gave me a rush.

I stepped out of the shower, the steam moving around me and fogging up the mirror. I wiped it off with a towel, then wrapped it around my body. As I felt the fabric against me, I wished it were a pair of rough, calloused hands instead. Those were what I longed to touch me. I could smell the scents of my shampoo, but I could also smell something savory, and I knew it must be whatever Colt had started making in the kitchen. Glancing into the mirror, I brushed my hair back, then I headed toward the kitchen to see what Colt was up to.

I could hear something sizzling and some pots and pans clanking. I found Colt standing at the stove, his back facing me. I stood there, taking him in for a moment. He was so focused as he moved his hands to flip the steaks. His muscles flexed with each movement, bringing a smile to my face. These discreet moments were my favorite. I loved when I could steal a quick admire without him noticing.

"Need a hand?" Colt turned swiftly, a grin spreading across his face.

"Yeah. Could you grab the seasoning from the cabinet? It's the one with the black lid." I nodded, moving toward where he had pointed. I grabbed the seasoning, my fingers brushing against the cool metal of the container. I turned back to Colt, catching a glimpse of him peaking at me. I quickly shook my head, focusing on the task at hand.

"Here you go, cowboy." I could still call him that since his dad wasn't here yet. That nickname would never grow old. He was stuck with it forever. "Anything else I can help you with?"

"I'm about ready, but if you could set the table, that would be helpful."

As I pulled out the plates from the cabinet and arranged them on the table, one for each of us, I thought about how hard it would be to contain myself at dinner. What if I smiled or laughed or even stared too long at Colt? Would Walt notice? I brushed those thoughts away, placing the last fork down.

I looked out the window, hearing the sounds of tires against gravel. Walt was home. My heart sank a little.

"Colt, your dad's here." He brought over the food, looking out the window as he walked over to the table.

"Great timing." His brow furrowed and his hand grazed my arm just as quickly as he pulled it away. "Just act natural. Everything's okay." I nodded, feeling the nerves of the situation. That was a lot easier said than done.

"Hey, dad." Colt held his casual tone, and I was a little envious of how he could flip a switch so perfectly.

"Smells good in here. What are you cooking?" Walt's eyes scanned the kitchen. I was already sitting at the table, waiting for the men to join.

"Just made some steaks and sautéed some veggies. Daisy helped a bit." Walt glanced at me as he sat in his chair at the table.

"Is that so?" He looked around at the food again, enough time for Colt to have a seat. "Looks like you two did a fine job. Hope it tastes as good as it smells. I could just about smell that when I got out of my truck." I chuckled. I appreciated this light-heartedness from Walt. It eased me a little. "Well, I'm glad Colt wasn't too bad of company while I was gone."

Colt and I exchanged a quick glance. Walt had no idea what kind of company his son had been while he was away at my dad's ranch. The flashbacks raced through my mind, the images of whipped cream, ice cream, and the ever so tasty chocolate syrup danced around, as did the way we cleaned each other. The best thing, though, was Colt telling me he would beg.

I jumped back in to listen to the conversation and to eat. Colt served the food.

"So, Colt...these steaks taste pretty good. How'd you make them?"

"I used that seasoning in the cabinet with the black lid. Just don't tell anyone my secret recipe."

"It'll be our little secret."

Walt winked at me and Colt, and the two of us exchanged another glance. My heart was racing but I knew there was no way he could have found out about the two of us, could he have? No. There was no way Walt knew about the deeper connection Colt and I had rekindled since I had been here.

We continued eating, the conversation flowing easily. Walt recalled a memory of us when we were kids one summer here on the ranch. It was one of those funny stories that never got old about when Colt had tried to build a treehouse, but he ended up managing to get stuck inside.

☐ ☐ ☐

Colt did have an adventurous side, but it couldn't compare to mine. It didn't even come close. On a summer afternoon at the ranch, Colt had decided to build a treehouse. He had so many ideas and I remember listening to him tell his mom and dad all about his plans. He was so excited. Colt gathered his supplies with his parents' help. They let him work on it with little assistance since he was eleven and had been helping his dad on the ranch for a few years now.

I had been on the ranch that day, but Colt had that look in his eyes that said he was on a mission so I didn't bother him. Colt climbed up the tree. I watched him from around the ranch while I was walking with my mom and listening to her talk to Rose. Colt looked about ten feet high and I was a little scared for him, but I knew he could do it. He had told me that he wanted to fill the treehouse with little treasures and that it would be our little, secret hideout. I liked that idea, and I liked that he was including me.

Colt was hammering away. As he worked, I could see how focused he was. The day was halfway over and he seemed to have a lot of it already constructed. He finally took a break to come inside and eat a sandwich with me, but not before he took a second to look at his craftsmanship.

"How's it coming along?"

"It is going so good, Daisy! Soon, we will be able to play in it! I will let you know when it's finished so you can come up and see it."

Before long, Colt was back outside and continuing to work. He was about finished, and that is when he found a small problem. Colt hadn't made himself anything that he could use to get down. He was stuck. He decided to finish the work on the platform and then make a roof to help keep the sun out.

Then, things took a turn. He reached for another branch but lost his balance, ending up wedged between two thick limbs. Panic set in. We were all outside on the porch when it happened.

"Help!" We heard his scream and went running toward him. *"Daisy! Mom! Dad! Help me! I'm stuck!"* His voice echoed. The sun was getting lower and he was scared. He looked down and saw all of us. He must have been so relieved.

"Colt, are you okay?" His mom asked, worried.

"Yeah. I'm just stuck."

"Don't worry, son. We'll get you down." Walt turned toward us. *"I'll go grab a ladder."*

"I'll come with you." Both our dads took off toward the barn.

"Daisy?"

"Yes, Colt? I'm here. You were too adventurous today. You know, everyone can't be like me." I saw him let out a small laugh. Laughter was the best medicine.

They brought back the ladder and pulled it out near the tree.

"I'm coming up." I watched as Walt climbed to the top. *"Try to swing your legs over to me."* Colt was hesitant and I could tell he was still afraid.

"Come on, Colt! I want some ice cream and we can't go get any unless you're down here!" I was looking for any way to distract and ease his mind a little.

Colt followed Walt's directions, managing to get himself unstuck between the two branches. Slowly but surely, he climbed down the ladder, holding onto his dad.

"Are you good?" His mom hugged him.

"Yeah, I'm good." I looked over at him.

"Next time you're going to do something like that, maybe think about how you're going to get down before you climb so high up."

◻ ◻ ◻

"I like that story." I smiled, remembering that day so clearly.

"Yeah. It's too bad that the storm a few years back tore it down. I thought that thing was going to last forever up in that tree."

"It survived that long?"

"Sure did." The conversation continued for a few more minutes, then Walt decided to head to bed.

Chapter Twenty-Five

Colt

I couldn't believe my dad remembered all the details of that story. It was so long ago, but I guess it was a little bit of a scary moment. I had been scared and a little embarrassed that I had been so stupid to not think of how I was going to get down once I got up there. After that incident, I always thought things like that through before doing anything.

My dad decided to go to bed, so I started cleaning up the dishes. I was glad that Daisy and I were finally alone again. I was sure that I would be wishing for that a lot more for the rest of the summer with her.

Daisy came up beside me, gently brushing her hand against my back, taking a towel in her hand.

"I'll help by drying them." I smiled at her.

We did the dishes in silence, and I just admired the way that being in her presence brought so much comfort to me. Daisy was impeccable and this evening between us was picture-perfect.

"Hey?"

"Hm?"

"So, what do you want to do now that we have some time to ourselves?" There were a lot of things I wanted to do, but I couldn't risk it all right now, especially with my dad just in another room.

"Do you want to go out on the porch for a bit?"

That was probably a safe option for us. My dad usually slept through the night until six a.m. when he got up, but being outside would give us some more relief and security.

"I could use some fresh air." I

I wanted so desperately to take her hand in mine, but I couldn't risk my dad seeing us. We walked out onto the porch, me quietly shutting the door behind us as not to disturb my dad. We took seats in the rocking chairs. My dad had built them for my mom. She always wanted a pair of them and a porch swing, and anything she wanted, my dad made happen.

"It's nice being back here." I turned, facing her. She was looking out toward the fields. "I've...missed this. I guess I never really realized how much."

"Yeah...I've...I never realized how much I missed having you around this place until you came back. I could feel it the moment I saw you, struggling with the gate...our hands brushed against each other when I came over to help you, and I...I felt something." I probably sounded crazy to her. "It sounds crazy, doesn't it?"

"You felt that, too?" I nodded, a surprised look on my face.

"Can I ask you something?"

"Sure."

"Why did you never come back here? I mean...you came here for my mom's funeral, but your dad said he never saw you otherwise."

"He came to visit me once, but I knew he felt so out of place that he wouldn't be back." I could see the hurt in her eyes. I felt so bad for her. I knew the death of her mom hit her hard. It me hard, too, when my mom passed. I was thankful for the twenty years I had with her, but Daisy only had sixteen years with hers. She didn't have her mom by her side for the rest of high school, her graduation from high school or college, or when she moved for college. I had my mom through high school. I never realized my situation could have been worse. "Sometimes I wish he had come back...maybe shown me a little more support."

"But why didn't you come here? It works both ways... doesn't it?"

"I was struggling. I guess...in ways...I still am." She paused for a moment, then stood and walked over the wooden railing. She folded her arms and propped herself against it. "After my mom died, I felt like a piece of me was missing. She was the rock, and then she was gone, just like that. I told you I have blamed myself."

"Yes, you did. But Daisy, I told you it wasn't your fault." I stood up and walked over to her, leaning against the railing beside her. "That's the truth. What happened is not your fault."

"Okay."

"Can I tell you something?"

"Yes."

"Your dad did want to visit you more."

"What?"

"I heard him and my dad talking. He told my dad that he wanted to go visit you again, but he wanted you to come home, and he didn't know how to get you to do that."

"Why does he want me here so badly?"

"Is it that bad being here?"

"This is where it all happened...all the pain. This place reminded me so much of my mom and being at the ranch with my dad; it just reminds me so much of her and what happened. I hate that feeling. I hate that pain. I left because I was struggling, and that's why I never looked back."

"Your dad was struggling, too."

"I guess I've not been the best daughter. I just wish he had tried to talk to me. He left that all up to me." We didn't speak for a few minutes, just stood on the porch. I glanced at her a few times, then finally placed my hand on hers.

"Daisy, I know we have to keep this relationship between us hidden, but I can't help how I feel about you. It feels so right." I leaned toward her, eager to feel her touch. She leaned in, too.

"I feel the same way, cowboy, but you're going to have to learn to keep your hands to yourself unless we are for sure alone." She backed away, and that only made me want her more.

"Daisy?" She turned her head. "I promise that I am going to make this summer unforgettable." She smiled, and that was like one huge green flag. It was my time to go. I moved in close to her, wrapping one hand around her waist and the other against her cheek. We stared into each other's eyes, getting lost. I pushed her toward the wall of the house beside the front door.

"Colt..."

"Mm, mm." She knew she only uses my real name when she is mad at me. I wanted her to say it again, but the right way this time.

"Cowboy..." I saw the teasing look on her face and I gave in.

My heart was racing, and my gaze was locked onto hers. There was such an intensity that shivers went down my spine. Holding her in place with one hand on each side of her, I moved my head and admired her whole body.

"I've wanted this for a while. My dad couldn't go to bed

soon enough." Her cheeks flushed.

I didn't give her a chance to respond before I pressed my lips on hers. The kiss was electric, a fire igniting between us. I moved back only for a second to let her breathe before diving right back in. I moved my hands slowly down her body as I kissed her, feeling every inch of her. She was melting into me, her hands now fisting my hair.

I knew she wanted more, and I wasn't about to stop just yet. I kept kissing her, this time agreeing to not stop until she used words to tell me she needed a breath. I could feel her soften beneath me. She was letting her guard down and I felt so privileged to be in her presence for this moment. I pulled her even closer to me, as if I were trying to make us one.

I lingered longer on her lips, taking in her taste and savoring every moment. I pulled back and searched for her eyes, asking for permission to continue. She nodded, and I planted kisses all the way down to her neck. I could feel her shiver as she leaned her head back. I now had perfect access to continue pleasing her. I pulled back again after continuing for a while longer and gave her a quick breath as I returned to her lips. The passion was as strong as ever. The world around us was gone, and all that mattered was the rhythm of our hearts beating in sync. The porch had now become our private sanctuary under the stars.

Chapter Twenty-Six

Daisy

I walked outside, seeing the sun peeking over the horizon and casting the beautiful golden tones across the ranch. The view was beautiful. The warmth from the summer sun only added to the warmth of last night's rendezvous lingering on my lips.

Colt and I shared something electric and magnetic, drawing us to one another. I felt something between us all those years ago, but what I felt then could never compare to what I feel now.

There was a thirst only Colt could quench.

There was hunger only he could satisfy.

It was both thrilling and terrifying knowing we had to keep us a secret from everyone, including his dad.

As I walked toward the barn, I could hear the whinny of the horse, the cattle in the distance, and the soft wind rustling. Walt had taken Colt out early, and I knew my first task was always to check on the horses and clean out their stalls.

Just thinking about Colt made my heart race, and trying to contain myself was proving harder than I thought. But if this is what I had to do to keep having scenes like last night and at the bar, then it was worth it. Oh, it was so worth it. Colt's smile made me feel like I could melt, and the way he looked at me reminded me of how he used to look at me- like I was the only girl in the world.

I brushed it off, knowing I needed to change my focus.

Today was busy. I cleaned out the horses stalls first, then carried a bucket of grain and gave each of them the right amount. I carried buckets of water to refill their water troughs, knowing that I would be thirsty, too, in the summer heat. I took some time to brush each of their manes, knowing how much they enjoyed it. Even with this familiar routine, my mind was elsewhere.

The heat of Colt's body pressed against mine and the way his lips moved against my skin made me forget everything and everyone. The world had disappeared, and we had been hidden in our little piece of paradise...our own little piece of heaven. Colt was intoxicating, but I knew the risks involved with us. He made a promise to his dad before I got here and I didn't want to cause any trouble. I would keep my feelings buried when we weren't alone.

As I worked, I caught a glimpse of Colt across the yard. He was busy with equipment, and for a second, I forgot what I was doing, getting lost in admiring the way he was moving and thinking of how his rough hands felt against my body. Walt was nowhere in sight.

"Hey, Daisy!" My heart fluttered, and I tried to keep my expression neutral because, although I didn't see Walt, that didn't mean he wasn't close by. "Need a hand?"

"Uh, sure." Colt started walking closer to me so we didn't have to shout. "Your dad said I needed to check on the cattle. That's where I was headed."

"Let's do it together then."

We walked side by side, and I could feel the tension between us. The thrill of our secret added a little extra excitement to our relationship, and I couldn't deny that it did feel kind of good.

When we reached the pasture, I noticed Walt in the distance. He was checking out some fence, and my heart dropped a little. I was really hoping we would get a moment alone today.

"Don't worry, Daisy. We'll be fine." Walt started moving closer to us, and I could feel my hands start to sweat. I wiped my forehead.

"I should probably get back to work." I created some distance between the two of us.

"Okay. Let me know if you need anything." I nodded.

"Will do." I forced a smile, trying to hide how freaked out I was. I couldn't believe that I just did that. Everything was fine, yet I couldn't even manage to stand near Colt while his dad walked over. How dumb was I?

The rest of the day dragged on, filled with plenty of work to be done. I finished all the tasks Walt had given to me on a piece of paper in the kitchen when I woke up, and I was tired. I took a moment to lean against the barn to cool off. I took a deep breath, wondering where Colt was. It had been a little bit since I had seen him, and I hadn't seen Walt in a while. Just then, I heard footsteps.

"Hey." I looked up and saw my cowboy.

"Hey."

"My dad went to the bar for a drink. He's meeting your dad there. I thought maybe we could go for a ride on the horses…if you're up for it?"

"Yes. That sounds nice."

"Let's go before it gets too dark."

We saddled up the horses, and I was eager to get some time alone with Colt. We rode Shadow and Domino in the open fields, feeling the gentle breeze.

"Let's race to the creek!" My competitive spirit was coming out. Colt laughed, and the horses under us galloped ahead. We raced side by side, feeling the thrill, excitement, and freedom of it all. Up ahead, I could see the creek sparkling in the fading light. I felt a rush of joy. I wanted every day to be like this with my cowboy. We slowed once we reached the creek.

"That was fun."

"It's even better if you win." I winked at him, knowing that I was always the fastest one.

"We should do this again soon."

"Definitely." We shared a moment of silence, and I knew I wanted to apologize to Colt for earlier. "Hey, Colt?"

"Yeah?"

"I'm sorry about earlier."

"What do you mean?"

"When you offered to help me out with the cattle…"

"Oh."

"Yeah. I'm sorry about that. I was quick to run off, and I shouldn't have done that."

"Daisy, I understand."

"Really?"

"Yes."

"It's hard burying my feelings."

"It's just as hard for me." There was more silence. "I want to just reach out and touch you, and sometimes I feel like I'm close to doing that, but then I remember we can't. Moments like this, though, make it all worth it."

"They do."

"I told you that I would make this the most unforgettable summer for you, and I still promise you that." I smiled at him. He always kept his promises…well, except the one about nothing happening between the two of us.

"Come here, cowboy." He moved his horse closer to mine, just close enough so we could reach out and touch each other. Our hands still on the reins, he took one hand and placed it on my leg. He smiled back at me.

"What do you want?"

"You know." I was teasing him again, and this was becoming one of my favorite things. We leaned toward each other, letting our lips meet. It was a soft kiss, not like the one from last night.

"Happy?"

"Yes, but…"

"But?"

"It's been a long day."

"One more?"

"One more." We leaned toward each other once more and let our lips connect. I was happy. For the first time in a long time, I was happy.

Chapter Twenty-Seven

Colt

The sun rose over the ranch. I woke up to the crowing of the roosters and the faint smells of the world outside. I grabbed breakfast, then slipped on my boots and headed out the door. My dad was already out in the fields. I was falling a little behind this morning. I joined him, helping with some of the morning chores.

"Colt, come over here. I need your help."

"I got it." I grabbed the door of the gate, closing it quickly. We had to wrangle the cattle and check on a few that were sick, making sure to give them the required medicine to help them get better.

"I need you to help me with them. They have to be held still so I can inject them. They have to get this medicine to help with their respiratory infections. Come on. We need to get this done so none of them get any sicker."

"I got it, dad."

"You ready?"

"Yes." My dad took the syringe and injected it.

"Easy now, girl." He gently rubbed her. "Good job. Now, let's move on to the next one."

As we worked side by side to give each of the sick cattle their injections, I couldn't help but think about Daisy. Since she had been back here, I had seen her love for this place blossom again. I understood why she had left and moved to the city. Pain is hard. It is especially harder to face it head-on rather than run away from it. I knew I would do everything in my power to keep my promise to her and make this the most unforgettable summer for her.

Once the chores were done, I decided it was time to find Daisy. I hadn't seen her in a bit, where I was so focused on helping my dad, but there was something I wanted to ask her. I walked over to the barn and didn't see her. Usually, she likes to hang out here if she has any free time at all. I thought about it, then made my way to the house. Once inside, I saw her coming down the hall.

"Oh, Colt. You scared me."

"Sorry."

"I just had to run inside to use the bathroom quickly. Are you hungry? I figured while I was in there, I would go ahead and make myself a sandwich. Can I get you one? I can make one up for your dad, too."

"That would be great, but could you make mine and yours to go?"

"To go?" She looked at me, confused.

"I thought we could go fishing."

"Fishing?"

"Come on. There's no way it's been so long that you've forgotten what fishing is."

"No, I haven't." She laughed lightly.

"Well?"

"I would love to go with you."

I wanted to kiss her, but I was going to save it until we were alone by the water. There was a small pond with just enough fish that we could catch from time to time and make a meal on, and I couldn't think of anything better to eat on a summer day than some freshly caught fish. We headed out, stopping by to drop off a sandwich for my dad.

"Daisy made us all a sandwich." He looked down, noticing our sandwiches in our hands.

"Where are you two headed off to?"

"Well, since we finished with the cattle and Daisy has finished everything with the horses, I thought she could go with me and help catch some dinner."

"Fishing?" I nodded.

"Well, make sure she doesn't scare them off. I want enough to eat." I nodded, offering a crooked grin.

Once we reached our fishing spot, I set up the rods while Daisy explored the area. She picked up a couple of rocks and skipped them in the water. I watched her, captivated by the way she moved. She was so carefree and adventurous, and this moment reminded me of when we were kids, and we would go fishing.

□ □ □

Daisy and I were sitting at the edge of the creek with our feet dangling over the water. She moved her feet back and forth to create tiny ripples in the water. The two of us had only been fishing by ourselves a few times. Our parents were nervous about us being around the water, but once we were old enough- I was fourteen and Daisy twelve- our dads convinced our moms that it would be okay.

"Do you think we'll catch anything this time?" Daisy asked,

her eyes sparkling. She held on to her fishing pole tightly, not wanting the same mishap from last time to happen again. I shrugged.

Going fishing with Daisy was special. It was just the two of us. We could sit and talk a little, or not say anything at all, and it was so peaceful.

She brought me peace.

She brought me comfort.

"We might catch something. I sure hope so."

"You had pretty good luck last time. Remember that big bass you caught?"

"Sure do! That was the biggest one I have ever caught." She turned her head back to face the water, watching her line in the water, hoping she would get a bite. "I really hope you get one today."

"Me, too. I hope mine is bigger than that bass you caught, too." I chuckled as she rolled her eyes. She was funny like that. She had pouted when I caught the bass, and she didn't have anything to show off from our fishing trip.

"What's that?" I noticed her pulling something out of her pocket.

"These are going to do the trick!" She held up a small container full of colorful worms.

I leaned against a rock, watching my line in the water, occasionally stealing glances at Daisy's way. She was beautiful. She was stunning. I knew there wasn't any such thing as perfect, but Daisy sure was the closest thing to it.

"It's so nice out here. I love fishing with you, cowboy."

"Yeah, you aren't too bad of company out here. But fishing is one of the best ways to spend a summer day."

We waited patiently for a while longer, and I was starting to lose all hope that we would catch anything for supper. I felt kind of bad because I knew how badly Daisy wanted to catch something.

After coming back empty-handed last time, she looked upset. She was trying to hide it, but I could see right through it.

"I think I got one!" I jumped. Daisy had so much excitement in her voice.

"Come on. Reel it in." Daisy had both hands on her pole, reeling it in. She was so close. "You can do it. Yeah. Just like that." *Daisy had the most determined look on her face, pulling with all her might.*

"Look! Colt, look!" She held up the end of her line, a fish hanging off. "I did it! I finally caught one!"

"You sure did. Looks like it might be a little bigger than the one I caught last time." *She was so proud, but there was no way she was as proud as I was of her.*

Daisy deserved this.

Daisy deserved the sun, the moon, and the stars.

☐ ☐ ☐

"Come on, Colt. Let's see who can catch the bigger fish this time. You remember I did last time."

"How could I possibly forget?"

We smiled at me, and I knew she was up for a challenge. I grinned, accepting it. We both cast our lines into the water. For a while, there was silence. The only sounds were of Mother Nature. As the afternoon was coming to an end, we were starting to think we wouldn't catch any.

"Colt!" I looked over at Daisy, reeling in her line.

"You've almost got it!"

Once she had it, she took the fish and held it up, letting me know she caught the first one. She stuck her tongue out at me, and I knew I needed to catch one quickly or else I wouldn't be hearing the end of this. She put it in the bucket, then threw her line back out. It was only a few minutes later when I caught one.

"Look here, Daisy. Two can play at this game." We smiled at each other.

"Just wait. I might have a secret weapon up my sleeve." This felt so natural, so right, being here with her. It felt just like old times.

"I'm really glad you're here this summer. I know you coming here wasn't what you had originally wanted, but you must admit that you're enjoying being here now."

"I am. I have missed this place, Colt. I have missed you." I could see the sincerity in her eyes.

"I've been thinking?"

"You? Thinking? Don't hurt yourself." I laughed.

"I've been thinking about us."

"And?"

"What are we going to do once summer ends?"

"Let's not worry about that. I don't want to talk about it." I nodded. "Let's just enjoy the summer. Remember, you promised me the most unforgettable one."

I nodded again, giving her a slight smile. I looked out at the water. A worried feeling came over me, and I could feel a little pressure in my chest afterward. What would happen between us when summer ends? Our time together will be up, and reality will set in. Daisy will be leaving to go back to her place in the city soon and resume her life there, and I will be here.

I will be at my family's ranch.

I will be at the Texas Rose Ranch.

I will be in Garrity Valley, Texas.

Our summer has once again been filled with talks, smiles, laughter- and this time, more. It has been as it once was. The thought of her packing up all her things and leaving is starting to weigh heavily. There will be physical distance between us again, but what if this also brought a different kind of distance? What if she decides it is too hard to try something long-distance? What if she decides to end things with us? I have been feeling that this means as much to her as it does to me, but what if she doesn't really feel that way? What if this is just a summer fling to her?

I brushed my thoughts away, knowing that worrying would do me no good. All I could do right now was to cherish the time that we have spent together and cherish the time yet to come for the remainder of the summer.

Chapter Twenty-Eight

Daisy

The sun was starting to dip below the horizon, and I knew we needed to start heading back before it got too late. Walt was surely starving by now, and we had just caught supper.

"Looks like we caught enough to eat." Colt glanced down at the bucket of fish, a proud look on his face.

"Yep. Your dad will be happy about that."

"He is probably waiting for us. We'd better head back." I nodded, and we took off walking back.

"I can't wait to eat. Who's going to clean them?"

Colt laughed a little, probably remembering that although I didn't mind baiting a line with worms, reeling in the fish, or any other aspect of fishing like that, what I refused to do was clean a fish. I had watched him, Walt, and my dad clean them before, but I knew I could never do it.

"My dad might handle it while we shower."

"Okay. And you need one. You stink." I held my nose for a

second, showing him how smelly he was. Truthfully, part of the smell could be coming from the fish, but that wasn't as funny as this.

When we got back to the house, I could smell the familiar smells again. This place brought contentment that I hadn't felt in a very long time. I missed that feeling. Walt was sitting in a rocking chair on the porch.

"How'd fishing go?" Colt held up the bucket so his dad could see inside. "Looks like you did good."

"We caught plenty to eat." Walt opened the door for us, both men letting me go in first.

"Here. Let me have that." Walt took the bucket from Colt's hands. "You two need to go shower. You smell. I'll take this and clean them and get them frying for supper."

"Thanks, dad."

"Yes. Thank you, Walt. I appreciate it."

"Still don't like to clean a fish, Daisy?" I shook my head no.

I hurried to the bathroom, turning the shower on to heat a little bit. I watched the steam rise as I took my clothes off. I lifted my shirt to my nose, and Walt was right. It did smell. I guess that's a perk for fishing. I hopped in the shower, letting the water run down my face as I wiped away the day. Something was loitering in my mind, though.

This summer has been amazing. It has been one of the best times I've had in years. It might just be one of my favorite times, ever. But the lingering words Colt asked me earlier stayed in my mind. What would happen once summer ended? I had no way of knowing. There were so many possibilities. I know I love being here. Except for the start of my arrival and that one disagreement between Colt and me, I was happy. Even with all the hard work to do around here, day in and day out, I have felt joy. That was something I hadn't had in my life in a while, and I was starting to get that back. I knew that Colt liked me. He showed me that in so many ways.

He showed me he liked me every time I talked to him, and his attention was only on me.

He showed me he liked me when we kissed, and I could feel the passion.

He showed me he liked me when he made me smile.

And when he made me laugh.

And when he made plans for us to do things together.

But did he love me? Did Colt love me? That was the biggest question of all and I wasn't sure he was there yet. I mean, we have not been together long, so how could he…right?

And did I love him?

I hopped out of the shower and put my clothes on. I could smell the fish in the kitchen, and I was hoping it was ready. My stomach growled. I was so hungry and eager to eat.

"It smells good in here."

"Wait until you taste it." I sat down at the table, and Walt placed a plate in front of me. "I bet you haven't had freshly fried fish in a long time, have you?"

"No, sir. I haven't." Walt took a seat beside me, and I heard footsteps. I turned and saw Colt turn the corner.

"Come sit. It's time to eat, son."

We all started to dig into the plates in front of us. The aroma made my mouth water. I was anticipating this meal. It had been a long time since I had eaten anything like this. You can't get food like this in the city. This is prime, country cooking, just like my mom used to make.

"Wow." I continued chewing the food. "This is so incredible, Walt. It's better than I remember." He chuckled.

"Glad you like it."

"You know, I haven't been fishing in a bit. Last time I went, I didn't catch a thing. Maybe I should have sent Colt here instead." He shook his head and took another bite of the fried fillet.

"Yeah, I've been pretty lucky lately." I knew what he meant, and it made my heart flutter a bit. "Maybe I can show you a few tricks sometime. I hear Daisy may have some, too."

"What do you mean?"

"Come on now. You must remember. You pulled that bag of colored worms out of your pocket last time we went fishing. We were fourteen and twelve then."

I was surprised he remembered that. I mean, even remembering our ages.

Did Colt pay that much attention?

"I remember." I turned to Walt, who was now speaking. "You came back and told me you needed some of those magic worms Daisy had." We all laughed. "Maybe you two can go back out fishing at least once more before Daisy has to leave at the end of summer. I wouldn't mind another meal like this."

Walt had no idea of the weight of his words.

"Yeah. That would be nice." I looked down at my plate, finishing my last piece.

Chapter Twenty-Nine

Colt

The clock struck ten, and my dad had settled in his room for the night. He was completely oblivious to what was about to happen between Daisy and me. She was standing in the door frame, and I towered over her, my arm placed above her head and propping myself up, my head slightly leaning into her figure.

"I can't wait any longer."

"Can't wait for what?" She knew exactly what I meant. She was just playing with me, and I didn't want any games right now. I only wanted her.

"I want you. All of you, darlin'."

"All of me?"

"Can I take it? Can I take what's mine?" She paused, biting her lip as if she were contemplating what to say.

"I don't think I should let it be that easy for you." Was Daisy McClain playing hard to get? And why was that even more tempting?

"What do you want me to do, then?"

"You remember the evening in the kitchen?" I nodded. "I want you to beg, just like you said you would."

"Beg?"

"Yes. Beg."

"Okay." I got down onto my knees like I had in the kitchen, setting the tone. I looked up into her eyes, seeing her smile from ear to ear.

"Please, darlin. Let me touch you. I need to feel your warmth. I need to feel your touch. I need to feel our bodies together. I need to hold you close and feel your heartbeat in sync with mine. I need a kiss from you. Can't you see, darlin'? I need you. I need to drown in every. Single. Piece. Of. You." I was grazing my hands along her body as I spoke, trying to tempt her. "Please, let me. I promise to be gentle." She grabbed me by the shirt collar, pulling me up to meet her.

"I need you, too, but don't you dare be gentle." She had a hunger in her eyes that I had never seen before. I saw the mischievous look on her face, and I was ready to dive right in.

I reached out to tuck a piece of loose hair behind her ear. I could feel her breath jump as I closed the distance between us.

Before I knew it, I had her shoved up against the wall, my lips on hers. I felt a rush of adrenaline that only tasting and feeling Daisy could tame.

Just as quickly as my lips found hers, the kiss deepened. All the tension from having to keep our relationship and feelings a secret was being released. Just like on the porch, her hands found my hair. I wrapped my arms around her waist, lifting her off the ground and making my way over to the couch. It was set perfectly where we were hidden from the hallway, just in case. I could feel her warmth against me, and my heart was racing even faster.

I lay her on the couch, placing myself on top of her. Our lips parted only long enough to do so and then they were right back to where they belonged…together. I looked at her, feeling my heart pounding.

"Darlin'…"

"Cowboy…"

I felt the heat radiating off her. It made my head spin. Like every other time we were together, even as kids, the world faded away. All that mattered was the way we held each other, the way her body felt against mine, and the way her lips tasted.

I slid my hands down her body, landing at her hips. I gripped her tightly, again having that overwhelming need to consume her. We were so close, yet so hidden, and that added a little excitement to it all. I knew it was risky with my dad just down the hall in his room, but it only fueled my desire. I pulled myself back on my hands to get a look at her.

"You good?" She nodded, and I had a newfound urgency.

I claimed her lips as mine again, giving her all the passion I had inside of me. She wrapped her legs around my waist as I lifted her. The world outside didn't exist. We were all there was. Each touch from her sent waves down my body. I pressed her up against the wall again, my hands exploring each of her curves.

"We shouldn't."

"Don't worry, darlin.' My dad is a heavy sleeper." I couldn't let this moment pass. I was craving her. "Just a little longer?" She nodded, tilting her head back.

I trailed my tongue down from her lips to her neck. She gasped and arched her back a little more as I found her sweet spot just below her ear. The way I had her pinned and the way she looked right now, I felt myself losing control, if I actually had any left in me at this point.

"We should be careful."

"I think being careful is almost the same as being gentle, and you didn't want that." I looked at her with determination. "I can't help myself. I need you, darlin."

She pulled me closer, our bodies forging together. The kisses grew more intense, my promise to her that there would be more where this came from. I knew we were playing with fire right now, but I didn't care.

Nothing or no one would stop me from taking what was mine-my sweet, darlin.' In this moment, wrapped in each other's arms, I was savoring every second.

Chapter Thirty

Daisy

Walt was in bed, it being nearly ten o'clock. I had no idea what was going to happen between Colt and me, but I was eager to find out. I stood in the doorway, watching Colt. He noticed me standing there, a little smirk forming on his face. Then, he came close and did that thing you see in movies and read about in books where the guy leans over you, his arm propped up above his head. He leaned his head toward me a little, and I could see why girls like this.

"I can't wait any longer."

"Can't wait for what?" I had an idea of what he meant. I just find it funny to play with him.

"I want you. All of you, darlin'." The way he called me darlin' sounded like music to my ears.

"All of me?"

"Can I take it? Can I take what's mine?" I bit my lip, growing the suspense, and I knew it was killing him. Playing games with Colt Hogan was my favorite pastime.

"I don't think I should let it be that easy for you." Making him work for? Yes.

"What do you want me to do, then?"

"You remember the evening in the kitchen?" He nodded. Of course, he remembers that. How could either of us forget an evening like that? "I want you to beg, just like you said you would." It had honestly been a big turn-on for me, and I wanted to see it again-right here, right now.

"Beg?" It was more of a playful question coming from him, and I knew he was about to do it.

"Yes. Beg."

"Okay." He slowly got down on his knees like he had that evening in the kitchen. He looked up at me, meeting my eyes, and I smiled. He was giving me exactly what I wanted.

"Please, darlin. Let me touch you. I need to feel your warmth. I need to feel your touch. I need to feel our bodies together. I need to hold you close and feel your heartbeat in sync with mine. I need a kiss from you. Can't you see, darlin', I need you. I need to drown in every. Single. Piece. Of. You." His hands traced along my body, and it helped the mood. I wanted him to touch me, and I couldn't wait any longer. I was about to give in. "Please, let me. I promise to be gentle." I grabbed his shirt collar, pulling him up to me.

"I need you, too, but don't you dare be gentle."

The last thing I want is gentleness.

I want rough.

I want to be desperate.

He pulled a piece of hair out of my eyes and placed it behind my ear ever so gently, and I was hoping that it was going to be the last gentle thing he did tonight. I let out a breath, and he closed the distance between us, shoving me against the wall. Our lips locked together.

With Colt Hogan kissing me, the world was jut standing

still.

I could taste him.

I could feel him.

The kiss deepened quickly, the thought of hiding to keep us hidden only intensifying it all. My hands found his hair, just like our scene on the porch. We continued kissing, and I could feel his hands wrapped around my waist. He lifted me and started walking. When I landed, we were on the couch, Colt on top of me. My heart was pounding even faster than ever before.

"Darlin'…"

"Cowboy…"

His hands moved down my body, stopping at my hips. I could feel his grip tighten. I looked at him, wondering how we got here…after all this time had passed. He leaned back on his hands, taking me all in. I watched as he licked his lips slightly.

"You good?" I nodded. I was so much more than good. Good didn't even come close.

I felt amazing.

I felt safe.

I felt wholesome.

Our lips locked again, and I felt like being devoured. There was so much passion in every kiss. I never wanted that feeling to go away. I wrapped my legs around his waist. He carried me to the wall again, pressing me firmly against it once more. His touch felt warm and rough, exploring every inch of my body.

I was starting to get a little worried that we were being too loud and that his dad might hear us. What if he walked in to see this? He would freak.

"We shouldn't." My body told a different story. My body said we should.

"Don't worry, darlin.' My dad is a heavy sleeper. Just a little longer?" I nodded, knowing I couldn't stop, and tilted my head back.

He trailed his tongue down from his lips to my neck. He was so close to my sweet spot, and once he hit that, it was game over. I gasped, arching my back a little more. He had found the spot. He remained there, kissing and gently nibbling.

It was better than anything I had ever experienced.

Colt was better than anything I had ever experienced.

"We should be careful." My words still didn't match my body language.

"I think being careful is almost the same as being gentle, and you didn't want that." He was right. I didn't want that when we started, and I don't want that now. I can't help myself. I need you, darlin."

I pulled Colt as close to me as I could. Our kisses were more heated, and I knew this wouldn't be the last one. We were wrapped in each other's arms, and my only wish was that it never had to end.

* * *

It was hard not to sleep in after the night I had, but I knew hearing a mouthful from Walt was never worth it. I headed out to the barn after I had my cup of coffee. I loved working with the horses, and that was honestly one of my favorite parts about working here for the summer, besides the ruggedly handsome six-foot cowboy I admire. The stalls needed to be cleaned before anything else. I didn't want to step in manure while trying to feed and water them, so I knew the horses didn't want to step in it either. I hadn't seen Colt yet, so I figured he was already out in a field somewhere working.

"Daisy?" I heard a faint call of my name but couldn't make out the voice. "Daisy?" I stepped out of the barn this time. It was Walt.

"Is there something you need me to do?"

"Actually, your dad needs a little help."

"Oh, no! Is he okay?"

"Oh, yeah. He's fine. He just called and said he needs a little help with the cattle today. Part of the fence needs fixing here, and Colt went to check it out. He should be back any minute. I just called him and told him to come back here."

"Are you going to my dad's then? Or sending Colt?"

"Actually, I need to stay here and fix that fence. You and Colt both go. It will be faster with more hands."

"You want me and Colt to go?"

"Is that a problem?"

"No, it's no problem."

I was a little surprised that he suggested Colt and I go together, but maybe this could be good. Oh, who am I kidding? Now, having to hide our relationship from my dad was going to prove a difficult task. I wasn't looking forward to that. I hadn't seen my dad since he stopped by and had supper with us.

"It'll be good for you to see each other, you know?" I looked up at Walt.

"Yeah. I hope so."

"Oh, look. There's Colt now." I turned and found Colt driving up on the side-by-side.

"Hey, dad. What's going on?"

"John needs some help with the cattle. I told him I would send the two of you to help. I'd go, but I'm going to stay and fix the fence." Walt placed a hand on Colt's shoulder, and they walked a small way away from me. I could see them talking, and I wondered what Walt was saying to him. Was it about me or my dad? Colt came over to me once they had finished, while Walt hopped on the side-by-side and drove out to the cattle.

"Are you ready to go?" I nodded. Maybe this encounter

with my dad wouldn't be as bad as I thought. I could only hope.

Chapter Thirty-One

Colt

I was out in the field, going around the fence on the side by side to spot the damage to the fence. My dad had let me know early that he wanted to me to run out and check it while he did a couple of things first and then he would head out and work on repairing the fence. I had just spotted the damage when my phone rang.

"Colt?"

"Yeah, dad? I just got out of here. I see the damage and…"

"Don't worry about it. I need you back here."

"Okay."

"Just go ahead and head back." I was a little worried by how that phone call went and the tone of his voice, but I was hoping everything was okay. I rushed back, eager to see what was going on.

"Hey, dad. What's going on?"

"John needs some help with the cattle. I told him I would

send the two of you to help. I'd go, but I'm going to stay and fix the fence." I was thankful that nothing was seriously wrong. He placed a hand on my shoulder, moving me away from Daisy.

"Listen, Colt. Make sure she doesn't dig herself a deeper hole with her dad, you know? I'm sending you to look after her and make sure she doesn't give him any of that attitude to make things worse. If I go, she will know why I took her along with me, so I'm sending you instead."

"I got it."

"She needs to finally talk to him, and this may be the chance to do that." I nodded and walked over to where we had left Daisy standing. I could hear my dad start the side-by-side and head out.

"Are you ready to go?" She nodded.

* * *

I knew John had been struggling a little bit lately and needed some help from time to time. My dad usually went over there when he needed someone. I occasionally went alongside him or in place of him when needed, but my dad usually liked to go. John and he were friends from way back. John hired help from time to time, but that doesn't come cheap. I was glad to have Daisy along for the drive out to John's, but I could see the nerves on her face. I hadn't seen this look on her face in a while, and I was concerned.

"Daisy, are you okay?" I waited a minute, and when I didn't get an answer, I repeated. "Daisy?"

"Hm?" She turned quickly towards me.

"Are you okay?"

"Oh. Yeah."

"I can tell by the look on your face that you aren't okay. Tell me the truth. What's going on inside that pretty little head of yours?"

"I'm just dreading this a little bit."

"Going back to the ranch or seeing your dad?"

"Um…"

"Both?" I nodded. "I haven't seen the ranch in seven years."

"You didn't see it when you came in for my mom's funeral?"

"No. We ate after, and that was it. He offered for me to stay the night there, so I didn't have to drive back to the city, but I turned him down."

"Oh. If you don't want to go…I mean, if it will be too hard for you…If you're not ready yet, you can fake getting sick, and I'll take you back, and you can go to bed and rest instead. I can handle helping your dad."

I made the offer because I wanted Daisy to know that she could count on me…that she could lean on me.

"I'll be okay. I need to do this." She nodded, and I placed my right hand on her inner thigh. She looked at my hand, placing hers on top of mine.

"Daisy, you don't have to hide it from me." She smiled, knowing I saw her trying to hide her tears. "Are you sure you're okay?" She nodded, and we got out of the truck.

I walked behind her, knowing how nervous she probably was after not being back here in so long. I knew she had spoken to her dad only once since being back here this summer, when he had come over one evening and joined us for supper. I knew she didn't feel the best after that conversation. I felt bad for her, knowing their relationship was a little strained, but I was glad I was here to help her in any way she needed.

Chapter Thirty-Two

Daisy

"Daisy, are you okay? Daisy?"

"Hm?" I turned to face him.

"Are you okay?"

"Oh. Yeah." I was such a bad liar. I wasn't okay. I was dreading every bit of this visit. I didn't want to go back there…I didn't think I could do it just yet. I didn't know if I was ready, and I had no reassurance of whether this would go well or not for me. What if it made things worse? What if I made things worse?

"I can tell by the look on your face that you aren't okay. Tell me the truth. What's going on inside that pretty little head of yours?" I wanted to take delight in the fact that Colt had just called me pretty, but that feeling just couldn't outweigh the heaviness of seeing my day today.

"I'm just dreading this a little bit." A little? Who was I kidding? I was freaking out at this point.

"Going back to the ranch or seeing your dad?"

"Um…"

"Both? I haven't seen the ranch in seven years." Seven years I had left this place and never looked back, and now here I was about to step foot on the same soil where my mom had died. That was hard to swallow.

"You didn't see it when you came in for my mom's funeral?"

I remembered that. It was a sad day, and it reminded me of being at my own mom's funeral. My dad asked me to come by the ranch to eat and stay the night, so I didn't have to make a trip right back to the city, but I didn't take him up on that offer. I could tell he really wanted me to stay and that it would mean a lot to him if I did, but I wasn't ready.

"No. We ate after, and that was it. He offered for me to stay the night there, so I didn't have to drive back to the city, but I turned him down."

"Oh. If you don't want to go...I mean, if it will be too hard for you...If you're not ready yet, you can fake getting sick, and I'll take you back, and you can go to bed and rest instead. I can handle helping your dad."

Colt's offer was generous. He was a kind person. He always had been. But I couldn't do that to him or my dad. I needed to bury my fears and go do the job Walt told me to do. I needed to face my dad.

"I'll be okay. I need to do this." I nodded, and Colt placed his right hand on my inner thigh. I loved the way his hands felt against me. I looked down at his hand, smiling slightly, and placed my hand on his. I knew Colt had my back.

"Daisy, you don't have to hide it from me." I smiled. "Are you sure you're okay?" I nodded, and we got out of the truck.

It hadn't yet registered with me that not only would I have to confront my dad after that last encounter we had and keep my relationship with Colt a secret, but I would also be back at the family ranch after seven years.

I hadn't seen the place since the day I left.

I felt panicky inside, rubbing my hands on my jeans to wipe away some of the sweat from them. I was shaking a little, trying my best to hide my feelings from Colt, who was sitting in the driver's seat beside me.

"Colt?" My dad spotted him as soon as he got out of the truck. I was coming up slowly behind.

"Hey, John. How's it going?"

"Could be better. I just need a little help with the cattle." That's when my dad saw me.

"Hey, dad."

"Hey. Walt sent you both over to help?"

"Yes. He did." I replied, feeling my palms sweat.

"What's he got going on today?"

"He's fixing a piece of fence. He wanted to stay and work on that." My dad nodded at my words.

"Yep. That's Walt, alright. That fence is like a baby to him. He's always taking care of it."

"You've got that right." I was glad Colt had stepped up to talk for a moment. I wiped my hands down my jeans, trying to wipe away some of the moisture from them.

"Well, let's get to it then." We followed behind him. Colt looked at me and mouthed the words, *you okay?* I nodded. We made our way over to the cattle in the corral. "I put the sick ones in here. They need some meds, but without anyone here, it's hard for me to hold them still and give them the shot of Cattle Master."

"Well, we're to help. Tell us what you need." Colt continued the conversation with my dad, and I was thankful for him.

"Can you try to hold them still while I inject them?" Colt nodded, and I wondered if my dad was only talking to him or me as well.

"Daisy, when I get them injected, can you help move them? That way, they don't get in the way or get injected twice?"

"Yes." I hated being short with him, but this wasn't the right time for me to talk to him about what had been weighing on me.

One by one, my dad and Colt gave the cattle the medicine while I wrangled them into the chute. Giving the cattle shots was a task that required both care and precision, and watching my dad expertly handle the syringes brought me back to my childhood. His hands were steady and confident, as I always remember so vividly. It reminded me of all the times I would spend right alongside him, helping him with any task so that I could learn all the ropes of ranch life. I knew we didn't have a big ranch like Walt's, but although our ranch was smaller, it was always peaceful and quaint, and not once did I mind that.

Every now and then, my dad would glance over at me, and I could see a little sparkle in his eyes. I wasn't sure what that meant. I wondered if me being here made him happy or if he knew we needed to have a conversation, too, and he is dreading it as much as I am?

Once we finished with the cattle, we sat on the fence, watching the cows graze.

"John, is it alright if I run inside? I need to relieve myself."

"Oh, yes. You go right on it. Help yourself."

Now that we were alone, it seemed like as good a time as any to have this much-needed conversation.

"So..." He turned his head towards me.

"So..."

"It's been a while since you've been here."

"Yes. It has."

"You know…I get why you haven't been back here." I looked over at him. "Daisy, I lost someone, too."

I think for the first time, that really sank in. I hadn't just lost my mom.

My dad had lost his wife.

His companion.

His confidant.

He had lost his best friend.

"I know, dad…I know."

"I miss her."

"I miss her, too."

"I'm sorry I didn't come to see you more. You were dealing with what happened in your own way, and I should have been there for you more."

"I should have come back here, too."

"You still can."

"I still can what?"

"Come back here."

I looked out into the fields again, watching the cows move along while grazing. My dad offering for me to come back here and stay was something a little unexpected. I have been on my own for seven years now, and I just felt like that's what it would always be like for me now.

The weight of his words lay heavy in my chest, thoughts racing through my mind.

Was I ready to leave the city?

Did I want to leave?

If I stayed, it could be better for Colt and me. If I left, I didn't know what would become of our relationship. Staying could also mean being around my dad more, which I liked the thought of. But then, what would I do for work? I wanted to take pictures and write, but could I really do that year? It had been a dream before, but I thought it was a lost cause after everything that happened.

It was a tough decision that I was going to have to think long and hard over.

I heard a noise and saw Colt coming out of the house. I was glad my dad and I had a few minutes to talk. I understand a lot more now.

"Hey?" I turned to look at my dad. A smile came across his face.

"Colt's nice, ain't he?"

"What?"

"I see the way he looks at you." The way Colt looks at me? Does he make it that obvious? "You used to be best friends, but I sense there's something more to it now. I laughed nervously, and I think I gave myself away right then and there. "Heck. I was right. Your old man may be old, but he ain't stupid." We laughed again. "Y'all ain't told Walt yet, have you?"

"No. Dad, can we keep this between us? Please?"

"Of course."

"It's just…complicated." Colt had now made his way over to us.

"You know?" I put my hand on my head, realizing he had heard our conversation.

"Yes. I could tell by the way you look at her. And listen… it's okay with me." He placed a hand on Colt's shoulder, gripping it slightly. "If she's happy, that's all that matters to me. Can I ask you one thing, though?"

"Sure."

"What makes it so complicated that you ain't told your

dad yet?" I wasn't sure how my dad would react, but I knew Colt. He would tell him the truth.

"Before Daisy came here, he asked me to promise him that I would keep it strictly business...professional...and that nothing would happen between me and Daisy."

"Oh?"

"Yeah. I guess I broke that promise."

"Well, son, you do need to tell him eventually. Got any idea why he made you promise that?"

"I don't know."

I have been wondering about the same thing since I found out, and I still don't have an answer.

"I think he thought he was protecting you."

"Protecting me? How?"

"We all saw how the two of you always hung around each other, ever since you were little, and how you wanted to do everything together. No one could separate you. And the way you two looked at each other then is the same way you do now." Colt glanced over at me, then we continued to listen. "Daisy lives in the city, and your dad was probably afraid that if you spent a lot of time together this summer, something could happen, and you'd get your heart broken. He doesn't want to see you get hurt, Colt."

"I didn't realize."

"Once you have kids of your own, you'll know how it feels to want to protect someone like that." We sat there for a few more minutes, watching the cattle. "Thanks, you two, for coming to bail me out today. You were of good help." I gave my dad a smile and he returned it. I had missed being able to talk to him.

By the time the sun began to set, casting a golden hue over the fields, we had spent the whole day with my dad on my family's ranch. I was grateful to Walt for telling me and Colt to come. It meant a lot to me to be able to reconcile with my dad. It was something my heart needed for a long time.

After spending this time here, I realized how much I had missed these moments. I enjoyed the work, the laughter, the talks, and the memories. I glanced over at Colt, busy teasing a calf, and felt grateful for this summer.

Chapter Thirty-Three

Colt

On the drive back, I wanted to check on Daisy and make sure she was okay. I knew she was struggling on the way there, and even though it seemed like she was okay when I came out of the house, I wanted reassurance from her.

"Are you okay?"

"Yeah. I'm good. I'm really good." I loved hearing her say that. I was so happy that she got some reconciliation with her dad today. I knew she needed that. They both needed that.

"So…your dad knows about us?"

"Yep. He's not going to say anything, though."

"You sure?" She nodded.

"I'm sure. Don't worry, Colt." Now look at who is consoling whom.

"My dad will probably have supper ready when we get back."

"Yeah. We've been gone about the whole day."

"I'm sure my dad won't mind that. He wanted the two of us to go."

"Can I ask you something?"

"Of course."

"What did your dad say to you earlier when he pulled you to the side?"

"Oh."

"Colt…was it about me?"

"Kind of."

"Would you tell me? Or is it supposed to be a secret?"

"I guess it's not really a secret."

"So?"

"He just asked me to kind of watch out for you."

"Huh?"

"He knew the situation with your dad had been strained, and he wanted me to make sure that you didn't spout off something and dig a deeper barrier between the two of you. He wanted you to go today to hopefully fix your relationship with your dad, or at least help it. He knew if he went that you would see through his motives, and if I went, it might be easier."

"Oh."

"He was just looking out for you."

"Like he was with you when he asked you to promise him that there would only be business this summer and nothing more?"

I rolled my eyes a little, knowing that Daisy was right. John was right. I knew when Daisy got here, before anything happened between us, that she would be leaving to go back to the city once summer ends. I went through with it anyway. I let my desires take over.

I went back on my word to my dad, and I made the first move by asking her out.

To the bar.

To dance.

And I kissed her.

I made the first move.

The thought of her leaving at the end of summer was becoming more and more real to me, and my heart hurt thinking about it. I didn't want her to go. I want her to stay…with me. I want her. I want us.

We pulled into the ranch, parking the truck beside the porch. I turned in my seat, moving my leg around so I could get a good view of Daisy.

"Daisy?"

"Yeah?"

"I'm glad things are good between you and your dad now."

"Me, too." Without thinking, I placed a hand on her leg. She looked down at it.

"Colt…"

"Daisy…"

"You two come on in and eat!" We turned quickly, getting out of the truck to see the front door swing open.

I should have been more careful, but I just wanted to tell Daisy how I feel. I want her to know that she doesn't have to go. She can stay. We can have a life together. I hope that is what she wants, but she does have a life in the city.

One thought weighed heavier than any other.

What kind of man would I be to ask her to give up on her dream?

We went inside and took a seat at the table where my dad had already laid out all the food. Fried pork chops, mashed potatoes, and corn. My stomach growled. I hadn't eaten since earlier in the day, and I was hungry. I was sure Daisy was hungry, too. I pushed the conflicting thoughts away and made myself a plate.

"So, how did today go? Were there a lot of them?"

"Ah, there weren't too many."

"Daisy, how was it?"

"Oh, it was good."

"It was good?"

"Yeah. It was. Thanks for sending me out there today." I glanced from Daisy to my dad and could see a smile form on his face. This was his doing. I knew how much it meant to Daisy, and because of that, it meant a lot to me.

"Not a problem, Daisy." I knew my dad wasn't going to pry and ask if they talked or what they talked about. He could tell the day went well, and that is all that really mattered to him.

"Well, you two...I don't know about you, but I'm tuckered out. Working on a ranch by yourself is a tough job."

"I'll grab the dishes, Dad." He nodded and stood from the table.

"I'm going to head out in the morning and take a few calves out to the sale. You two are alright to stay here and take care of things."

"We can do it, dad." He walked down the hall to his room. I turned to look at Daisy sitting across from me.

"So?"

"So?"

"We have a little time to ourselves, darlin'."

"Seems like we will have a little time to ourselves

tomorrow, too." She winked, and my heart fluttered.

"I have some ideas for that."

"Oh really?"

"Oh, yeah. Big plans there. But first, we have right now, and I want to do a little something."

"Hmm…what could you have in mind?"

"Wouldn't you like to know?"

"Let's go out on the porch, cowboy." I followed her outside, my head pressed gently on the small of her back.

Once out there, I pushed her against the wall, extending my left arm with my hand pressed beside her head. The roughness of the house contrasted with the softness of her body. I took my right hand and grabbed her chin, lifting her head up where her eyes stared completely into mine. I wanted her to see how I felt. I wanted her to see the hunger I had for her.

"What are you waiting on, cowboy?" I took that as permission, and I firmly let our lips meet.

I grazed my hand down her body, keeping a slow and steady pace. My fingers traced the curves of her waist, exploring the way her body was responding to my touch. She was melting against me, and I could feel my heart racing. She leaned into the kiss, deepening it. It only made me want her more.

Her fingers found their way to my hair, and I was sure this must be one of her favorite things. She had done this several times now when we kissed, and I was enjoying the way my loose curls were being gently pulled. With her hand in my hair, she pulled me closer. I moved one hand to lift her leg some. The kiss became more passionate. Each movement lit a fire inside of me.

I slid my hand down further, taking my time to save this moment. I felt her breath hitch with each caress. I moved my lips, trailing them from her mouth to her neck, planting soft kisses along the way. She gasped, arching her body toward me.

Each kiss was a promise of my feelings for her. That I cared for her and would continue to be there for her in any way she needed.

I pulled back slightly to gaze into her eyes. I could see the desire and tenderness in them. I was amazed at how much this woman had hold of me. She could ask me to do anything for her, and I would. I would run through fire for her.

"You have no idea what you do to me," I whispered, my voice low and husky. She smiled with flushed cheeks. I was so captivated by her.

"You make me feel alive." She whispered, her voice barely above a breath. I gave her a smirk and leaned in again.

I captured her mouth with his, pouring all my unspoken thoughts and feelings into the kiss. I was waiting for her response, and then her hands moved to my chest. She placed one hand on my chest, and I was sure she could feel the thump of my heart beneath her fingertips. How could a woman make me feel this way? No one has ever made me even a little excited, but Daisy sure can. She always made me feel electrified.

Every kiss and every touch reminded me of the undeniable connection we shared.

We couldn't be separated as kids, and we couldn't be separated now.

I clung to her.

My heart clung to her.

The porch once again was a little safe haven for a private sanctuary. It was a place away from everyone and everything-where it was just the two of us.

The sun was setting. A beautiful, golden hue captured the sky.

I pulled away and pressed my forehead against hers. We were both breathing heavily, needing to catch our breath.

"I don't want this to end," I whispered and looked up.

She nodded, and I could see how the look on her face had changed. I kissed her forehead softly. Daisy wrapped her arms around my waist, pulling her chest into me. I put my arms around her and held her tight. I could tell she was scared and afraid of what would come of this. The weight of summer ending was heavy on her, too.

"I got you, darlin'. I got you." She squeezed tighter, and so did I.

Chapter Thirty-Four

Daisy

The next morning, Walt had gotten up with Colt, and they had loaded the calves in the trailer while I was getting changed. I stood in the kitchen, a coffee in my hand, looking out the window as Walt drove out.

I thought of last night and how special each kiss with Colt is. I thought of all the things I love about him. The way his hair curls at the brim of his cowboy hat. The way he has that one scar, I rubbed the night at the bar. The way he keeps constant eye contact with me when we're alone. The way his hands and fingers move against my body to find all my curves. Every time he kisses or touches me, I melt. The way he concentrates when I speak, letting me know I have his full attention, is something I have longed for. It's like an addiction. He is so intentional with everything he does.

"Hey, Daisy?" I had been so lost in my thoughts that I didn't notice Colt walking back to the house and into the kitchen to where I was standing.

"Hey. How long is your dad going to be gone?" I took

another sip of my coffee. I was hoping he wouldn't be back anytime soon.

"He'll be late. He said not to wait up for him for supper, that he would stop and grab himself something on the way back." I nodded, curious about what Colt had up his sleeves. At supper last night, he said he had big plans, and I was eager to know what those were. He always had a way of surprising me. There was never a dull moment with him.

"What do you have planned for us?" The anticipation was killing me.

"So eager." I laughed, playfully hitting him in the shoulder. I set my coffee cup down on the counter, leaning against it. Both of my hands were gently holding onto the counter. Colt moved in closer to me and placed a soft kiss on my lips. Then, he stepped back, only making me want more.

"That's it?" He chuckled, and it was a little infuriating.

"For now? Yes. Now, go grab your bathing suit and meet me outside at the truck." I raised an eyebrow.

"Bathing suit?"

"You did bring one, didn't you?"

"Well, yeah, I did. I mean, I thought maybe at some point I would be able to go swimming in the river, but with all the work I just haven't had time to go yet."

"Well, hurry up and grab it so we can go."

"That's what your big plans are?"

"Oh, darlin', there's more than that."

I ran down the hall to grab my bathing suit. I was excited to see Colt shirtless again. I would be able to admire his muscles once more. I pulled the bathing suit out from my underwear drawer and ran out to meet Colt. He was leaning against his truck, the biggest smile on his face. I threw my bathing suit inside.

"We need to go check on the horses before we leave. I checked on the cattle when I was there helping my dad load up the calves, so that's not a concern."

"Okay. Let's giddy up, cowboy."

I winked at him and took off running leisurely toward the barn. I could hear him behind me, the sounds of his boots thumping against the ground. Colt brought so much excitement into my life. It was something I didn't know I needed. I stopped inside the barn, pressing my back against a stall door. Colt slowed when he saw me, and he slowly made his way nearer. He leaned in, and I kissed him first, a change from our usual. I pulled back and grabbed the shovel. He looked a little confused, and I must admit, it was kind of cute seeing him like that...wanting more.

"Come on, cowboy. I can't get you all distracted, or we'll never make it to go swimming."

He waited another second to make sure I was serious, then grabbed another shovel and started helping me. Once we finished cleaning out the stalls, I took on the task of feeding while Colt did the watering. We made a good team.

"I think that's it." He looked around at the horses, taking both our shovels and putting them back against the wall.

"One more thing." I walked over to him and planted another kiss on his lips. His hands started to move around my waist, and that's when I stepped back again.

"Oh, come on." Teasing Colt was more fun than I expected.

"We have places to be, cowboy." I took his hand in mine, and we walked to his truck.

* * *

The sun was out, and the warmth of the day was wrapping around me like a comforting blanket. I stood at the water's edge, listening to the sounds of the water gently flowing. Colt ruffled his hair and moved closer to jump in.

"Come on, Daisy!" He splashed water in my direction, holding that large smile on his face. I felt a few cool drops against my skin, and I couldn't resist any longer. I had to join him. I waded in and let the water cool me off. I shivered at first, but I quickly started warming up with the sun's rays hitting the water.

I submerged myself completely for a moment, then rose up and wiped the water off my face while flipping my hair back. I swam closer to Colt, wanting to be near him. Once I was close enough, he reached out for my hand and pulled me into him. Our bodies met, and everything faded away. We were two crazy kids swimming in the river, just like all those years ago.

□ □ □

Colt and I were in the river, cooling off from the summer heat. This summer felt different than others. It wasn't because we were both teens- me sixteen and him fourteen. It was because I was trying to balance the complexities of my feelings, knowing that our friendship was as strong as ever, but the fluttering feelings inside of me were more.

We were at one of our favorite spots. This part of the river was surrounded by trees, some leaning over the water slightly. The breeze passing through lifted the scent of the wildflowers.

My hair was in a tight bun- my attempt to cool off the best I could before Colt suggested we go for a swim to beat the heat. I took it down, dropping the hair tie on the ground beside me. Colt dove in first, and I stood at the river's edge, admiring how the droplets glistened off his sun-kissed skin.

"Come on, Daisy! The water's fine!" His words were playful, and the water looked so inviting.

I hesitated for a moment, feeling both excited and nervous. Colt and I have always been friends. He's really my only friend, at least the only one I share anything real with or hang out with outside of school. Lately, though, I had started to see Colt in a different light.

His laughter.

His smile.

The way his eyes sparkled in the sun.

The way he listened to me, hanging on to every word. I shook off the thoughts. I couldn't take it any longer, so I took a deep breath and jumped in. I was ready to join him and have some fun.

We swam, played games, raced, and tried to outdo one another with goofy tricks. At one point, Colt flipped off a rock, and it did make me a little nervous that he could get hurt, but I knew neither of us backed down from a challenge. We splashed water on each other, fighting playfully. The water was acting as a barrier between my feelings for him, but every laugh and moment together made those feelings stronger. Our connection was still growing, and all I wanted was to know if he felt the same way I did.

After a while of swimming and goofing around, we floated on our backs. I watched the clouds for a moment, then closed my eyes before the sun started to hurt them. Listening to nothing but the sounds of the water was so peaceful and calming. I suddenly felt some movement, so I rose up.

"Do you think we'll always come here?" *I felt nostalgia and uncertainty. I wanted to forever continue coming back to this spot with Colt. I wanted to keep doing all the things with him that we have been doing over the years.*

"I hope so. I really like this place."

This spot was special, and I wanted to tell him how much he meant to me, but no other words came out.

"So do I."

"I can't imagine summer without you."

☐ ☐ ☐

"I dare you to swim to that rock over there."

His face showed mischief, and his words proposed a challenge. I would never turn down a challenge. He pointed to a large rock a few yards away. I nodded, accepting it.

I swam hard and fast to get to the rock, feeling the heaviness of the water against me as I moved. Colt was following behind me, not yet able to catch up to me, despite his efforts. When I reached the rock, I rose from the water a bit to see him finally catching up. Before I knew it, he was right beside me, his breath heavy.

"Not bad, darlin."

I felt a blush on my cheeks. As he leaned closer, I could feel the tension building. The water rippled around us, and I knew something was about to unfold.

"We're pretty secluded here." The river was surrounded by trees that were currently swaying in the breeze.

"Yep. It's just us and the fish." With those words, he planted a kiss on my lips.

The kiss was soft and tender, mixing with the water to send a shiver down my spine. I softened against him, feeling the contrast of the cool water with the warmth of my insides. My hands found their way back to his hair, just where they seemed to be meant to be.

I wanted to lose myself in this moment.

I wanted to lose myself in him.

The world around us faded even more with each moment our bodies touched, and our lips met again. The sound of the water was a distant hum, and I felt weightless. I was surrounded by a sea of emotions. Colt wrapped his hands around my waist, my body pressed firmly against him. Every touch and every kiss felt like a promise that more was to come.

We pulled away for a moment, and I rested my forehead against his.

"Wow." I covered my mouth with one hand, not realizing I said that out loud.

"You know, I could get used to this." I smiled.

"Me, too."

I pulled back and splashed some water his way, giggling as I did so. He splashed some back at me, and we were lost in our playful banter.

Eventually, we swam back to the edge of the river. As we climbed out of the water, I could feel the droplets against my skin. I looked at Colt, seeing how his body was glistening. He caught me staring and raised an eyebrow.

"You like what you see?" I jokingly pushed him. He closed the distance, wrapping his arms around my waist.

"I think you know the answer to that." Before I could react, he pulled me in for another kiss, leaving me breathless.

We then packed up our things and headed to the truck.

"What's next, cowboy?"

"Just you wait, Daisy. I'm going to whip up something nice for supper."

"Oh, you're cooking?"

"Sure am. It's all part of my plan."

"Well, I hope the food is as good as last time you cooked."

"It'll be even better."

* * *

We drove back to the house in silence, stealing silent smiles across the cab. Colt gave me all the butterflies. He made me more excited than I was as a kid going to a rodeo, and honestly, I'm thinking about our future.

I spent the short ride daydreaming about what the end of summer would be like if I didn't decide to go back to the city. If I decided to stay.

The city and all its chaos, noise, and people was feeling so far away. This summer has been peaceful and relaxing, and a much-needed break for me from all my busy life. The air was so polluted there, and here it was fresh. I didn't hear the honking of car horns or all the chatter of people. I heard the rustling of the wind, the mooing of the cattle in the fields, and the clopping of horse hooves against the ground.

I thought about when I was last here, seven or some years ago. I thought about waking to the heat of the sun filtering through the window against my face. I thought about the smell of freshly brewed coffee in the mornings and the sound of a familiar laugh echoing through the house. Colt's laugh.

There was potential for us to build a life together.

With Colt, I knew there would be plenty of adventures and those special, quiet moments. We could work together on Walt's ranch or even help my dad out at his. We could do both. Make both our dads proud. We could have a family barbeque again, and it could be me, Colt, Walt, and my dad. It could be as close to old times as we could get. Our mothers wouldn't be there physically, but they would certainly be there in spirit. I can see our dads telling stories while we gathered on the porch, sure to share their wisdom and make us laugh. I could see myself planting flowers around the yard, riding horses with Colt, and sharing our dreams under the stars like we did as kids.

As the evening sun began to set, I felt a hint of longing. I knew my daily life of being on the ranch with Colt was fleeting, but the thought of a future with him filled my heart with joy. I wanted to hold onto this feeling. I wanted to capture it like a snapshot in my mind so it would stay there forever.

Staying here and building a life with Colt was a dream that I hoped could become a reality.

Chapter Thirty-Five

Colt

As I pulled the truck up to the house, the sun was beginning to set, casting a golden hue through the sky. I felt a rush of heat as I stepped out of the truck and headed to Daisy's side of the truck to open her door. I followed behind her to the door of the house, opening it for her. I quickly jumped back with the pang I had just felt.

"Hey!"

"Sorry, cowboy. I just couldn't help myself."

"Darlin', are you admitting you've been checking out my butt?" She grinned ever so slightly, her teeth biting on her lip. Dang, she was tempting.

"Sure am." I pulled her inside and pushed her against the back of the door. I leaned in, taking a moment to look at her before planting a kiss on her lips.

"Let's get cleaned up." She held a playful grin, playfully messing up my hair. Daisy nodded, my heart jumping at the sight of her. She walked down the hallway, and I followed behind, stopping at my room and watching as she continued to hers. "I'll hop in the shower first so I can go work on supper!" I no longer saw her, but I knew she was listening.

I went to the bathroom first to shower and change. I had left Daisy with plenty of thoughts to keep her mind occupied while she was waiting for me to finish. Honestly, she had left me with plenty, too.

I love the way she moves.

I loved the way she never backs down from a challenge and is always up for an adventure.

I love the way she makes me smile.

I love her laugh and the way she gets louder with each chuckle.

I love her confidence.

I love the way she makes me feel like a crazy, in-love teenager again.

After a few minutes, I emerged from the bathroom, steam flooding behind me. I peeked out the door and called to Daisy.

"Hey! I'm out now. You can go ahead!" She came out of her room and peered at me. I could see her throat bob as she swallowed. There was something undeniably intimate about this moment. The air was thick with unspoken words, shared warmth, and familiar glances.

I went back inside my room, changed, and ran to the kitchen to get the meal started cooking. I wanted it to be ready as soon as possible. I pulled out some steaks from the fridge and some green beans I had left thawing. I cut two potatoes down the middle, keeping them whole, and tossed them in the microwave to start cooking. I seasoned the steaks and slapped them on a pan with high heat, listening to the sizzling sounds, and put the green beans in a kettle with some salt and butter.

"Smells amazing in here." I turned and saw Daisy with her hair in a messy bun, a worn T-shirt, and shorts completing the look.

"Thank you. I'm not finished just yet."

"No worries. Don't get your panties in a wad, cowboy. I can wait." She pulled some plates out of the cabinet and placed them and some silverware on the table.

"You don't have to do that. I will get to it."

"Nonsense. You're cooking. The least I can do is set the table."

She came closer to where I was standing at the stove and wrapped her arms around my waist from behind. I could feel the weight of her head as she pressed it against my back, and I wanted to take her right then and there, but I knew it wasn't the right time.

"Hope you're hungry. Food's ready." She let go and made her way to the table, and I followed behind her with the food. "One more thing." I walked into the living room, returning with a candle. I grabbed the lighter from the top of the fridge and lit it, placing it between us.

"Look at you pulling out all the stops. Colt Hogan trying to be romantic?" I nodded, and I could see the way her face lit up. She was enjoying herself.

We started eating, giving quick glances and nonstop smiles. She was perfect. She was everything I could ever want in a woman. I had a plan for this evening, and I knew that I wanted to do this one last thing before we were too tired to stay awake any longer, and before my dad showed up later tonight. I scooted the chair beside me out a little and pulled something up from it, placing it on the table. Daisy looked down, and she knew exactly what it was.

"My journal?" I nodded. "How do you have it?"

"I found it after you moved away. I needed some space to be alone for a bit, so I went up into the tree house. I saw it there and picked it up."

I remember that day like yesterday. It was the day my mom died. I went out into the treehouse and sat there, wishing all the pain would disappear. I had lost my mom, and I didn't have the one person in my life who always made me feel comforted. I didn't have Daisy. That was one of the few times that I have ever cried.

I cried because of the pain.

I cried because of my mom being gone.

I cried because of all the things my mom wouldn't be here for.

And I cried for my lost friendship, the one I wanted back more than anything.

I cried for the love of my life to return.

"I thought I had lost it." I picked it up and handed it to her. I saw a look of fear flood her face.

"Did you read it?" My face lit up, a mischievous grin forming. I knew Daisy, and she wouldn't stay mad at me over something like this. She could never stay mad at me.

"You mention several times wanting to wear the cowboy hat." She covered her face partially with the book, trying to hide her rosy cheeks. "You know what they say about that, don't you?"

"What's that, cowboy?"

"If you wear the hat, you ride the cowboy."

"I've heard that before."

"So?" She raised an eyebrow.

"I've not worn your cowboy hat yet." She was telling the truth, but there was an easy solution.

"Well, we can fix that." I rose from the table, placing one hand on my hat to take it off and place it on her head, but I was stopped by her hand. I knew she was trying to stop me, and we both returned to our seats. "There's plenty of spots here on the ranch that I think could be christened." I winked.

"Maybe we could do that at one point."

"Check the page that's bookmarked." She looked down and then back up at me as if asking for permission. I nodded, then she opened the page.

―――――

I saw Colt again today. We went swimming. And I am here to admit that I am seeing Colt in a different light.

His laugh.

His smile.

The way his eyes sparkle in the sun.

The way he listens to me and clings to every word that leaves my lips.

We made the most of today and had a lot of fun. I enjoy every moment being with him. Every interaction throughout the day made my feelings grow stronger, but I wasn't ready to tell him.

Our connection is still growing, and all I want is to know if he feels the way I do.

He asked me if we would always come here, and I told him I hope so. That spot is special. Being with Colt is special. I want to keep doing things with Colt that we have always done. I always want to be in his life.

The last thing I told him was that I couldn't imagine summer without him, and that is true.

―――――

I finished eating while Daisy read through the page. Each entry in her journal was filled with memories and moments. Each entry was filled with details and feelings about me. When she finished reading, she looked up at me and we smiled at one another. Daisy needed me soft side right now.

"Looks like we ended up spending summers without each other." She nodded, and I could see tears forming in her eyes. Oh, no. I hated seeing her cry more than anything in this world. It hurt when we were kids, and it hurts now.

I stood up from my seat and made my way over to her. I got down in front of her and placed a reassuring hand on her leg. I put my other hand on her chin and moved her head up so she would look at me.

"Daisy, it's alright. I don't want you to cry. It was never my intention to make you upset by giving your journal back." I felt so bad and guilty for causing her to cry. I didn't want to cause her any pain. I never wanted to do that. Flashbacks of not telling her about my promise to my dad came back, and I couldn't stand the thought of hurting her anymore. I couldn't handle it.

"I know."

"Why are you crying?" I took my thumb and raked it across her cheek to get rid of her tears.

"Because it's my fault."

"What's your fault?" I was unsure what she was talking about, but I would try to fix it if I could.

"Why did we spend all those years separated and never see each other. That is my fault." She wiped her face, making the tears disappear. "I'm sorry."

"Daisy, it's okay." She put her head on my chest. "You needed time and space. I understand. You don't have to apologize to me for how you needed to heal. We all deal with things our own way. It's okay." She sniffed.

"So, you read it all?"

"Every word." I watched her look down at her journal. I took it gently from her hands and turned to another page. "I've had a really nice time with you today, darlin', but I am worn out. I will see you in the morning. Don't worry about the dishes. I will get them in the morning." I gave the journal back to her and placed a kiss on her forehead before going down the hall.

Chapter Thirty-Six

Daisy

We pulled back up to the house and all the thoughts that had been clouding my mind on the drive washed away. I looked at the beautiful colors in the sky that the setting sun was creating as I stepped out of the truck. Colt had opened the door for me, just as he always has. Again, he is a gentleman. Some would say a lost art. Colt followed behind me as we made our way to the house and opened the door for me. I looked down, taking in his backside, and I let my inner thoughts win.

"Hey!"

"Sorry, cowboy. I just couldn't help myself." I really couldn't. It was like a reflex, and it happened so quickly that there was no stopping me. I smacked him right on the butt with my hand, just playing around.

"Darlin', are you admitting you've been checking out my butt?" I grinned and bit down on my lip. Of course, I was teasing him. It was fun to mess around with him like this, and his reactions always made it better.

"Sure am." He pulled me inside and pushed me against the

back of the door. I looked into his eyes as he towered over me, and all those thoughts about our future rushed back. This felt like a small glimpse into what a future with Colt would look like. Finally, he placed a kiss on my lips. It was a soft, warm kiss that made me feel comforted and safe.

"Let's get cleaned up." I messed up his hair and nodded, then went down the hallway to my room. I could hear his footsteps behind me, stopping before I made it to my room. "I'll hop in the shower first so I can go work on supper!" I knew his footsteps had ceased at his door. I was already inside my room and couldn't see him, but I could hear his words.

I sat on the floor in front of my bed, sprawling my legs out in front of me. I was worn out. A day of swimming always did that to me. I raked my hand across my forehead and pushed my hair out of my face.

There were so many thoughts running through my mind, but I knew that I was in no shape to think about them at this moment. I was too exhausted and hungry. I sat there and peeked at my door.

"Hey! I'm out now. You can go ahead!" I stepped out to let him know I heard what he said, and I couldn't believe the sigh in front of me. Colt was standing there with only a towel wrapped around him. I swallowed hard.

He was breathtaking.

I could see his muscles, clear as day.

His longer hair dripped down his neck, lying on his head.

I turned and went into the bathroom, shaking my head at what I had just seen.

Colt knows me.

He makes me smile and laugh, just like when we were kids.

He makes me excited for the days to come.

He makes me see the future.

He calls me out on my crap, which no one else has ever done.

He is everything.

"Smells amazing in here."

I stepped out with a T-shirt, shorts, and a messy bun. I was going for comfort, even if Colt was preparing a meal for us. I knew he wouldn't mind what I was wearing, as long as I was there.

"Thank you. I'm not finished just yet." I glanced over at him, stirring something on the stove.

"No worries. Don't get your panties in a wad, cowboy. I can wait." I took some plates down from the cabinet, along with some silverware from the drawer, and set the table. I was hungry, and I would help if it meant I could eat sooner.

"You don't have to do that. I will get to it." He was sweet. I liked that he had planned this whole day for us. It made it that much more memorable.

"Nonsense. You're cooking. The least I can do is set the table."

I stood at the table, staring at him for a minute. He had this perfect, muscular, and rugged exterior, but inside, he was soft and gentle. I walked over to him at the stove and wrapped my arms tightly around his waist, laying my head against his back. I could feel the heat coming off him against my face.

"Hope you're hungry. Food's ready." I had been waiting to hear those words, but now that I was pressed against him, I didn't want to let go. I walked over to the table and had a seat while Colt brought all the food over. "One more thing." I saw steak, baked potatoes, and green beans. I wasn't sure what could possibly be missing. The food smelled amazing, and there was plenty for the two of us. I watched as he returned from the living room holding a candle. He walked over to the fridge and brought back a lighter.

"Look at you pulling out all the stops. Colt Hogan trying to be romantic?" He nodded, and I was sure my face was about to get stuck from the big smile plastered on it. Colt had really pulled out all the stops for this alone time together, and I couldn't be more grateful. He really surprised me today.

We started eating. The aroma from the food made my mouth water. It tasted just as good as it looked, which was saying a lot. I have never had anyone cook for me before besides my parents, so this was new. I glanced over at Colt a few times and caught him already looking at me from across the table.

Colt's muscles showed through his tight T-shirt, and I thought back to his shirtless body at the river. Colt took my breath away in more ways than one.

He reached over to the chair beside him and pulled it out. When he raised his arm back up, he laid something down on the table between us. I looked at it, believing that my eyes were playing tricks on me. It couldn't be.

"My journal?" He nodded. "How do you have it?" I haven't seen this journal since I was sixteen. How did Colt possess it now?

"I found it after you moved away. I needed some space to be alone for a bit, so I went up into the tree house. I saw it there and picked it up." I wonder why he needed space then. I wonder what was going on in life that he needed time to be away. I remember us playing up there as kids. It always felt like a safe place for us. We shared countless stories in it.

"I thought I had lost it." He handed it to me, and the realization set in that if Colt had my journal, he might have opened it. And if he had, then he may have read parts of it. I had written so many personal things in it- things about Colt, the way he looked, memories of us spending time together, and my feelings for him. I was horrified to find out, but I needed to know.

"Did you read it?" His face carried a mischievous grin. I

wanted to be mad at him, but I couldn't be. I probably would have done the same thing if the roles were reversed.

"You mention several times wanting to wear the cowboy hat." My cheeks were surely pink. I took the journal and covered the bottom half of my face with it. "You know what they say about that, don't you?"

"What's that, cowboy?" There was no telling what Colt was about to say. I was both nervous and scared.

"If you wear the hat, you ride the cowboy." I'm sure my cheeks turned a darker shade of pink. I knew exactly what he was referring to.

"I've heard that before."

"So?" I raised an eyebrow at his question, not going to give in.

"I've not worn your cowboy hat yet."

"Well, we can fix that." He rose from the table, taking a hand to lift his cowboy hat off his head. I pushed my hand out, stopping him. "There's plenty of spots here on the ranch that I think could be christened." He winked. I was going to stand my ground. Not yet. I wasn't ready just yet.

"Maybe we could do that at one point."

"Check the page that's bookmarked." I looked down and then back up at Colt. At first glance, I remembered what I had written about. He nodded. I felt weird reading through my journal after all these years, but I opened the page anyway.

―――――

I saw Colt again today. We went swimming. And I am here to admit that I am seeing Colt in a different light.

His laugh.

His smile.

The way his eyes sparkle in the sun.

The way he listens to me and clings to every word that leaves my lips.

We made the most of today and had a lot of fun. I enjoy every moment being with him. Every interaction throughout the day made my feelings grow stronger, but I wasn't ready to tell him.

Our connection is still growing, and all I want is to know if he feels the way I do.

He asked me if we would always come here, and I told him I hope so. That spot is special. Being with Colt is special. I want to keep doing things with Colt that we have always done. I always want to be in his life.

The last thing I told him was that I couldn't imagine summer without him, and that is true.

I glanced up at Colt, who took the last bite of his food. He smiled at me, and I smiled back.

"Looks we ended up spending summers without each other." I nodded, my eyes swelling with tears.

It was my fault we had lost touch.

It was my fault we had lost our friendship.

It was my fault we had stopped making memories with each other.

It was my fault for leaving.

It was my fault for never visiting.

I had no one to blame but myself.

Colt stood up from his seat and walked to me. He knelt beside me, placing a hand on my leg. He took his other hand and lifted my head with my chin.

"Daisy, it's alright. I don't want you to cry. It was never my intention to make you upset by giving your journal back."

"I know."

"Why are you crying?" He wiped the tears from my face with his thumb.

"Because it's my fault."

"What's your fault?"

"Why did we spend all those years separated and never see each other. That is my fault." I wiped my tears. "I'm sorry."

"Daisy, it's okay." I leaned into him, laying my head on his chest. "You needed time and space. I understand. You don't have to apologize to me for how you needed to heal. We all deal with things our own way. It's okay."

I sniffed. How could Colt be so understanding? He was so patient with me, and it is all I could ever ask for.

"So, you read it all?"

"Every word." I looked down at the journal, realizing just how many memories it must hold. I used to write in this all the time. It saw me cry and smile. Colt took it from my hands, flipping it to another page. "I've had a really nice time with you today, darlin', but I am worn out. I will see you in the morning. Don't worry about the dishes. I will get them in the morning." He handed me the journal. I gripped it a little tighter as he placed a kiss on my forehead. It was different than our usual kisses, but everything Colt did was meticulous. That kiss was what I needed right now. I needed that gentleness. I watched as Colt walked down the hall to his room. I looked down at the page, rubbing my finger across it, then read through the entry.

―――――

Colt and I went riding in his truck today. He has taken me for a few rides in it, and I know how much that truck means to him. It was his grandfather's after all. Colt is sentimental about things like that.

He took me out to see the sunset again. He has no idea how special that place is to me. He has no idea what kind of hold he has on me.

He could ask me to do anything for him, and I would. Of course, I would make it a challenge for him, but nevertheless, I would end up doing it.

Colt told me that he loved spending time with me.

Does that mean he likes me?

Does he have feelings for me?

I don't know if he does or not, and I am so afraid that asking him could ruin our friendship.

I can't lose Colt.

I will do whatever it takes to always fight for our friendship.

I need him around.

When I left the ranch to go home today, I gave Colt a hug and said goodbye.

As he walked into the house, I whispered, 'I love you.'

Maybe one day I will hear those words leave his perfect lips.

Chapter Thirty-Seven

Colt

I was standing there in the kitchen, watching the sun come up. It had just begun to rise over the horizon as I took another sip of my coffee. As I finished my coffee and got ready to start the day, I thought of last night and Daisy's journal. That journal was an unexpected find, but in a way, I felt it was necessary for me to find it. I held on to Daisy after all these years because of it. I went on dates, but I compared everyone to Daisy and the way she makes me feel. No one could ever measure up. I would read through her entries from time to time to remember our time together. Each time I read one, a smile formed.

I heard footsteps coming from behind me, getting closer. My dad walked into the room, pouring himself a cup of coffee.

"Morning, Colt." He took a sip.

"Morning."

"How'd things go with Daisy yesterday while I was gone?"

"It was pretty good. Daisy and I got the work done, no problem." He raised an eyebrow like he was suspicious, but my expression and tone didn't falter. "Really, dad. It was no problem."

"Glad to hear it. I won't lie to you, son. I was a little worried."

"Why?"

"I was worried she might give you an attitude or something, and things would be slacking around here some. You know how she can be. Your mother thought the world of her, but she knew how to handle her. Your mom knew all the right things to say and do." My dad never really spoke of my mom, so this was a surprise to me. I liked hearing him talk about her. It meant he was remembering her and hadn't forgotten.

"I know, Dad, but Daisy did just fine. We did just fine." He nodded.

"Good." He took another sip. "You know, I've noticed Daisy seems not to be minding working here as much as she first did. She doesn't complain so much now. Have you noticed?" Of course, I have noticed. She has lost the attitude for the most part, and I was to thank.

"Yeah, now that you mention it, I have."

"Well, maybe it was seeing her dad that helped, or maybe she got used to it again, but whatever the reason, I'm glad. It's a good thing."

"Yeah. She does seem to like it more. Maybe she's not letting the bad memories trample the good ones."

"Wouldn't that be the dream?"

"I miss Mom."

"Me, too, son. Me, too." He finished his coffee, we standing side by side and looking out the window at the fields.

"So, how did it go yesterday selling the calves?"

"It went well. I sold most of them at a good price. The

market's been decent lately, so I can't complain."

"That's good."

"We should have extra cash heading into fall because of it." I nodded. My dad always liked to put a little back for fall and winter, just in case something came up.

"You have your eye on anything to use some of the money for?"

"I was thinking maybe we could finally get that new tractor we saw a while back. We could put so much down on it, and then that would help with paying it off faster."

"That would work."

"I would leave some, just in case."

"We could get a lot done with it. I like grandpa's old tractor, but it's about seen its days."

"Yeah, it has. It's been a good one, though." He put his empty cup in the sink. "But first, we have some work to tackle today. Daisy can manage the horses again, but I noticed the hay needs to be restacked. It's starting to get a bit chaotic in the barn."

"Sounds like a plan."

"If you help me out with the hay, it shouldn't take too long to get it finished."

"Of course I'll help. Think you're up to see who can stack the hay the fastest, old man?"

"Are you challenging me? I may be old, but I can still whoop you any way."

"Prove it."

As we both headed out the door to make our way to the barn, I noticed my dad smiling. His smile had faded once my mom died, and for a while, I forgot what he looked like with one. I was glad to see it back.

"You know, son, I appreciate you taking care of things while I was gone."

"Dad, it was no problem. It's just part of the ranch. We all pitch in, sometimes a little extra, when we need to."

"It means a lot." He placed a hand on my shoulder as we were standing just inside the barn. "I know I've not told you, but I'm proud of you. Your mother would be proud of you, too."

"Let's get to work, then. I've got some showing you up to do." He laughed, and we both started stacking the hay, quickly glancing at one another to see who was going faster.

The sun was now high in the sky, showcasing the beautiful colors of summer over the fields. The sweet smell of fresh hay filled the air as we continued stacking the bales, and the sound of rustling straw accompanied us.

"Better keep going." My dad winked. The challenge was still going strong. My dad was as tough as they came. I loved him, even if he could be a bit of a hardball sometimes.

"Better remember to lift with your legs, not your back." I winked back at him. I watched as he lifted the next bale with ease, not showing any sign of weakness.

I mimicked his movements. The bales were heavy, and this was not a fun job that anyone wanted to do, but it came with working on and running a ranch. It was one of the toughest jobs.

After each stack, I felt a sense of accomplishment knowing that my dad is proud of me. That meant a lot to hear from him. My mom had said it plenty of times when she was alive, but my dad had never uttered those words. We continued working with rhythm-lifting, tossing, and stacking the bales on the wooden shelves that lined the barn.

"How many bales do we have left?"

"Getting tired, son?"

"Not a chance. I am just curious, is all." He nodded, teasing me.

"We've got to keep going to make sure we have enough for the fall and winter. It's a big job, but we seem to be managing pretty well." I wiped the sweat from my forehead and kept on stacking.

The sun was beating down as we maintained a steady pace, stacking the hay. My dad stopped to take a drink of water, and I followed suit. I think the challenge of it had finally died down, and we were both ready to have this job behind us. To pass the time, my dad started telling me stories about his childhood.

"Back in my day, we didn't have all these fancy machines. We only had our hands. It was all about teamwork and getting your hands dirty. It was a lot of what we are doing right now."

I clung to every word, soaking in all the knowledge and life lessons he was trying to teach me. I had missed getting to talk to my dad like this. He had been so sad for so long, nearly depressed at some points along the way. I wasn't sure what had changed with him, but I was happy to see him like this and to be able to talk to him in ways I was unsure I would be able to ever again. My dad had such a strong work ethic, one that he instilled in me at an early age, and it was something I wished to instill in my children one day.

We stacked the last few bales, and I felt pride in knowing that I had accomplished a difficult task with my dad. We had accomplished a lot by doing this and the barn looked so much better organized this way. It was good to see us prepared for the fall and winter seasons.

"Good job, son." He patted me on the back. "I don't know about you, but I think I deserve a break." I nodded in agreement.

We stepped outside the barn, taking a moment to look back inside at the bales we had stacked before staring out at the open fields. This was the best view. There was so much peace in it, and yet, so much freedom. There was nothing but the sounds of nature to soothe the soul.

Just then, we heard clopping against the ground. Daisy was coming in from the distance, riding Domino. Since the first time I had her ride Domino, she has really taken up with the horse. I liked seeing him being ridden. It was good for him.

Daisy's hair was blowing in the breeze, her curls bouncing with each stride. She approached the barn with a sense of grace and confidence.

She was beautiful.

She was stunning.

She was breathtaking.

"Look at her go. She really knows how to handle that horse. I'm glad she's taken up riding again. You two used to always ride together, with your mom's, too."

I watched in awe as Daisy dismounted and led Domino into the barn. I wanted to rush to her and feel my hands against her, but my dad was right here, and that would not be a smart thing to do. She brushed Domino's mane, taking so much care with each stroke.

"Maybe should help her out."

"Why don't you go help her? I'll go inside and make us all a sandwich."

I watched my dad turn away and waited until he was out of sight before heading into the barn to greet Daisy. I must have startled her by the way she jumped as I put my hands on either side of her hips and spun her around to face me.

"Colt!"

"Shhh…"

"What on earth! You can't scare me like that." I kissed her lips.

"We don't have much time."

"For?" I winked, then put my lips back on hers. I moved them from her mouth to her cheeks, and then to her neck and chest. I wanted to taste her, even if it could only be for a minute or two. "Okay...okay, Colt. We'd better stop before we get caught." She was right, so I nodded as I backed away.

"Still good, though?"

"Always."

Chapter Thirty-Eight

Daisy

I had gotten up before Walt and Colt to get a head start. I wanted to watch the sunrise, and the best way to do that was from a horse. I saddled up Domino and took off into the fields, knowing a perfect spot that Colt and I had escaped to as kids, our moms going with us on a few occasions.

The morning air was crisp, and everything around me was only beginning to wake up. I felt a slight breeze blowing my hair, feeling cool against my skin. I felt so much freedom riding, freedom that I have never felt anywhere else. The soft rustling of leaves in the wind and distant sounds of birds chirping filled the air. Each hoofbeat resonated with the earth, and I felt each one in my chest. I felt in sync with Domino.

There were so many thoughts running around in my head. The day yesterday with just Colt and me was about as close to perfect as you can get. Each moment we spent together was a treasure. I had never been on a date, except with Colt, and seeing him be so meticulous with planning made it so special and meaningful. I could tell he had put a lot of thought into it. I hoped for more days like that with him.

I wondered if I did stay here, if that would be what it could be like. If being near Colt every day could always feel that good- if it could always feel like coming home, wrapped in warmth and comfort.

This was the hardest decision I had ever had to make. When I left Garrity Valley for Dallas seven something years ago, I didn't have someone else to worry about. I knew my dad would be alright on his own, so I did what I thought was best for me. Now, though, I had to consider someone else and their feelings. That made the choice so much more difficult. I didn't want to hurt him. I could only imagine what it did to him when I left without a word after all those years of friendship, and I was afraid of what leaving him might do to him.

I couldn't decide what to do, stay or leave, so I did what my dad always told me when you were stuck between a rock and a hard place. When in doubt, let your horse do the thinkin,' he'd always say.

As Domino and I made our way through the dew-kissed field, we reached the top of the hill with the best view of the sunrise. I halted him. You could see so much from up here. The horizon began to light up with hues of orange and pink. The sun was slowly rising, casting a warm glow over the ranch. This was one of the best views, and one of my favorite things about being in the country. I couldn't help but smile, feeling the gentle breeze as I watched the sun come up. Mornings were always my favorite. It was a moment of tranquility before everything woke up and started stirring. I closed my eyes for a moment, soaking in the beauty and peace of it. This was my sanctuary, a place I could come to be one with my thoughts, escape, and find solace in nature's embrace.

As the sun continued its rise, I felt a renewed sense of hope. I wasn't sure what was going to happen or what decision I was going to make, but I knew that Colt and I would find time to talk about it. I knew we could make that decision together.

I moved the reins to get Domino going again, this time headed back to the ranch. I needed to feed the horses and make sure they all had water, my first tasks of each day, since I had been on Texas Rose Ranch. I took the journey back slowly, wanting to savor the quiet for a little while longer.

When I finally saw the barn come into view, I could see two figures standing right outside it. Walt and Colt were watching as I made my way closer. My hair was blowing in the breeze with the bit of speed we had picked up. I finally gained my confidence back with riding, and I was proud of myself for that.

I glanced at Colt briefly, trying not to let Walt catch me staring. I saw his curls, his muscles, and the sweat beaming from him. No doubt he and Walt had been working hard this morning. I liked how hard Colt worked, and I had his dad to thank for that. I couldn't blame Walt for wanting to start early. It meant if you kept a good pace, you may not have a long day, and if you were lucky, you would get the toughest chores out of the way before the heat of the summer really picked up in the middle of the day.

I dismounted and led Domino into the barn. Rewarding Domino for letting me take him out so early, I brushed his mane, taking so much care with each stroke. He was so gentle.

The next thing I knew, I felt hands against my waist. I jerked as those hands spun me around.

"Colt!"

"Shhh..."

"What on earth! You can't scare me like that." He kissed my lips.

"We don't have much time."

"For?" He winked, then put his lips back on mine.

He moved them with such rhythm, from my mouth to my cheeks, then to my neck and chest. I didn't know how he could make me feel like I was floating with every kiss, every touch.

"Okay...okay, Colt. We'd better stop before we get caught." He nodded and backed away. He knew I was right, even if this was what we both wanted to be doing.

"Still good, though?"

"Always. So, where'd your dad go?"

"Inside to make us all sandwiches."

"Kind of early for that, isn't it?"

"Ah, he said he needed a break, so he's not in any hurry. He knew we'd be a bit. He told me to help you out. I know you went riding to see the sunset this morning, so you probably still need to feed and water the horses."

"How'd you know what I did?"

"Well, besides the fact that you made it out of the house before we did, it was always one of your favorite things."

He remembered so much about me, like he had kept a list in his head all this time, hoping one day he would be able to put it to good use. It made me feel a little guilty that I had ever tried to forget this place. No matter how hard I tried, though, I couldn't forget Colt. I didn't want to. He had once been my go-to person, and there were too many memories there to wash away.

Colt was shoveling out the stalls while I gave each horse food and checked their water. I loved moments like this, being able to slow down with the hustle and bustle of life. The sunlight filtered through the wooden slats, and I was starting to feel the heat. I rubbed Domino on the nose, feeling a little mist as he neighed, then walked back to hang up the bucket. I picked up the water hose and sprayed a little in Colt's direction.

"Hey!"

"What?" I was definitely flirting with him.

"You'll get some back."

I sprayed him again. He ran towards me, trying to take the hose from my hand, but we ended up spraying it everywhere. It was a good thing Walt was in the house, so he couldn't see us. He wrapped his arms around my waist, moving me around to try to free my hands. I held on a little longer before dropping the hose. Colt walked over and turned it off.

"Told you you'd get some, too." We laughed, but it was cut short.

Suddenly, a loud, whiny sound broke the lightheartedness between us. We turned our heads toward the sound. Titan jolted, and his ears pricked forward. Colt tried to react quickly, while I was unsure of what to do. Titan knocked over a bucket of feed, and Colt walked over to steady him. Out of the corner of my eye, I spotted a small snake slithering across the barn floor. It was little and harmless, but the sight of it startled Titan.

"Colt!" The snake was small, but I still didn't like them. I was with Titan on this one. Colt stepped back with the urgency in my voice. Titan was dancing around nervously.

"It's just a snake. He's okay."

Titan didn't listen, though. He continued moving around, pure chaos ensuing. His instincts kicked in as he tried to escape. Titan moved, showing pain in his hoof. Colt rushed to him, trying to calm him down more. I froze. What was wrong? What had happened? Was he hurt? I walked over to the stall. During it all, Titan had stepped on a loose nail sticking out.

"No, no, no, Titan!" Titan was still agitated but slowly coming down from the rush of the incident. I brushed his mane, trying to keep him calm so Colt could take a look at the injury.

"Shh, you're alright, Titan. We got you. You're safe." I continued brushing him, speaking softly. I could feel him trembling underneath me.

I peered down to Colt handling Titan's hoof and could make out a small cut on his leg from where he had stepped on the nail.

"We need to get him treated." Colt looked at me with concern, and I was scared. It had been a long time since I had to deal with anything like this. It made me nervous.

"Let's get your dad." I think Colt could see my jitters, so he shook his head in agreement.

"Go get him. He'll be able to help." I dashed out of the barn, running as fast as I could to the house. I found Walt sitting in the kitchen, drinking some water.

"Walt! Walt!" He rose quickly, walking over to me and putting his hands on my shoulder.

"What's wrong?"

"It's Titan! He…he…" I was out of breath and couldn't get the words out.

"Slow down, Daisy. Take a deep breath." I did, Walt coaching me through it. "What happened?"

"Titan got spooked by a snake and hurt his leg. There's a cut on it. Colt needs help treating it."

"Show me."

Walt's expression went from confusion to concern as we made our way to the barn, me running in front of him. When Walt walked into the barn, he went straight to Titan and Colt, assessing the situation.

"Alright, let's get a good look at him." Colt held the horse steady while Walt examined the cut. "It's not too deep. We need to clean and bandage it." He looked up at me. "Daisy, can you grab some clean water and a cloth?"

"Yes!" I hurried to gather the supplies. I wasn't good in a crisis. Colt always was, which made us a perfect pair. I could lean on him during times like this. I returned in a flash with the supplies. Walt cleaned the wound while Colt continued to keep Titan calm.

"You're a good boy, Titan. Just a little bit longer." I walked close enough to rub Titan on the nose while Colt spoke to him.

"There we go. He'll be fine." I looked at Titan's leg, seeing the bandage wrapped around it. "He just needs some rest. No need to worry."

"Thanks, dad." Walt patted me on the shoulder.

"You did well coming to get me, Daisy." He looked back at Titan. "Just keep an eye on him for the next few days. Hopefully, that snake won't be back, and if either of you sees it, then we need to get rid of it. We don't want anything like this happening again." We both nodded, and Walt walked back toward the house. "I was about to make those sandwiches. You two come inside and eat when you're ready."

Once Walt was out of sight, I leaned into Colt. I placed my head against his chest and instantly felt hands wrapping around me. The feeling of him holding me tightly made me feel safe, calming my nerves.

"You alright?" He pulled me back, a hand of his on each of my shoulders.

"Yeah. I'm okay. I don't know how you do it."

"Do what?"

"Stay calm. I was a nervous wreck. I didn't know what to do."

"I guess it comes with being used to this way of life. There are so many things that could happen, and you can never be prepared for them all. What do you say we go inside and eat, and once we're finished, we can rest a bit on the tire swing? Promise not to push you too high." He winked, trying to make me feel better, and it did.

"That sounds nice."

Chapter Thirty-Nine

Colt

As we walked into the house, I could smell the food. Glancing at the table, my dad had three sandwiches there, him already eating his.

"Hey, you two. Made you both one."

"Thanks." Daisy picked up a sandwich, both of us taking a seat at the table with my dad.

"Hope you're hungry. I made your favorite, Colt, turkey and cheese with a little bit of mustard."

I took a bite. My mom used to always make fun of my dad when he made a sandwich. She always said turkey and cheese with mustard was kind of weird. She wasn't big on mustard. She preferred mayonnaise.

"You know, Daisy, Colt used to beg me to make him this sandwich all the time when he was little. He couldn't say sandwich, so he called it a sam sam."

I used to find that story embarrassing, but as I stole a

glance at Daisy while she laughed at my dad's joke, I wasn't ashamed. The way she lit up the room made my heart race. She had a smile like a starry night sky- beautiful and captivating.

I glanced back at her, seeing that she still had a little bit left to eat. I sat there in silence, waiting for her to finish, but not rushing her. I was filled with a rush of excitement and nerves. I was going to share a moment with her, even if it was for a short while.

"It's been a wild morning. Y'all go take a break for a bit. I'm going to ride out and check on the cattle in the far field." I watched as my dad rose from the table and headed outside. I listened for the sound of the side by side starting, and when I heard it, I turned to Daisy.

"Do you want to go outside for a bit? We can go to the tire swing now." I wanted to steal a few moments for just the two of us.

Daisy nodded, then we made our way outside to the tire swing hanging from the big oak tree in the front yard. It was swaying slightly in the breeze. Daisy sat down, and I gently pushed her, keeping my promise not to push her too high. Her hair flowed back against the slight wind, and I could hear a gentle laugh from her. It instantly took me back to when we were kids.

☐ ☐ ☐

I was leaning against the big oak tree, listening to the slight creaking sound of the tire swing. Daisy was laughing as we enjoyed the serenity of a little haven on the sprawling ranch. She had raced me to the swing, obviously beating me, but I let her win. I didn't mind pushing her on it. It made her happy, so it made me happy.

"Push me higher, Colt!"

As a kid, she was always so full of adventure. She never backed down from a challenge, and I wondered if she would always stay like this.

She was so unique and special, and I loved that she wanted to spend time together. Even after all these years, she never grew tired of me.

I saw the sparkle of excitement in her eyes as I grinned. I dug my boots into the ground to give her that extra push, and I felt joy seeing how happy she was soaring higher into the sky.

"Look! It's like I can touch the clouds!"

Her laughter echoed like music to my ears. I watched her in awe, mesmerized by how carefree she was. She had a way of turning the simplest moments into something magical. I would do anything to hear that laugh and see her smile.

With each sway, she threw her head back and closed her eyes, like she was savoring the feeling. I felt so strongly for her, wishing that I was brave enough to confess my feelings to her, but no matter how hard I tried, I couldn't get the words out. Honestly, sucking it up was okay. I would rather be Daisy's friend and get to spend these amazing times with her than risk it all with her and have it blow up in my face.

I couldn't lose her.

I wouldn't survive without her.

She was my comfort, my joy, my safe place.

She was the moon and the stars.

She was a light in the darkness.

She was everything to me.

As I continued pushing her, I imagined what it would be like to fly and be able to freely explore the world. I dreamed of things like that, but not as much as Daisy. The truth is, although I thought about getting away and seeing other parts of the world, I would never do it. I didn't need to do it, and I didn't really want to.

I would gladly stay here for the rest of my life, as long as Daisy was here with me. She was my anchor. She was my best friend, partner in crime, and the one person who truly understood me. We shared secrets, dreams, and plenty of adventures together.

She was all I needed in this world.

With her, I knew I would be happy.

"Hey, Colt?" I was so lost in my thoughts that I hadn't noticed she had stopped swinging.

"I'm sorry. Let me push you again."

"Hold on." I moved to face her and noticed the look on her face had changed. Her head hung low, and my heart hurt seeing her like that.

"I wish things could stay like this forever."

I felt a pain in my chest. I wanted that, too. I wanted to stay with Daisy forever. The days she wasn't at the ranch with me, I felt like I could hardly stand it. I just wanted to be with her, spend all my time in her presence.

"Me, too. We'll always be friends, Daisy. You can always count on me."

"Good." Daisy smiled, and her laughter returned as I pushed her once more on the swing.

☐ ☐ ☐

"This is nice...just us." I nodded, knowing exactly what she meant. Moments like this made the secrecy worth it. As hard as it was, I could see the silver lining in it. I pushed her again.

"I wish we could be open about this. About us. I mean, it hasn't been that bad. I just really want to show you off."

"Show me off?" I tried to make a joke, but she wasn't ready for it. I could tell she was serious. "I know. We just have to keep being careful and keep this hidden for a little while longer." She nodded.

"Then you'll tell him?" I sighed.

My stomach still did flip flops every time I thought of telling my dad.

After talking with John, I realized why he did what he did, but it didn't make the idea of having a talk with him any easier. I always found it hard to talk about real things with my dad, something we never really did much as I grew up.

I wanted to sit and hold Daisy in my arms. I squeezed my hand into a fist. Not being able to touch and be with her in the ways that I want, publicly, was so debilitating.

I pushed her a few more times, thankful that I was at least able to touch her in this way. I wanted so much more, but stolen glances and little moments were all we could have right now. Soon, it will change.

After that, I knew we needed to get back to work. My dad hadn't shown back up from the field and checking on the cattle yet, but I knew it was only a matter of time. The last thing I needed was for him to see me gawking at Daisy.

I helped her off the swing. We walked to the barn, side by side, our hands grazing each other's, sending a shiver down my body. It was a small, intimate touch, but it still made me feel excited and aroused.

Our relationship is a secret, but it isn't something I take lightly. It is important to me. It is precious. It was like we were in our own little world, nestled inside the ranch, with only us living in it.

As we drew nearer to the barn, I was determined to keep this secret hidden, at least for a little while longer. I knew that at first it seemed kind of fun and dangerous, but it was weighing on both me and Daisy. I knew she didn't want to keep this up much longer.

I knew I would eventually have to come clean to my dad about it all, but I wasn't ready just yet. I needed a little more time. I hoped he would understand, but for now, I was willing to do whatever it took to protect our relationship and Daisy. I didn't want my dad to say something to upset her when he found out. I wanted him to accept her- to accept us -but it was all a guessing game at this point.

Chapter Forty

Daisy

We made our way outside to the tire swing. It had always hung in the same place from the big oak tree. Colt's mom had his dad install it right there so she could see him from the porch or if she were inside the house. It was the perfect spot. She loved watching us play. I sat down, and Colt pushed me gently. I laughed lightly, feeling the breeze against my skin.

"This is nice...just us." He nodded.

"I wish we could be open about this. About us. I mean, it hasn't been that bad. I just really want to show you off." I wanted nothing more than to be with him, openly. I wanted people to notice that we were together.

"Show me off?" He tried to make a joke, but the lingering thoughts made it kind of difficult to find laughter in the moment. "I know. We just have to keep being careful and keep this hidden for a little while longer." I nodded at his words. This had become harder as the days passed.

"Then you'll tell him?" He sighed, but I pretended not to

notice. I didn't want to start overthinking.

All I wanted was for Colt to man up and tell his dad. It was his place to tell him, not mine. He made his dad a promise and broke it, now he needed to own up to it. He needed to have a talk with him. Maybe he would understand. Maybe he wouldn't be as hard on Colt as he thought.

I wanted Colt to sit with me, wrap his arms around me, and just be free. I wanted to be free from the chains and shelter of having to keep a secret. I closed my eyes for a moment as I briefly felt Colt's hands against my back as he pushed me again, letting out a deep breath.

I had been paying attention to see if Walt came back, but I hadn't yet seen him. I knew he would be back soon since he had already been gone for a bit.

Colt walked in front of me and helped me off the swing. We walked to the barn, side by side, just as when we went anywhere together as kids. I felt our hands grazing each other's. It was a small thing, but it was a sweet, silent moment.

"Hey, Daisy?"

"Hm?"

"You haven't checked on the chickens, have you?"

"No, not since I've been here. Your dad hasn't asked me to do it."

"Yeah. He really likes chickens, so he usually does that himself. My mom always loved them."

"They probably remind him of her."

"Yeah. She collected them. That's why there's some in the house."

"I've noticed them. I think the black and white one with the cowboy hat, boots, and bandana is my favorite."

"She liked to find the ones that were unique and different."

"She had a good eye for them."

"What do you say we go take a look at the chickens?" I nodded.

As we approached, I could hear the clucking of the chickens echoing in the air. I was excited. I hadn't been around chickens since the last time I had been at Texas Rose Ranch. We didn't have chickens, but I always saw them here. I spotted the chickens with their glistening feathers in the sunlight. They scurried around, pecking at the ground below.

Colt opened the door, and as we stepped inside the coop, I could smell hay and fresh straw. I looked around at the ground, trying to avoid most of their little drops. Colt filled the feeder with grain while I checked the water buckets. I carefully made sure their water was clean before adding fresh water for them to enjoy.

"Look at them go!" Colt chuckled, nudging me slightly.

One hen pushed her way to the front to get to the food. I smiled, enjoying the sight of our feathered friends. It had been a long time since I saw chickens. There weren't any in Dallas, but Garrity Valley always had them. It was something else I really loved about this place…Something I had missed and not even realized. Sometimes, it's the little things that bring the most joy.

Being with Colt made everything more fun. I watched as he made sure everything was just right. He was so meticulous. It was one of the things I admired most about him.

"Let's see if we can find any eggs." I nodded, hoping I would find more than him.

We wandered around, checking all the spots. From experience, even if you have a nice box made with hay or straw in it for them to lie in, you will always have at least one that decides a random spot on the ground is a better place. Hunting eggs was almost like a treasure hunt.

"Got one!" I held it up to show Colt.

"Nice one! I don't see any more lying around anywhere. Maybe the rest were smarter and actually lay in the boxes."

"Let's check." We walked over to the boxes, and all but one of them had at least one egg inside.

As we gathered the eggs, we were careful not to crack them. A good thing about being on a ranch like this was being able to get some food like this without having to go to a store. I never did like going shopping, and even after moving away, I still only went when it was absolutely necessary.

I glanced over at Colt, who was still collecting eggs, being so careful and attentive as he placed each one in the basket he was holding. I loved these moments with Colt. They felt timeless. I wanted to bottle little moments like this up so I could go back to them later and relive them all over again. Eventually, we finished our egg hunt. Colt set the basket down and began counting the eggs.

"Twenty eggs, Daisy!"

"Do you all usually get that many?"

"Yeah, it's usually around that many this time of year."

"That's a lot!"

Working with the chickens today was another way for us to bond. It had always been a strong one, and getting that back has been great. It has meant a lot to me that Colt and I could put the past behind us and be like this together. He was wonderful. We have been creating some more memories that I can look back on and hold near and dear to me.

As we walked back to the house, I wanted to reach over and take his hand, but I could see his dad in the barn and knew that wasn't the best idea. However, I still smiled and felt grateful that I had someone so special in my life who would make saying goodbye so hard.

Chapter Forty-One

Colt

When we got back to the house, I took the eggs inside and sat them on the counter while Daisy waited on the porch. We still had a few chores left before calling it a day. My dad hadn't been able to get around to tending to the garden yet, so he had mentioned it to me earlier. I was excited to get to do it, though. My mom always did this part, and after she passed, my dad wanted to keep it up.

Before Daisy came for the summer, my dad and I had planted vegetables. The garden was starting to get a bit overgrown and the weeds needed to be pulled so we could properly check on the plants.

"So, what's next?"

"With how busy things have been, no one has tended the garden. Some weeds need pulled and then we can check on the vegetables we planted."

"Want me to help?"

"Of course. I remember how much you used to talk about

your mom's garden."

"It was always a big one. I loved getting to eat fresh vegetables. Sometimes I would sneak a pepper or tomato from the garden and eat it before my mom got a chance to take it inside and wash it."

"I did that, too, sometimes. They taste better when you grow them rather than buying them, don't they?"

"Absolutely."

I grabbed a bucket and Daisy followed behind me as we made our way to the garden. I gave her a pair of gloves I picked up from inside the house. I started pulling the weeds, reminding her how to do it. I was sure she probably didn't need a reminder, but I gave her one anyway. It was basically an excuse for her to admire me. Once she started pulling the weeds herself, I admired how focused she was, her brow slightly furrowing as she concentrated on the task at hand.

"Colt, do you guys ever make salsa?"

"Yeah. Sometimes we do. Why do you ask?"

"My mom used to make the best. It was perfect for a summer day."

"She always did cook the best."

She smiled and I could see a mix of sadness and joy on her face. I felt peaceful as we worked together pulling weeds and tending to the plants.

"Are you hungry?"

"Yes! I wonder what your dad is cooking this evening. I'm sure it'll be good regardless." We chuckled, knowing my dad cooked well for a man. It was nice that he never taught us gender roles, only life skills. That was another thing I wanted to instill in my children someday.

"Let's go dump these buckets and we can go inside and clean up for supper."

"I know we've been busy today, Colt, but I have enjoyed it."

"Me, too." She gave me a soft smile, and I could feel the heat between us. She was beautiful, in more ways than one.

We walked over to the barrel and dumped the weeds inside. We burned them with other garbage from time to time in the barrel to dispose of them easily. I glanced at Daisy, fighting the urge to place a kiss on her cheek. The sun glistening off her made her beauty shine even brighter.

"Are we all set?"

"Yep. We can go in and clean up."

"Good. I need a shower." As we walked toward the house, Daisy leaned over to me. "Thank you for today. I needed this. Just this time together. It helped me not be taken away by my thoughts."

"You're welcome, and I know what you mean. I promise you; everything will be alright." She nodded and I could see a hint of relief on her face.

As we entered the kitchen, I was taken aback by the delightful smell filling the air. I saw my dad stirring a pot on the stove, a big smile on his face.

"You two look like you've been working hard."

"We got to the garden and got those weeds pulled."

"I appreciate that. I just haven't gotten around to it with everything else."

"No problem. Daisy liked getting her hands dirty." My dad had turned his back to continue stirring the pot on the stove, and that gave me the perfect opportunity to wink at Daisy after my joke. She hadn't spoken, just stood there listening to our conversation.

"The food will be ready soon."

"I need to go shower first." My dad turned to Daisy.

"Of course. Yeah, you both need to go wash up. Supper will be ready when you get back."

"Daisy, you can go on ahead and I will go after." She nodded and walked down the hall.

"How did things really go today after the snake incident?"

"Things went good."

"Daisy didn't mind pulling the weeds?"

"No, she did good."

"Well, I'm glad to hear it. You dumped those weeds in the barrel, didn't you?"

"Yep. Both buckets were full."

"The garden look better now?"

"Yeah, it looks a lot better. I checked on the plants and they all looked good. Daisy was talking about when her mom used to plant a garden and make things from the vegetables."

"I'm sure she's probably thought a lot about her since being back here."

"Yeah. She has mentioned her a couple of times to me."

"I'm glad she and John had a nice talk. They got along alright from what you saw?"

"Yeah. At first it was a little awkward, but I went in to use the bathroom and came out and they were talking."

"You got some good timing." We both laughed. My dad was good at jokes sometimes.

"Things seem to be better for them now."

"I was hoping they would reconcile after she went. Thanks again for going with her, and for being back up here. I'm glad I have you around."

"Me, too, dad."

I heard footsteps and turned to see Daisy coming into

view.

"Your turn."

I headed down the hall, brushing my hand against her as I walked past, and my dad had his back turned toward us. I went into the bathroom and took a quick shower, eager to eat.

When I got back to the kitchen, the dinner table was set. I felt a sense of comfort when my dad made a meal like this. It reminded me of my mom and when she used to cook. The table had stew and bread, and the smell was amazing. As we ate, I couldn't help but steal glances at Daisy. She was making conversation with my dad, but I had no idea what they were saying because I was so focused on the food and trying to get a peek at her.

She was a breath of fresh air.

She made me want to be around her every minute of every day.

She consumed me and filled my soul with such a fire that I couldn't explain.

She meant more to me than anyone ever has.

As we finished our meal, my dad walked over to the sink to do the dishes. Daisy helped him clear the table, and I watched how her movements were so graceful and effortless. She made everything look good. I felt pride when I thought about how we are partners now. I wanted to be her partner for life. The day had been filled with lots of work and a crazy situation with Titan, but we had so many special moments. With Daisy, there were always positives. There were always times to look back on, laughs to have, and smiles to give.

We settled into the living room. The sun had set, and the air had cooled a little. I sat next to Daisy on the couch since my dad had gone to bed. I felt so much peace being so close to her. There was no place I would rather be. I brushed my hand against her hand, glancing up to meet her eyes.

Every day with Daisy was an adventure, and I wanted to experience that every day of my life.

Chapter Forty-Two

Daisy

In the shower, I thought about the ups and downs of the day- how I started off watching the sunrise on Domino, how poor Titan injured his leg from getting spooked by the snake, Walt making us sandwiches, Colt and I enjoying a quick break on the tire swing, getting the garden fixed up, and now supper.

When I first came back to Garrity Valley, I wasn't excited. I didn't want to be here. I didn't want to do all the work that came with running a ranch. I didn't want to get back on a horse. I didn't want to do chores. I didn't want to do any of it.

I had been so angry with my dad for forcing me to come here, but now, we had reconciled. I was really happy about that because even though he gets on my nerves, I still want my dad in my life. I have missed having him around.

And Colt and I started talking again and now look at us. We are in a relationship. Yes, it is a secret. Yes, we still have some things to talk about and to figure out before summer is over- which it will be very soon- but we would figure that all out together.

I scrubbed the shampoo through my hair, then let the water wash it out. I stood there, lost in my thoughts, for a few more minutes and let the water drip down my body. I got out, dried off, and slipped on some clothes. I hadn't taken nearly as long of a shower I normally would take, but I could smell the food, and I knew Colt still needed to shower before we ate.

When I walked down the hall toward the kitchen, the aroma of the food was even stronger. I was starving, so I let Colt know he better hurry up. The smell was not helping my hunger.

"Your turn."

Colt headed down the hall. As he passed me, he brushed his hand against mine. I closed my eyes for a second, breathing in his scent. I longed to be able to touch him and be with him openly.

"Hey, Daisy. Do you care to set the table? I'm about finished here."

"Of course. I don't mind." I walked over to grab some plates from the cabinet and silverware from the drawer, taking my time to set the table. "I hope Colt hurries up. I'm ready to eat."

"Hope you like it."

"What did you make?"

"Stew. I have some bread to eat with it."

"That sounds so good. I could smell it from the bathroom." Walt chuckled.

Walt placed the food on the table, and we sat down. Colt came into view, sitting in the chair across from me. I could feel Colt's eyes on me, stealing sneaky glances when he knew his dad wasn't looking. I noticed how his lips were turned to one side and teasing me in a way that sent shivers down my spine, causing my whole body to tremble.

"So, Daisy, what do you think?"

"It's very good, Walt. Where did you learn to cook like

this?"

"My mother and grandmother taught me. They always made sure to teach my brother and I things. They wanted us to be able to cook if we never found a woman to put up with us." We both laughed.

"Did they say that?"

"Oh, yes, they did." We laughed again.

As we finished our meal, Walt walked over to the sink to do the dishes, and I helped him clear the table. Colt was now standing, leaning against the wall that went into the kitchen- the same one he had pressed me against during one of our hot and steamy make out sessions.

There had been so much to do on the ranch today, but I didn't seem to mind it. I was with Colt, and any time spent with him was always a good time. I liked getting to see how calm he was during the snake incident. I was a nervous wreck, but he was the calm to my storm.

Walt finished the dishes and said he was going to bed after the long day. I'm sure he was even more tired than me, as he is older.

The sun had now set, and Colt and I settled into the living room. Colt plopped on the couch beside me. He brushed his hand against mine, moving his eyes up to meet my own. The atmosphere was relaxed, and I laid my head on his shoulder.

"Hey, Daisy. Do you want to step outside for a minute?" His voice was low, but I caught a smile on his face.

We walked outside, hand in hand, and I felt the slight coolness of the air against my body. The porch creaked beneath our feet as we leaned against the wooden railing. The stars were out and shining bright, casting a glow in the night sky. The view was breathtaking. Colt turned to me.

"Is it just me or does it kind of feel like we're in a movie?"

His voice was still barely above a whisper.

"It does…like a secret romance movie."

We leaned closer and I could feel the tension growing between us. He had a warmth radiating off him, and I knew his arms would feel like a comforting blanket wrapped around me. He brushed a strand of hair behind my ear. The simplicity of the touch sent shivers down my spine. Our gazes locked, and everything else faded away.

"Daisy, I know we are keeping this a secret, but I can't help how I feel about you." A lump caught in my throat, and I was unable to find words to reply to him.

Before I could find the words to say, Colt leaned in closer. His lips brushed against mine in a soft, passionate kiss. He had a hand on each side of my face. The kiss deepened as he pulled me in closer to him, and all my thoughts and worries faded away.

The kiss felt right.

His touch felt right.

My feelings for Colt felt right.

Being with Colt felt right.

We pulled away, our foreheads resting against each other. We were both breathless. I heard the faint sound of the TV from inside, and I was reminded that we needed to be careful about our secret rendezvous.

"We should go get some sleep." I knew that's what we needed to do.

"Yeah, it's been a long day." He kissed me on the cheek one last time before we made our way into the house.

I hoped our secret was just the beginning, and I couldn't wait to see where it would lead.

Chapter Forty-Three

Colt

The next morning, I lingered around in the house for a little longer so I could see Daisy before we had to start working around the ranch. My dad had already gone out because he wanted to check on Titan's leg. He said he would go ahead and do the feeding and watering for the horses and for me to let Daisy know when she came out of her room.

"Colt? What are you still doing in here?"

"I wanted to see you before we headed out, just in case we didn't get a chance to be alone today."

"Oh, really?" I walked closer to her, wrapping my arms around her waist and pulling her in close.

"Yes, really." I kissed her on the neck and when I raised my head up, her cheeks were a perfect rosy red. "My dad went to check on Titan's leg and said he would take care of the horses this morning."

"Oh, that's nice of him."

"I'm sure there's plenty of other work to be done around here today."

"Isn't there always?" She walked closer to the door, me following behind. "Colt?"

"Yes, darlin'?"

"Do you think we could maybe go to my dad's today? I'd like to go see him and maybe help him out a little bit."

"I'm sure if I ask my dad about it that he wouldn't mind. He'd probably like it that you were spending time with your dad."

"Maybe we could spend a little time together, too, since my dad knows about us? What do you think?"

"I think I could easily pack us some food and we could have a nice picnic after we help your dad with some things."

"A picnic?"

"What? Do you not like the idea?"

"Oh, no. I like it. I just didn't picture you as a picnic kind of guy."

"I'm just full of surprises."

"Yes, you are." She leaned in and placed a kiss on my cheek.

"I'll go out and talk to him. We did so much around here yesterday. I think the only thing is to just feed and water everything. He did mention he was going to check on the garden and maybe a little fertilizer to it to help the vegetables we planted. He should be fine with it. I'll come back in and let you know." I had the door halfway open now.

"Colt?" I turned back, one foot inside the door and one foot outside of it. "Thank you. I really appreciate you. You have been so good to me."

"You don't have to thank me, Daisy. You deserve all the good in the world and more. You deserve nothing but the best."

She smiled at me, tears forming in her eyes. I hated to see her cry, so I quickly ran out to talk to my dad after saying, "I'll be right back. Help yourself to some of the bacon I fried this morning while you wait."

Once outside, I put a hand on my chest, feeling how tight it was. Daisy had a way of making me want to forget about everything to just spend all my time with her. She made me happy and excited. She made me crave things I have never wanted before. I continued walking toward the barn, moving my hand off my chest.

"Hey, Colt."

"How's Titan's leg doing?"

"Seems to be pretty good. I was going to go out for a ride later once I took care of the horses and cattle. I'll probably ride Domino. I wouldn't want to put too much strain on Titan. He still needs some rest. Would you want to come along?"

"Actually, I came to ask you something?" My dad rose from his kneeling position beside Titan.

"Oh, yeah? What's that?"

"Well, it's about Daisy actually."

"Alright."

"She mentioned to me that she would like to go see her dad. She's still nervous about talking to and being around him since they only recently have rekindled their relationship. She asked if I would go with her. I wanted to see if that was okay with you before we went. Daisy said she would like to help him out around the ranch some. If we are needed here today, I can tell her we should wait another time."

"If she wants to go see her dad, then I think that's a fine idea."

"Really? She'll be happy to hear that."

"You go along with her and make sure everything's good.

Hopefully they can keep building their relationship back. I know how much John has missed her. You know, he once mentioned the idea of selling his ranch?"

"What?"

"He said it was small anyway and he wasn't sure that Daisy would ever come back after being gone for so many years. He didn't see any reason to keep it."

"But he loves that place."

"That's what I told him. He decided to keep it and held out hope that she would eventually come back. I know he's glad she's here. It'll be a nice surprise for the two of you to go over there. You two don't worry about rushing back here, either. Let those two have their time together. They both need it."

"Thanks, dad. I'll go let Daisy know and we'll head out."

I walked back to the house to tell her the good news. Daisy was still inside, standing in the kitchen, sipping away at some coffee. I stopped in my tracks for a second, taking in how the morning glow was casting a shadow on her face. She is breathtaking. I cleared my throat, getting her attention.

"Oh. What did your dad say?"

"He said we were good to go."

"What did you tell him?"

"I let him know that you had talked about going to see your dad and help him out a bit, but that you were still a little apprehensive about going since you two just reconciled. I told him you asked me to go with you because of that."

"And he said that is okay?"

"He did. He said that since we did so much yesterday, besides tending to the animals, there's not much to do today. He's going to work in the garden some today is all."

"So, when do we leave?"

"As soon as I get this bag packed for our picnic."

She smiled softly, taking the last sip of her coffee. I grabbed some chips from the cabinet and made two sandwiches to go. I threw in two waters as well. This was going to be a good day. I could feel it.

I looked back up and saw Daisy leaning against the counter. She had the prettiest smirk on her face, and it made my heart skip a beat. She could make the simplest things feel like the biggest things. She was amazing in every way, and I was lucky enough to call her mine, even if it was in secret for now.

Chapter Forty-Four

Daisy

As Colt drove down the familiar winding road to my dad's place, I stared out the window, taking in the beautiful scenery. Excitement and nerves filled me, but I was eager to see my dad again. The sun was fully out now, and a warm glow was cast over the land. I couldn't help but smile. The family ranch wasn't that big-just enough room for a couple of horses and a few cattle-but it was special. It brought a sense of comfort and coziness. I was glad to be back, and I was ready to continue rebuilding the relationship between my dad and me. It had been a long time coming.

As Colt pulled into the driveway, I could feel my heart racing. I glanced at Colt, who was adjusting his cowboy hat. He looked so calm, and it was almost a little infuriating, but I loved that he could be the calm to my storm any day.

"You ready for this, darlin'?"

"Yes."

"Don't forget. You have a nice, romantic picnic waiting for you once we finish the work." He smiled at me, and it only fueled my excitement. This was going to be a good day; I just knew it.

I stepped out of the truck, taking in a deep breath. I could smell the wildflowers and grass, reminding me of so many memories. I had a lot of fond memories here growing up, and I was glad that my mind wandered to those instead of the really bad time.

I looked around to see my dad, but he was nowhere to be found. As I walked closer to the front door, I felt anticipation. Neither me, Colt, nor Walt had let my dad know about the two of us coming here, and I was hoping he would be happy to see us.

"There's my girl!" I looked up and saw my dad swinging the front door open, a wide grin lighting up his face.

He pulled me into a warm hug. There was so much strength in his arms, and I was instantly reminded of how much I missed this connection. Colt was standing back, giving us a moment. My dad quickly turned to him, though, extending his hand.

"Colt! Glad you could make it."

"Sorry, this is a little unexpected, dad."

"Y'all are welcome here any time."

"We thought we would come help you out today."

"Yeah, my dad has it all under control back at Texas Rose."

"Whose idea was this?" Neither of us spoke, but from dad's reaction, I'm sure that somehow Colt let him know it was my idea.

"Well, follow me."

We made our way to the backyard, where my dad was ready with a list of chores for us to do. My dad and I are both really trying, I feel a lot of gratitude because of it. I want to support him, and I want him to support me.

"These weeds need to be pulled. I know the garden isn't very big, but I still like to keep it up." Just like Walt, my dad kept the garden going because it was one of my mom's favorite things.

We spent the next little while working together, pulling out all the weeds from the garden to tidy it up. It was nice to have this time with my dad. With so many years apart, I was starting to think that we would never get to do things like this again.

"What else do you need, dad?"

"Well, the shed needs to be cleaned up, and I need to fix a place in the fence."

"We can help you with that, no problem." My dad smiled back at me, then we all three headed toward the shed.

We stole glances at each other while working side by side. The shed was a mess, and I could only imagine how hard it had been for my dad to keep this place running by himself. I knew he enjoyed this place, and he would never want to give this up. It meant too much to him, and I knew it reminded him of my mom.

We took a break, and I saw my dad wipe sweat from his brow. He looked so content and pleased.

"You know, it feels good to have you both here. I like having some help around here."

"Didn't you have someone hired? I thought my dad had said something about it."

"I did, but they found work elsewhere that paid better, so it's been a one-man job around here for a while."

"I hate to hear that. You know, if you ever need any help, you can always call me or my dad. One of us will come lend a hand." My dad placed a hand on Colt's shoulder.

"I know. You are good people, you and your dad. Y'all have bailed me out plenty of times."

"Well, I appreciate that, John."

"I have missed this, though. It's nice to have some help around here, and it's even better when my daughter comes and helps." I smiled at him, receiving that warm smile from him that was always there to lift me up as a kid.

"I've missed it, too, dad. I'm really glad we're doing this." This felt like a turning point in our relationship, and I was welcoming it with open arms.

"Well, I'll finish up here. You two go off somewhere."

"What?"

"You know what I mean. You two need some time alone together. Plus, I did notice what looked like a packed lunch when y'all were getting out of the truck."

"You were spying?"

"Oh, no. I just notice things. Now you two run along."

"We won't be gone that long, dad."

"Take all the time you need."

We walked back to the truck, leaving my dad to finish the fence himself. Colt grabbed the bag he had packed with sandwiches, chips, and some fruit, along with the water I threw in there, and we headed off in the field.

Seeing my dad and Colt interact today has been special. I could be open with him about mine and Colt's relationship. I always wanted my parents to love and to accept who I was dating, and it was kind of fitting that my dad was the only one who knew about us being together. He has been amazing during this, and he has been so supportive. Having his approval means a lot to me.

As we sat down to eat, Colt spread a thin blanket down onto the grass. He emptied out the bag, handing me a bottle of water and a sandwich, and placing the chips and fruit in the middle of us. I looked around us and felt so much peace being surrounded by only Colt and nature.

We enjoyed our food, Colt casually feeding me a grape every now and then. Each time, I looked into his eyes and saw a sparkle. His face was lit up with the biggest smile, and his eyes were only on me. He never took them off me.

It made me feel special.

He made me feel special.

"This is perfect."

"It is. So, what gave you the idea to have a picnic?"

"Honestly, I thought of it on the spot. I knew we both wanted to spend some time alone together, and I knew how much you loved being out in the field, enjoying the view. I thought this would be a good way to do those things."

"Well, you did good, cowboy." He grinned, and it was everything I could do to hold myself back. All I wanted to do was kiss him.

Suddenly, I gave in to temptation. I giggled a little as I settled on his lap, a leg on either side of him. I forgot all about the picnic for a moment as our lips met. At first, the kiss was slow and teasing. Then, it deepened with a hunger that I felt with every kiss and touch from Colt.

My fingers simultaneously found their way to his hair, intertwining between the strands, as my lips continued to taste his. I pulled him closer as I felt his rough, calloused hands around my waist, his thumbs rubbing circles on my skin.

Our kiss broke, and I was absolutely breathless and flushed. I looked at Colt's face and could see that he was the same, hearing his heavy breathing and noticing the red tint to his skin. I rested my forehead against his, placing a hand on his chest where his heart would be. We were in sync as I felt the pounding in his chest.

"Wow." I looked up at him.

"Well, cowboy. What do you think?"

"I think you sure know how to take my breath away…in a good way." He reached up and gently brushed a stray strand of her hair from my face, placing it behind my ear.

He held me tightly for a moment, and I buried my face in his neck. I took in his familiar, woodsy scent. I felt the strong, solid strength of his body against my own. I was captivated by him and by his touch.

I carefully turned around, so I didn't knee him between the legs. I lay against him, my head on his lap where I could look up at him or out at the scenery around us, and my legs extended out from me on the blanket. Colt placed an arm around my hip, and I nestled against him, feeling so much safety and comfort in his presence. The world was fading away again, and I was cocooned in a bubble of love and affection held by him. I closed my eyes for a moment, taking in how calm I felt.

Colt leaned down and kissed me softly, a tender peck that spoke volumes in this moment. Colt was being so gentle with me, allowing me to take control, and I was thankful for him.

I thought of all the reasons why Colt was so special to me and why I felt so safe when I was with him.

He listens to me.

He cares about me.

He doesn't judge me.

He makes me feel good about myself.

He is encouraging.

He is adventurous.

He is caring.

He makes an effort to plan things and make our moments together meaningful.

He takes an interest in what I'm doing and how I'm feeling.

He treats me like I matter.

He understands me.

Most importantly, he makes me feel seen.

He feels like home.

As our lips parted, I felt the deep connection between us. I felt so much peace and contentment wash over me, and I knew in that moment that I was exactly where I was supposed to be- in the arms of the man I was falling in love with.

Colt continued holding me, and I wanted to stay in this little world with him forever. I felt his grip tighten, like he was afraid to let go. I snuggled even deeper in his embrace, letting the security wrap around me. I was so content, and knowing that we had to get up soon made me want to cry. I wasn't ready to let him go just yet.

Coming back here, I found something truly special in Colt.

I found someone who had the potential to be in my life for a long time…maybe even for the rest of my life.

Chapter Forty-Five

Colt

The day was a blur after our romantic time together at the picnic.

It was now the next morning, and the morning sun was casting a long shadow across the ranch. Daisy emerged from her room, her hair still lightly damp. I smiled at her as she made her way to the front door where I was standing. I opened the door for her, leading her towards the barn.

"Dad's already out there." I nodded in its direction. "You know he gets up before the chickens even think about it." She chuckled a little, and the sound of her laughter filled my soul.

As we approached the barn, we found my dad tinkering with the old tractor. His hands were covered in grease and dirt as he expertly adjusted the carburetor. His brows were furrowed as he concentrated. I couldn't wait until we could afford a new tractor. We had both spent a lot of time working on this one, and it was about time for an upgrade. I was tired of it breaking down and costing us parts.

My dad looked up, a smile softening his rugged features as he saw us standing there near him.

"Morning, you two. Sleep alright?"

"Yep." Daisy nodded, agreeing with my answer.

"How did it go at your dad's yesterday? I didn't get a chance to ask you two about how it went last night." I looked at Daisy, wondering if she was going to answer. I noticed her lips parting, so I stayed quiet.

"It went well. We helped him in the garden. I know he keeps that up because it was one of my mom's favorite things." She paused for a moment, then continued. "We helped him tidy up the shed and get it organized, too. He needed some help with repairing a small part of the fence where the cattle are." She glanced at me. I remembered that was the moment I stole her away for our romantic picnic rendezvous. "Colt and I aided in the repairs to it."

"Well, I'm glad you two got to go over there and help him out for the day."

"He told us about the help he had leaving for other work. Walt, has my dad been struggling?"

"Ah…" My dad scratched his head, not wanting to answer. "He was doing pretty good running the place with the help he did have. Since they're gone now, he has called on me and Colt sometimes for a little help. It's not a big ranch, but neither you nor your dad is getting older. A little assistance is good for us. I don't know what I'd do without Colt here."

He placed a hand on my shoulder, squeezing it. It felt nice to have him say those words and give me some credit for all the effort I put in and the work I do around the ranch. I want to take over someday. That's the dream.

"Alright, enough talk. We've got work to do. Colt, I need you to go check the fence and cattle. You can take the side-by-side down there. Daisy, can you help me with the horses?"

"Of course."

I heard a bark and looked around to see Hank stepping into view. He never strayed far from my dad.

"Oh, alright, Hank. You can help with the horses, too." My dad knelt down and rubbed his head. He moved his leg a little, letting us know that the head scratch was hitting the right spot.

I grabbed food and water and loaded it into the back of the side by side. I was eager to get started. Once I arrived, I filled up the troughs with food and water, then slowly drove the side-by-side around the fence, making sure there weren't any problem areas. We had one heifer that liked to try to break through it often, and it was better to check the fence daily and be safe rather than sorry. I didn't catch anything wrong with it.

I paused for a moment and watched the cattle as they ate. Growing up here, Daisy and I talked about seeing other places, but I never did want to go. Being around life like this all the time, I didn't see why anyone would ever want to leave it. I understood why Daisy left, though. There was a lot of heartbreak, and she always had that strong, adventurous side that wanted to explore the world.

□ □ □

I was fifteen and Daisy was thirteen. She was sitting on the tire swing at the big oak tree, me pushing her gently. The gentle breeze felt cool against my skin and the only sounds were of the horses whining. Daisy leaned her head back as I gave her a push, her arms briefly letting go of the swing as she came back to be level with the earth beneath us.

"You know, cowboy?"

"What's that, Daisy?"

"I've been thinking about all the places I want to see when I grow up."

"Like where? Looking around, this is the best place to be. Here, you don't have anyone to bother you, and you can be surrounded by

nature, horses, and cattle all day. You can go riding when you want, and there are so many things you can do and have here that you can't anywhere else." She ignored my comment and continued.

"There is so much out there. New York City would be fun to see one day. It's so big and the buildings are so tall there."

"Yeah, but it would be really crowded there with all the people."

"Exactly! I want to see the bright lights, the street performers, and all of the sights it has to offer. I want to experience it. The Statue of Liberty must really be a sight!"

"You and your big dreams. What else?" I pushed her again, and she kept talking about all the places she wanted to see someday.

"The beach! I've never been. People at school talk about going on vacations in the summer."

"I've heard them."

"You could go swimming and build sandcastles. You may even see a dolphin! That would be awesome!"

"What if you got sunburnt?"

"I'll wear sunscreen. That's beside the point. Don't worry, though. I'll bring you along so you can help me build that sandcastle. Maybe I can bury you in the sand, too."

"You wish."

"Wouldn't the mountains be nice to see? We could go hiking. We could have a picnic up there, too, as we took in the view from the top."

"A picnic?"

"We could explore caves and look for cool rocks. At night, we could lie under the stars."

"You've really thought this through, haven't you?"

"I guess so. I just think it would be fun to see other places besides here...only if you go with me, though." I smiled. I liked the

fact that she included me in all her plans. "Garrity Valley is my home, and I will always come back to it. It would be nice to visit some other places in my life."

◻ ◻ ◻

The sun had now climbed high, and the earth felt like it was baking in its rays. The side-by-side bounced against the ground as I headed in the direction of my dad and Daisy. I could see some dust flying up as I moved along. The air was thick with the smell of leather and sweat as I got back to the barn. I ran a hand across my forehead, wiping away the perspiration.

I slowed the engine as I approached. My dad and Daisy were still inside, standing in the doorway now. My dad was leaning against Titan's stall, and Daisy was in the center, her hands moving with gentle ease as she brushed Domino's mane. Domino shifted and snorted softly, but Daisy's calm voice soothed him. Sunlight seeped through the cracks of the barn, beaming off her face and illuminating the dirt on the group inside.

I cut the engine, the sudden silence allowing me to hear the horses. Daisy looked up, her eyes meeting mine, and a smile formed on her face.

"Hey." She called out, her voice carrying across the distance between us.

"Back already?" I nodded to answer my dad's question. I hopped out of the side-by-side and walked over to them.

"The fence looked good. I left them eating, and the water troughs full of water."

"Good to hear."

"So, what's next?"

"Can you two pick up sticks from the yard? I need to mow, so I'm going to go work on that. After that, could y'all go feed and water the chickens and collect the eggs?"

"On it, Walt."

"Got it, dad."

Daisy and I headed straight to the yard, me pushing the wheelbarrow behind her so we could throw all the sticks in for easy collecting and disposal.

"Come on, slowpoke." I looked up at Daisy after that remark.

"Excuse me? You know I could run circles around you with picking these up." I waved a stick around as she scoffed.

"You're on."

We worked in a comfortable silence, stealing glances at one another to see the progress each of us was making. Neither of us wanted the other to outdo ourselves. Daisy scooped up the sticks swiftly, but with my longer legs and arms, I clearly had the advantage. Daisy was more methodical, scanning the ground and carefully picking up the smallest bits of debris.

"Looking good, team." We both looked up at my dad's words. "Looks like I'm ready to start. Take the wheelbarrow and dumb all the sticks in the barrel." I nodded and started wheeling it over, Daisy following behind me.

"Looks like it might have been a tie."

"That sounds good to me."

Together, we unloaded the sticks from the wheelbarrow to the inside of the barrel. This would be good to lay on a bonfire. I was hoping we could have one soon. A little over half of the barrel was filled, and we walked back to the barn so I could put the wheelbarrow back inside. I felt a smack on my butt and jolted back.

"Hey!"

"Don't worry. Your dad is on the mower and can't hear a thing. He's concentrating too hard to be looking over here at us." I shook my head at her but still smiled. I liked that she did it without warning. She kept me on my toes.

"I'll grab the basket from the barn." Daisy headed over to grab it while I grabbed the feed bucket and filled a jug of water.

I made sure to keep a couple of steps behind her as we headed to the chicken coop. Inside, the smell was a mix of dust and crap, and the air was filled with feathers and clucking. I hoisted the feed bucket, scattering grain across the floor.

"Alright, y'all. Food is served." I heard squawks as the chickens ran toward the scattered piles of feed.

I walked over and refilled their water. Daisy was already kneeling by the nesting boxes, placing eggs in the basket she had in her hands. I checked the boxes on the opposite end of where she was, placing those inside the basket along with the others.

"How many do we have?" We stood up, and Daisy started counting.

"Twelve eggs. Not bad at all."

***

That evening, we were all sitting out on the porch. We had accomplished quite a bit on the ranch today, and I was glad that I could experience this time working alongside Daisy. I wondered what it would be like to work with the person you were in a relationship with after seeing my parents and Daisy's parents working together all those years. Experiencing it now was nothing short of amazing. We balanced each other out, and it was always fun being around her.

"Well, kids, I've got to head out." I turned to him. "I've got some business to take care of."

"Business?" I raised an eyebrow. "What kind of business, dad?"

"Nothing you need to worry about, just something I need to get done. Don't wait up on me. I may stop at John's before I come back." I nodded, and my dad headed to his truck.

We watched as he drove down the driveway, dust flying behind the tires. As he went out of view, there was silence in the air. The only sounds were those of the crickets chirping. I turned to Daisy, an intense gaze forming between us.

"Well, Daisy. I have a proposition for you."

"Oh. I'm intrigued." She leaned against the porch railing, biting her lip on one side. She was doing things to me just by the way she was looking at me.

"What do you say we head into town and go to the bar for food, drinks, and I have a dance or two in me. I heard the bar has a live band playing tonight." I winked at her.

"Hmm…I don't know." I twisted my head, knowing she was messing with me. I stepped closer, placing a hand on her cheek. "Of course I'll go. I could use a night out. You, too, cowboy." She leaned forward, kissing me on the cheek. I wasn't about to let her tease me like that, so I grabbed her face, pulling her lips to mine.

"Go get cleaned up. We leave in twenty."

"On it, cowboy."

I quickly showered, knowing that I could be in and out faster than it would take Daisy to pick out clothes to wear. Her last outfit stole the show, so I was curious what she would have on tonight.

I slipped on a light blue button-up, rolling the sleeves up to my elbows, and a clean pair of jeans. I pulled on my boots and added my cowboy hat to finish the look before heading out of the room toward the living room to wait for Daisy. I was hoping she would be quick. I was eager to eat, but I was even more anxious to see her.

I heard footsteps, so I turned toward the hallway. When Daisy walked into my view, all I could do was stare. She had on this dress, a perfect shade of blue, mimicking the colors of the night sky with its dark and blue and shimmering effect. It was short, but it didn't show too much. She had on some short, black boots, and her hair was down. I admired how her bouncy curls flowed down her body. She was glowing. Her makeup was simple, and I recalled how she never wore a lot. She liked the natural look. She was effortlessly stunning, like she just threw it on and walked out the door. I looked her up and down as she came closer to me. My breath caught as I looked at her, every curve making me ache with how beautiful she is. She was a dream, my dream, and didn't even know it.

Chapter Forty-Six

Daisy

Colt was standing near the door, and he looked so handsome. The light glimmered off my dress, and I watched as his eyes drifted down and up my body. He was taking me all in, and I didn't mind it. I liked it. The dress hugged my curves perfectly, and I knew he was admiring the fit.

I walked as close to him as I could without running him over. His eyes never strayed from me, and I was enjoying how captivated he was. I leaned against the doorframe, a playful smirk on my lips as I looked into Colt's eyes.

"What do you think? Is it too much? I can change." I looked down at the dress, teasing him. He didn't speak. Instead, he grabbed my arm and pulled me into him.

"Not too much." His lips crashed onto mine, and his hands made their way to my hips. He tightened his grip, and I was afraid that if we didn't stop that we would never get to the bar and get any food.

"Better slow your roll, cowboy. I'm hungry."

"For?"

"Food."

"Well, then, let's get you to the bar and get some food in your stomach." He opened the door for me, and I followed him out, making sure to stop at the passenger door of his truck so he could open it as well. I didn't dare mess with his manners.

The engine hummed softly as Colt headed out the gravel drive toward the main road. As we approached town, neon lights were blurring into streaks of color. The windows were partially down, and the cool night air whipped through my curls. He had the radio on, and I hummed along with the tune.

"Excited?" I glanced over at him.

"Are you kidding? I'm starving." I laughed.

"Oh, so I'm just a good meal to you, then?" I laughed again, playfully hitting his shoulder.

"I could use a good dance or two. It's been way too long since we did that last." I turned my face to look out the window, letting the wind hit my face. "Thanks for offering to take me out tonight, Colt. I needed a nice outing. It'll be fun."

"Anytime, Daisy." He smiled, and it made me feel warm inside. "Besides, I could use a good dance or two myself. Who knows how it will end?" He winked, and I remembered our last rendezvous at the bar, and how hot the kissing was between us that night. I had craved him that night so much, for the first time since I had been on Texas Rose Ranch this summer.

As we pulled up to the bar, the sight of neon lights made me excited and reminiscent. The music spilled out into the parking lot, a welcome invitation with each vibration., My eyes lit up. I couldn't wait to get inside and let the night unfold.

The moment we stepped inside the bar, the wave of sound and energy enveloped us. The sights of people dancing on the floor and the smell of alcohol consumed me. Colt led me through the crowd of people dancing, his hand gently guiding me until we arrived at the corner booth.

"This is perfect." I slid into the booth across from Colt, seeing the waiter coming toward us.

"What can I get the two of you?" Colt looked at me to answer first.

"Burger and fries for me."

"I'll have the same, and two Michelob Ultras." She jotted the order down in her notepad and took off.

We waited for the food, watching the people dancing and having some conversations.

"I guess the burger and fries were pretty good last time?"

"Oh, yeah. I like it. That's why I got it again." I glanced back at the people dancing and spoke again. "Where do you think your dad went?"

"Honestly…" Colt rubbed the back of his neck and adjusted his hat. "This isn't the first time he has done this."

"Really?"

"I followed him once to see where he was going."

"And?"

"He went to this little spot right outside of town that he and my mom used to go together sometimes. He parked his truck and sat on the tailgate. It looked like he was talking a little bit, but I couldn't hear him. I stayed far enough back where he couldn't see me. I left, and any time he mentions something vague, I know that's where he's headed off to."

I wiped my eyes where tears had formed. I noticed the waitress carrying our food and drinks out of my peripheral vision. I grabbed the beer as soon as she set it on the table, and Colt grabbed his.

"This is exactly what I needed. Good food, good company."

"To nights like these," Colt chimed in.

"To nights like these."

As the last remnants of our food disappeared, a surge of energy filled me. *Boot Scootin' Boogie* by Brooks and Dunn blasted through the speakers.

"Okay." I wiped my mouth with a napkin. "I'm ready to dance." A group of people was on the dance floor, dancing to the music.

"Line dancing?" Colt raised an eyebrow.

"Absolutely. Come on, don't tell me you're too cool for this." I took his hand, and he gave in to me, letting me lead him to the dance floor to join the crowd of honkeytonkers.

We jumped in, moving in unison with the others, creating a flurry of cowboy boots. I fell into step with ease. I loved this song, and I had taught myself this line dance years ago, back when I was hoping that Colt would ask me to dance at some point. I glanced over at Colt, who was a little less graceful. I laughed lightly and watched as he found his rhythm.

With each repetition, Colt's confidence grew, and he managed to throw in a couple of hoops and hollers in my direction. The energy of this place was infectious, and I was extra thankful for this time with Colt tonight. I liked seeing his playful, carefree side. I got lost in the moment, letting everything else go. It was just us and the music.

The lights overhead beamed onto the dance floor. Everyone here seems so carefree and filled with excitement. Colt has the biggest smile on his face, really enjoying himself. My face was surely flushed, but I didn't care. I threw my head back, laughing and having fun.

As the song was nearing its end, everyone cheered. I felt a surge of adrenaline, and I saw Colt wiping sweat from his forehead. I gave him a high-five.

"You good there, cowboy?"

"Oh, yeah. Never been better."

"I'm going to run to the restroom." He nodded, and I went inside. I wiped away the sweat and checked my face. I let out a deep breath, trying to slow my breathing.

As I emerged from the bathroom, my eyes scanned the room for Colt. When they landed on him, I saw a woman beside him. She was all smiles and fluttering eyelashes, leaning in close, with her hand resting on his arm. I saw her lips moving, an invitation in her eyes as she moved her arm to gesture to the dance floor.

I realized the band was starting to play a slow song. Filled with annoyance, I wanted to go up to her and tell her to stay away from my cowboy, but instead, I stayed still and watched. I was curious how Colt would respond.

Before I could step forward, I saw Colt remove the woman's hand from his arm. He gave her a polite, yet firm smile, and made his way over to me. His sweet and sexy smile was plastered on his face as he took my hand in his.

"Daisy, would you do me the honor?" I nodded, smiling back at him.

As we made our way to the dance floor, I caught a peek at the woman who had just been near Colt. Her face fell at the sight of us. I would be lying if I said I wasn't happy about it. I was thrilled.

Colt chose me.

He keeps choosing me.

We started dancing, my arms around his neck and leaning on his shoulders, and his hands perfectly fitting on my waist. We started swaying to the sounds of *There's The Sun* by Zach Top.

"I love this song."

"It's a good one, for sure."

"Who was that you were talking to?" I nodded my head toward where I had seen the two of them standing.

"I don't even know her name. I couldn't even get a word in, honestly. She only asked me to dance. And I declined. I only want to dance with you."

"She's not your type?" He shook his head.

"My type currently has her hands around my neck."

In Colt's arms, the world seemed to shrink. All the noise and people around us faded away. I felt one of his hands move from my waist, pressing gently against the small of my back. I let him lead, guiding me in a slow, rhythmic sway. I breathed in, taking in the scent of his cologne- still the same, woodsy scent he had always worn -and felt so much comfort. Looking up at him, his eyes had a hint of a sparkle in them. He had such warmth inside his eyes that were radiating, making me forget any doubts I ever had about this working between us.

I will be leaving tomorrow, and I had pushed that thought into the back of my mind, not wanting to think about it. I didn't want to think about leaving my home again, and Colt.

As the music continued from the band, Colt pulled me in closer, his head resting on top of mine gently. I let one hand slide down to his chest, and I could feel the steady beat of his heart in sync with mine. It was comforting and a reminder of our special bond.

The song was nearing its end. Colt moved his head off mine and tilted my chin up with his hand. His gaze was intense and loving. Time stopped as he leaned in, his lips meeting mine in a soft and tender kiss. So many unspoken feelings were in that kiss, and I was afraid time was almost up for me to spill my heart out to Colt, letting him know exactly how I feel. Our connection, though, was evident. A spark ignited within me, leaving me breathing heavily and wanting more.

"Come on." Colt took my hand and led me to the door.

Outside, the night air was a good contrast to the humidity of the summer day. It had started to get warm inside the bar. The live band had clearly drawn in a lot of people tonight, and I could feel the heat from that many being gathered in one place.

Colt led me to his truck, and I remembered this scene all too well. He leaned against the hood of the truck, turning to face me. He had an expression of pure desire and hunger that mirrored my own. We both wanted more than the kiss we had inside. With one small tug, he drew me to him. I watched him look at my lips, and I took my own peek at his.

"Darlin', I'm dying from the lack of the sweet taste of your skin on my lips."

I wasn't sure of anything else he could say that would make me feel the way I was feeling in this moment. It was the perfect chance, and I took it. I threw my arms around his neck and eagerly rushed my lips onto his. The kiss was anything but gentle.

It was passionate, fiery, full of longing and need.

His hands roamed my back, and I could feel a tingle down my spine. With each touch, we pulled the other closer, like we were trying to become one. Nothing else mattered but his touch and the feel of his lips on mine. There was electricity running through my body, and I could feel the undeniable pull that drew us together.

Colt could very well be my forever.

Chapter Forty-Seven

Colt

Last night, after we got home, I kissed Daisy goodnight outside in my truck. My dad was home in bed when we got back. The realization that summer is over hit me hard as I lay in bed, and I knew I wasn't ready for the next morning.

The sun peeked over the horizon and cast a golden glow across the ranch. I was out on the porch, leaning against the wooden railing with a coffee in my hand. I needed some time to myself while my dad was off with the cattle. I looked out at the fields, the world just beginning to wake up. The sounds of nature around me filled the air, but it couldn't take away my thoughts. They were heavy as I thought about Daisy and how quickly our time together had slipped away, leaving nothing but sweet memories that played out in my mind.

I knew Daisy was only supposed to be here for the summer, but with how things have played out the past couple of months, I was hoping it wouldn't end here. We talked a little about it, but nothing completely concrete. We both had been living in the moment and enjoying each second that we spent together.

Now, though, Daisy had to leave to go back to Dallas. The thought twisted in my gut, and I felt sick. I couldn't shake the feeling of dread that filled me. We had a romantic time at John's at our picnic, and just last night, we shared a moment in the bar. It was the perfect reminder of that first moment we truly gave in to temptation and let ourselves give in to each other. We have shared more laughter, secrets, and kisses that have lit a fire within me that I haven't felt since the two of us were kids and spending as much time as we could with each other.

The reality of distance loomed over me like a dark cloud. I took another sip of my coffee, letting the warmth seep into me. Although nothing could create the heat I felt when I was around Daisy.

Leaning against the wooden railing, I replayed moments from this summer that we shared in my head. I thought about riding horses together, taking her out in my truck, going to the bar, dancing, the picnic, swimming together...so many memories were made that changed our relationship and that let our once strong friendship blossom into something more. I thought about the way her laughter echoed in my ears, the way her smile brought me joy, the way her eyes sparkled in the light, and the way her lips were so soft against mine.

I smiled, thinking about all the kisses we shared, especially that first one outside the bar against my truck. It was the best kiss I've ever had, and it made me want her even more than I did when we were younger. That night felt like a dream; it was perfect. But dreams have a way of colliding with reality, and the reality is that Daisy has her place and job in Dallas. She has a life there, and who would I be to ask her to give it up?

I sighed, rubbing the back of my neck. I set the coffee cup on the wooden railing and took off my hat, then ran my other hand through my hair. I heard the creaking of the wooden boards under me and turned to see Daisy coming out to join me. Her hair caught in the morning light, and after all this time, she was still taking my breath away. She is beautiful. She is stunning. I looked her over and saw the sadness in her eyes. Maybe this was weighing as heavily on her as it was on me.

"Hey." She spoke softly.

"Hey." I forced a smile, not sure what to say. "Sleep well?"

"Not really. A lot on my mind. You?"

"Same thing."

"I kept thinking about today and leaving."

"Me, too. It's going to be tough without you around. This summer went by too fast, didn't it?"

"It did." She waited a minute and spoke again. "Colt, can we talk?"

"Yes, of course." My heart was racing with anticipation. I was curious about what she was going to say. I wanted her to stay, but I wanted it to be her decision. We moved over to the rocking chairs on the porch, sitting down.

"I know we haven't been together that long, but we have a history, and what we have is real. Do you agree?"

"I do."

"I want you to come clean to your dad about us." That thought shook me, making me anxious.

"You want me to tell him that we've been seeing each other, keeping it a secret from him?"

"Yes, Colt, I do. He deserves to know."

"What if he doesn't take it well?"

"Then we will figure it out if we get there. He might surprise you. My dad told you that your dad was protecting you from getting hurt. He might surprise you with his reaction. He may understand, Colt."

"You think?" She nodded her head.

"After that, we can talk and figure out where to go from here." I didn't speak. I wasn't sure how to even go about starting this conversation with my dad. "It's up to you to show him that you're serious about us. It's up to you to tell him. I'm not going to make you or pressure you. It all relies on you now."

"Okay."

She walked back inside, and I turned to see a couple of bags sitting by the door. She has already packed her stuff, ready to go. Why would I go and tell my dad if she was going to leave anyway? It would only show my dad that he was right after all for telling me to promise him that this summer would just be work, and nothing more, between Daisy and me.

I wasn't sure what to do. I wanted Daisy and I didn't want this to end. Her words felt like she might want to stay, but there was still question about that seeing her bags already packed and at the door. I didn't ask her what she wanted. Maybe that was my mistake.

Chapter Forty-Eight

Daisy

We had one last kiss in Colt's truck last night, and I wanted to sit there and let time stand still in that moment. I didn't want this to end between us. This had been the best time of my life, even if it didn't start that way.

I got up the next morning after barely sleeping with the thought of my leaving the ranch, my dad, and Colt. I needed to have a conversation with Colt and see where his head is at.

I wanted him to say he wanted to be with me.

I wanted him to tell his dad about us.

I wanted him to ask me to stay.

I was only supposed to be here for the summer, and at first, I absolutely hated being here. Colt even called me out on my crap one night. I never expected to enjoy being here again, and I definitely didn't have Colt and me forming a romantic relationship in the cards. I wanted us to be together all those years ago when my crush had just started to form and we were basically inseparable, but it never happened.

It was time for me to go back to my place and job in Dallas. I still had my stuff there. Yes, I could find a job here. Maybe I could write about and take pictures of the people here, like I always wanted. That was always the dream, and I know that's why my dad got me to come back here in the first place.

I thought about the day we helped my dad and he told me he knew about us. I thought about us having a picnic at my dad's. I thought about the bar and riding horses. I thought about us swimming together and how it reminded me of when we did that as kids. I thought about every single moment between us over this summer.

There were so many sweet moments of laughter and smiles, and some intense moments of kissing that lit a fire in me that I had never felt before.

I had packed up my stuff, because I did have to go back, whether it was to stay for good or to come back here and placed them by the front door. I looked out on the porch to see Colt rubbing his neck before taking off his hat and running his fingers through his hair. I loved the way his hair was slightly longer and curled toward the brim of his hat.

"Hey," I spoke softly.

"Hey." He smiled, but I could tell it was forced. "Sleep well?"

"Not really. A lot on my mind. You?"

"Same thing."

"I kept thinking about today and leaving."

"Me, too. It's going to be tough without you around. This summer went by too fast, didn't it?" That was the understatement of a lifetime

"It did." I needed to have the conversation with myself, and it needed to be now. I couldn't put it off any longer. "Colt, can we talk?"

"Yes, of course." We walked to the rocking chairs and took a seat beside each other.

"I know we haven't been together that long, but we have a history, and what we have is real. Do you agree?"

"I do."

"I want you to come clean to your dad about us." I could only imagine how he felt when I said those words, but he needed to do it. This had been put off for too long, and now the summer was over.

"You want me to tell him that we've been seeing each other, keeping it a secret from him?" Yes, that's exactly what I want. I want you to stand up for what you want and believe in.

"Yes, Colt, I do. He deserves to know."

"What if he doesn't take it well?"

"Then we will figure it out if we get there." I leaned forward in the chair, "He might surprise you. My dad told you that your dad was protecting you from getting hurt. He might surprise you with his reaction. He may understand, Colt." We had no way of knowing how Walt was going to react, but if Colt didn't tell him, we would never know.

"You think?" I nodded.

"After that, we can talk and figure out where to go from here." He didn't speak. I knew he was just trying to process everything. "It's up to you to show him that you're serious about us. It's up to you to tell him. I'm not going to make you or pressure you. It all relies on you now." I couldn't do anything. Only Colt could do something now.

"Okay."

I walked back inside. I wasn't sure what Colt was going to do. I could see the fear and anxiety plastered on his face during our conversation. I was afraid he wouldn't tell his dad. That made me want to cry.

I just wanted him to come clean.

I wanted him to fight for me.

I wanted him to fight for us.

I wasn't sure what was going to happen, but I was supposed to leave in about an hour, so I was hoping to get some information soon.

Walt let me off the hook from doing any work around the ranch this morning so I could pack. There was one thing I wanted to do before I left, though. I waited until Colt had brought his coffee cup inside and disappeared around the ranch before I went outside. I wasted no time heading straight for the barn to saddle up Domino. I wanted to get in one last ride.

"Can I join you?" I turned around to face the familiar voice.

"Dad? What are you doing here?"

"Can't a father come see his baby girl before she leaves?" I gave him a big hug. "Now, can I ride with you?"

"I'd like that."

Out in the field, surrounded by only the sounds and smells of the nature around us, I was enjoying one last ride. This time, it was with my dad. I glanced over at him as we rode, side by side, and could tell he wanted to say something. He had something on his mind.

"I know you have something to say."

"Yes, I do."

"Say it." I pulled on the reins to get Domino to stop, and my dad did the same with Shadow.

"Are you really going to leave?"

"What do you mean? We both knew I only agreed to be here for the summer."

"Yes, that's true...but haven't things changed?"

"You mean with me and Colt?"

"Well, yeah, honey. You two seemed awfully serious when I saw you. Are you not going to see that through?"

"I told him I wanted him to tell his dad. I told him that this morning. He walked off, and I don't know if he was going to come clean about us or not. I saw so much anxiety and fear in his eyes…I just don't know, dad. I don't know."

"Do you want to stay? For him?"

"I do. I've liked being back here, even if I wasn't too happy when you first got me to come here."

"I've enjoyed having you back here. What about your job?"

"I could always find another one here. Maybe I could give that writing and pictures a chance here."

"Your dream always was to do that for the people here. I hated to see you give up on that."

"Maybe I can get it back. I just have to wait and see what Colt is going to do. I can't just up and leave there without any sort of notice, anyway."

"I know. Things will work out, honey."

We circled around and rode the horses back to the barn. I was grateful for my dad giving me this summer back in Garrity Valley. Without that, I wouldn't have had this reconnection with Colt, and it developed into a relationship, and my dad and I wouldn't have rekindled our relationship. This summer was a new beginning for me, and I had my dad to thank. We got off the horses, took off their saddles, and put them back in their stalls. I gave my dad one last hug.

"Well, it's time for me to go."

"Let me help you with your bags." We walked to the house, Walt sitting in a rocking chair and Colt leaning against the wooden railing. My dad carried the bags out to his truck, putting them in the back. Walt stood up.

"It's been nice having you here, Daisy." Walt gave me a quick hug. "You can always come back here and see us. Don't be a stranger."

I looked over at Colt, who was still standing in the same spot, looking out at the fields. He didn't look at me, and that was all I needed to know. I walked off the porch and got into my dad's truck. I waved back at Walt as we drove off, then wiped a tear from my eyes.

Chapter Forty-Nine

Colt

I watched Daisy as she walked down the steps and got in John's truck. I wanted to say something, but I couldn't find the words. I hadn't told my dad. I hadn't asked her how she felt. I was letting her go, and my heart was aching with heartbreak as I watched her leave. My dad came over beside me on the porch, placing a hand on my back.

"She's gone, son."

"I know. She just left. She has to go back to the city."

"Does she, though?" I rose from where I was propped against my arms and looked at my dad. What was he saying?

"I know, son."

"What?"

"About you and her. You two must think I'm stupid for not knowing what is going on around here. I know everything that happens on this ranch." I couldn't believe what I was hearing.

"I'm sorry about breaking my promise." I rubbed the back

of my neck. "Why didn't you say anything?"

"I thought you'd come tell me at some point. You never did, though. I only had you make that promise to protect yourself. I knew you liked her when y'all were younger, and it hurt you when she left. I didn't want you to have to go through that again. There's been enough heartbreak in this family, and if I could help prevent any more, that's what I was going to do."

"I know why you did it, Dad. I understand."

"Do you love her?"

"Love?"

"Yes, son, love. Do you love her?"

"How do you know that? How did you know mom was the one?" My dad walked inside the house and returned with a picture of his and my mom's wedding day. He handed it to me, and I studied it, remembering how amazing my mom was.

"When you're around that person and you want to be better for them, when their happiness makes you happy, when you want to do things for them, when you want to spend all your time with them and when you're not with that person all you think about is being with them…that's love."

I looked back at the road leading to the highway, and I felt a pain in my chest. Daisy was gone. All the words my dad said ran through me, and all I wanted to do was go back and tell her how I felt. I want her to know I love her. I want to spend my life with her. I don't want to lose her again.

"I don't want to lose her again, dad. What do I do?"

"Well, son, let me give you some advice my dad once told me. Speak your mind, but ride a fast horse. The summer's over now, and Daisy doesn't work here anymore. Go get your girl."

If I tell Daisy how I feel, she may still decide to stay in the city, but if I don't tell her, I will live with that regret and the what ifs for the rest of my life. She needs to know how I feel.

"I'll be back." My dad nodded, and I think he knew exactly what I was going to do.

I ran to the barn and quickly saddled up Shadow. I kicked him into high gear, and we ran through the yard and down the driveway, heading straight to the highway. I was going to get my girl.

When I finally spotted the truck, I kicked Shadow into gear again. I tried waving my hand, but John didn't see. I turned Shadow to get him to go to the passenger side of the truck where Daisy was. I waved two times, and then she spotted me. I saw her put a hand on her dad's arm, and then I saw the brake lights come on. I slowed Shadow and took him off to the side of the road near Daisy's door. I hopped off and walked closer as I saw her get out.

"Colt! Are you trying to get yourself killed?"

"No."

"That was reckless."

"Daisy, my dad knows. He knew all along." I waited for her to speak, and when she didn't, I continued. "I need to get something off my chest. I want to be better because of you. Your happiness makes me happy. I want to do things for you. I want to spend all my time with you, and all I do is think about you when we aren't together." John was now outside the truck, leaning against the side. I knew he was listening but trying to give us space, too. "I don't know about you, Daisy, but this summer wasn't just some fling to me. Yes, it was fun, but it meant more to me than that... it meant more than rekindling our lost relationship. Being around you means more to me than the entire world. We're inevitable, darlin'. That's why we finally had this time together again, after all these years apart." I took her hands in mine. "I would crawl to the depths of the earth for you. Death couldn't keep me from you. I did something reckless to get to you before you got too far down the highway, to bring you back to me. For good. You are my perfect reminder that through all the hurt and hard times, there is good. There can still be paradise on the other side." She looked at me, eyes and ears completely focused. I could tell she was still processing what I was saying. It was a lot. I wanted her to hear me loud and clear. I wanted her to finally see exactly how I felt. "Do you remember when we first went swimming together? We were goofing around, splashing each other with the water, and challenging one another to do dumb crap. You looked at me and I felt it. I just let myself see you, and what I saw...was a girl who could absolutely infuriate me, make me smile and laugh, and hope for the future. A future with you. Daisy, you are my God given solace."

I watched as her eyes swelled. Then, tears streamed down her face. I took my thumbs and gently raked them across each cheek to wipe the tears away. I left my hands there and raised her head up so her eyes could meet mine. Then, I closed my eyes and let my lips find hers. I could find them in the darkest parts of the world. I could find Daisy in any life. I would crawl to her as I took my last, dying breath. She meant everything to me, and I was so glad she finally knew it.

"I love you, darlin'."

"I love you, cowboy."

Afterword

I am beyond trilled to finally have this debut novel in your hands. I have been thinking about this for a while, and I finally hopped in the saddle and wrote this book. Here's to always following your dreams. I hope you love Colt and Daisy as much as I do.

Acknowledgement

Thank you to all my family and friends who have hopped in the saddle right along with me during this journey. Y'all have been amazing and I could not have done this without you. I love y'all.

A special thank you to Katie Diggle with Scripted Waves for working with me throughout this process to make my book cover come to life, as well as anything else I have needed. I am thankful for all your help.

Lastly, thank you to all the cowboy romance authors who have strengthened my love even more.

About The Author

Alicia Vanover

Alicia Vanover is an author of small-town cowboy romance who loves good book boyfriends and the strong heroines who make them yearn. She lives in Kentucky where she has been reading since Kindergarten.

She loves baking, cooking, teaching, reading, country music, and all things western. She has an old soul and a soft spot for anything that sounds like 90s country.

Printed in Dunstable, United Kingdom

67464612R00161